He has no redeeming qualities. And you'll love him.

D0913556

DOVER THREE

A DOVER MYSTERY

Joyce Porter

This edition published in 2020 by Farrago,
an imprint of Duckworth Books Ltd
13 Carrington Road, Richmond, TW10 5AA, United Kingdom

www.farragobooks.com

By arrangement with the Beneficiaries of the
Literary Estate of Joyce Porter

First published by Cape in 1965

ISBN: 9781788422062

Cover design by Patrick Knowles

*Thanks to the generosity of the inheritors of the late Joyce Porter, royalties from this publication
go towards the work of The Friends of Friendless Churches (Registered Charity 1113097).*

*The Friends of Friendless Churches rescues and campaigns for redundant religious
buildings threatened by demolition, decay and unsympathetic conversion.
The Friends care for many former places of worship in England and Wales,
preserving them for the local community and visitors to enjoy. Without this work,
all of these buildings would no longer be here, or open to the public.*

For more information, visit www.friendsoffriendlesschurches.org.uk

Have you read them all?

Treat yourself again to the first Dover novels –

Dover One
A housemaid has disappeared in remote Creedshire, but why should Dover, of all people, be called upon to find her?

Dover Two
This time Dover may have two murderers to catch, if, that is, people would only stop distracting him.

Dover Three
Obscene poison pen letters in the little village of Thornwich lead a shaken Dover to a most unlikely killer.

Turn to the end of this book for a full list of the series, plus – on the last page – the chance to receive **further background material**.

Chapter One

'Prevention,' said Dame Alice, 'is better than cure. You're not going to argue with that, are you?'

The man she was addressing shook his head and cowered even further behind his desk. After half an hour of Dame Alice's undivided attention he had had most of the argument knocked out of him.

'In that case,' said Dame Alice, pulling on her gloves with an air of high satisfaction, 'we needn't waste any more time discussing it. Let me know the minute you've made the necessary arrangements, and remember, speed is the most important thing now.'

The man behind the desk pulled himself together and made a last-ditch effo t to get her to see reason. He was, after all, a chief constable, and when it came to police matters he ought to be given credit for the fact that he knew what he was talking about.

'It can't be done,' he muttered and ducked instinctively as Dame Alice jerked her head and snorted with exasperation.

'What can't be done?' she demanded with justifiable irritation. Really, these men! One sometimes wondered if they obstructed every suggestion on principle.

'Scotland Yard,' explained the Chief Constable unhappily. 'They wo 't come, you know.'

'And why not?' she asked. Typical! You beat them hands down on the main issue and then they started trying to trip you with a lot of footling, minor details. Well, let the old fool get on with it! Dame Alice was nursing an ace up her sleeve with which she would fell this bumbling idiot to the ground when the time came.

Mr Mulkerrin, the Chief Constable, sighed. Women! Always interfering and poking their noses into other people's affairs. Look at Dame Alice! Mr Mulkerrin did, and was not reassured by what he saw. She ought to be sitting at home knitting instead of ranging round the county trying to teach every hard-working officia she could lay her hands on how to suck eggs.

'Well,' said Dame Alice, 'I am waiting.'

Aw, drop dead! Get stuffed! Put your head in a bucket three times and pull it out twice! Go for a long walk on a short pier!

'It's a simple matter of police procedure, Dame Alice,' explained Mr Mulkerrin meekly. 'We can only call in Scotland Yard to deal with cases of serious crime which we can't handle ourselves. Well, now' – he risked a patronizing smile – 'you can hardly call this a serious crime.'

'Can't I?' retorted Dame Alice indignantly. 'Let me remind you that I, personally, have been involved in this revolting business, and I can assure you I regard it as a very serious matter indeed.'

'A few poison-pen letters.' Mr Mulkerrin shrugged his shoulders.

'Hundreds of poison-pen letters!' Dame Alice corrected him firml . 'Nasty, obscene epistles which have been arriving by every post for a month now, and whose author your policemen so far have proved themselves completely incapable of finding '

'The e are no clues!' protested Mr Mulkerrin, furious at finding himself on the defensive once again.

'Fiddlesticks!' snapped Dame Alice. 'The e must be clues. Your men are just too stupid and incompetent to find them, that's all. Gracious heavens, there aren't more than four hundred people in the entire village. An intelligent child of fi e could discover the culprit, and at considerably less cost to the ratepayers,' she added spitefully.

Mr Mulkerrin scowled. That was a typical woman's blow, right below the belt. Amongst her other numerous activities, Dame Alice was a county councillor of antique standing and currently the chairman of the Standing Joint Committee. Mr Mulkerrin had several pet plans on the boil for improving the amenities of his force (and, of course, improving its efficiency) but without Dame Alice's support he could kiss his dreams a sweet goodbye. He switched the conversation on to another track.

'Scotland Yard wouldn't touch it with a barge-pole,' he said. 'They only send their people out on murder cases and things like that. The 're all high-ranking, senior detectives, you know. They won't waste their time on a tuppence-ha'penny case like this. Besides,' he added quickly, 'even if they would come, which they won't, the County would have to foot the bill.'

'We will cross that bridge when we come to it,' said Dame Alice.

'But they *won't* come!' insisted Mr Mulkerrin. Damn it, didn't she listen to anything you said?

'They will,' said Dame Alice with a smug smile. 'I've already arranged that. Perhaps you didn't know, Mr Mulkerrin,' – the smile was very sweet now – 'that the Assistant Commissioner for Crime at New Scotland Yard is a very dear friend of mine.' Dame Alice produced a simper which made the Chief Constable's blood run cold. 'A *very* dear friend of mine! We knew each other years ago – long before either of us was married. I telephoned him last night and explained the whole situation. He quite agreed with me that while on the surface it might *look* a very trivial matter, there could be ugly and dangerous developments if the perpetrator of these disgusting missives was not found quickly. I had to tell him, of course, that your men had been working on the case for four weeks without any sign of success. He seemed very surprised. I asked him to help us. He was quite agreeable, but pointed out that the assistance of Scotland Yard must be requested by the local police.' Dame Alice fi ed Mr Mulkerrin with a steely eye. 'I told him there would be no difficult about that. He is expecting you to ring him. No doubt you know the number.'

'It's all very irregular,' muttered Mr Mulkerrin, conceding victory but doing it as ungraciously as possible. 'And anyhow,' he added with a flash of truculence, 'I don't see what a couple of bogies from London are going to find out in a place like Thornwich. It's obviously a job for local men who know the district – and the peculiarities of the inhabitants,' he concluded, getting a dig in on his own account.

'Poppycock!' said Dame Alice. 'It's no good whining about it. You've had your chance. This man is obviously just too clever for you. We need real experts on the job. Now, I hope you've got everything straight. I've got to go now – I've got an important meeting and I'm already late for it – so you can telephone the Assistant Commissioner right away. Just mention my name. You'd better give me a ring this evening at home and let me know what's happening.'

No one will ever know how Dame Alice managed to persuade the Assistant Commissioner at Scotland Yard to send two of his detectives down to Thornwich to investigate an outbreak of poison-pen letters. The e were, of course, several theories, mostly scurrilous and ranging from a sudden onslaught of dementia praecox to simple blackmail. Whatever the reason was, it left the Assistant Commissioner in a filthy temper. He swore at his secretary, kicked his desk, rang for an underling and shoved the whole business into his lap.

'It can't be done, sir,' said the underling, happy to be able to disoblige.

'It must be done!' roared the Assistant Commissioner, adding a few colourful epithets to drive his point home.

'I just haven't anybody to spare,' insisted the underling, who was actually a deputy commander.

'Don't give me that crap!' snarled the Assistant Commissioner. 'I know how many men you've got and I know how much ruddy work they do! I wasn't born yesterday, you know.'

'Well, there's Chief Inspector Dover, sir.' The suggestion was made with the utmost caution.

The Assistant Commissioner's face turned an alarming purple. 'You're joking, of course,' he said in a strangled voice. 'I thought I told you to get rid of that fat, stupid swine months ago!' The sentence finished on an ear-pie cing squeak of fury.

'I've tried, sir,' said the Deputy Commander unhappily, 'but nobody'll have him. I've offe ed him to every single division in the Metropolitan area. The 're all short-handed and none of 'em'll touch him. I can't understand it.'

'I can!' said the Assistant Commissioner grimly. 'Why don't you promote him? He'd have to go then. We've no vacancy for a superintendent at the Yard, have we?'

'We've no vacancy for a chief inspector, sir, either,' the Deputy Commander pointed out sadly. 'Dover's supernumerary to establishment and has been for years. H Division lent him to us when we were short-handed during that Mullen's business. And then they wouldn't take him back again.'

'Selfish blighters!' said the Assistant Commissioner, speaking from the bottom of his heart. 'I can't think whoever promoted him to Chief Inspector in the first place '

'Well, you did that, sir.'

'Eh? Oh, but that was just to help old Gooch out in J Division. He threatened to cut his throat if I didn't get rid of Dover for him. Kicking him upstairs was the only way.'

'Oh, quite, sir.'

The Assistant Commissioner lapsed into deep thought. After a few moments he glanced wickedly at his subordinate. 'D'you think we dare, Tom?'

'I don't see why not, sir.' The wicked grin was returned. 'This Chief Constable is hardly in a position to cut up rough about it, is he, sir? I mean, the whole thing's so irregular anyhow.'

'Yes,' agreed the Assistant Commissioner doubtfully. 'That last chap – what was his name? – he wrote me a very nasty letter. Very nasty. Can't say I blame him,' he added after a pause.

'Actually, it would fit in very well, sir – sending Dover on this poison-pen case. He's on light duties at the moment.'

'Not again!' groaned the Assistant Commissioner, clutching his head in both hands. 'What the hell's supposed to be the matter with him this time?'

'His stomach, sir. Same as usual. He was in my offic this morning telling me all about it. He was asking for a job, too. One that'd get him out of London for a bit.'

'Ho, ho!' scoffed the Assistant Commissioner. 'Very funny! Now pull the other one.'

'No, seriously, sir. The doctor turfed him out of bed and put his missus in. Said she was exhausted and needed a rest: Her sister's coming over to look after her. Apparently our Wilf can't stand the sister at any price, so any excuse – even work – to get out of London would suit him down to the ground just now.'

'But he didn't actually *ask* for a job, though, did he?' insisted the Assistant Commissioner.

'Well, no, sir – not in so many words. That would be expecting too much, wouldn't it? But I think he'd go all right – without all the usual screams about victimization, overwork, cooked rosters, and all the rest of it.'

'OK!' The Assistant Commissioner made up his mind quickly. 'Send him! And if they don't like it, they can lump it. Who generally works with him?'

'Detective Sergeant MacGregor, sir, but he's asking for a change.'

'Huh!' snorted the Assistant Commissioner. 'He'll be lucky! We aren't running an academy for sensitive young ladies. Do him a world of good working with Dover. Knock a few corners off him. Broaden his outlook. Teach him how the other half live.'

'Yes, sir.'

'Right!' The Assistant Commissioner leaned back in his chair with the air of a man who's done a good day's work. 'Tha 's settled. Well, don't just sit there, man! Get moving!'

Chief Inspector Wilfred Dover cleaned a hole in the steamed-up window of the bus with his handkerchief and peered through. It was pitch-dark outside. Occasionally a flur y of thin snow or sleet pattered against the outside of the glass.

"Strewth!' said Dover in tones of deep disgust. He scowled at his companion as though it was all his fault.

Sergeant MacGregor sat silently by his Chief Inspector's side, and suffe ed. They were the only passengers on the bus and they made an incongruous pair. MacGregor was young, tall, slim, rather handsome and a very snappy dresser. He was keen, too. He wanted to get on in his chosen profession. That was why he was always whining about having to work with Chief Inspector Dover. Prolonged association with Scotland Yard's worst detective just wasn't doing Charles Edward MacGregor's career any good at all. Detectives, like most other people, are judged by results, and Dover's results were very poor. Of course, he did manage to solve some of his cases – not many, but some. MacGregor didn't mind being associated with the successes, it was being associated with a lengthy list of crashing failures that worried him. Besides – well MacGregor prided himself on not being a snob, but really, it was rather embarrassing to be seen about with a lout like Dover.

The Chief Inspector was a big man, and fat – six foot two and turning the scales at seventeen and a quarter stone. Some coarse-minded colleague had once said that he looked like a pregnant hippopotamus, but this was generally agreed to be grossly unfair to that animal. It was true that most of Dover's excess burden of fat had settled below waist level and well to the fore, but his face had a most un-hippopotamus-like appearance. For one thing it was too pale, except around the extensive, overhanging jowls which were permanently sown with dark stubble. Dover had a big, flab y face in which the features – small button nose, tiny rosebud mouth and piggy little eyes – were almost lost in the wide expanses of pasty-coloured flesh. On top of his head was a thin covering of dark, dandruff-bespeckled hai .

Dover's figu e generally might be considered to constitute a tailor's nightmare, but luckily no tailor was ever called upon to answer the challenge. When he bought a suit – a very rare occurrence – he bought it off the outsize peg, and it looked like it. He favoured blue serge, which soon acquired a disgusting patina of grease and dirt. He usually wore an enormous dusty black overcoat and a bowler hat. This latter was no frivolous, guardee affair with a smart curly brim, but a heavy, solid, utility job, designed to protect Dover's cranium from the onslaughts of the wicked. Th ow in a grubby shirt with a too-tight collar and a tie whose original colouring was now quite unidentifiable, and the elegant Sergeant MacGregor's feelings arouse some sympathy.

Not that Dover in his turn was too enthusiastic about consorting with young MacGregor. He considered his assistant more than a bit of a cissy and frequently asked his superior officer how they thought MacGregor could dress so expensively on the pittance he received as a detective sergeant, second class. 'Stands to reason,' Dover was wont to say in the quarters where it would do most harm, 'the young pup's taking a bit on the side. You don't find me coughing up forty quid for a suit and I'm a chief inspector. Where does he get the money from, that's what I want to know.'

The bus was now churning painfully along in bottom gear. MacGregor shivered and pulled his overcoat collar up round his ears. It was bitterly cold and only the driver baked by his overheated engine, was making the journey in any comfort.

'How much longer are we going to be?' Dover twisted round awkwardly in his seat and bawled the question at the conductor.

That young man stopped writing things in a little notebook and stared out of the window in his turn.

''Bout half an hour,' he announced. 'It's a long pull up to Thornwich. 'Course, with a decent bus you'd do it in half the time. Not that you'll find this company wasting its money on decent buses. Not them! Or on anything else. Squeeze every last ha'penny out in profits, they do, so they can run around in their posh limousines. They don't worry about decent working chaps like you and me and Fred up front there getting stranded out in the dark and cold with nothing but a lot of frozen sheep to keep us company – not them, they don't! We're expendable, we are, mate!

They weigh up what we're worth against the price of a new set of piston rings and, take my word for it, brother – you and me and our wives and kids come a hell of a long way down on the list of priorities!'

'Ask a silly question and you get a silly answer,' observed Dover in a loud voice. Both he and MacGregor had been at first surprised, and then outraged by the bus conductor's unexpected tirade. 'Decent working chaps like you and me' indeed! Dover scowled blackly. He had had a hard day and he didn't suffer the proletariat gladly at the best of times.

The bus conductor, sensing that his audience wasn't exactly with him, lapsed into a moody silence and started writing in his little notebook again.

Dover's stomach rumbled loudly.

'Hear that?' he asked MacGregor with gloomy triumph. 'It shows I'm hungry. Regular meals, that's what the doctor said I had to have.'

MacGregor nodded and hoped they weren't going to have another session on the vagaries of Dover's stomach. Coming down in the train had been bad enough. Dover had started off by insisting that a rather fetching and very surprised young lady should give up her seat by the corridor to him in case he had to make a quick dash to the toilet, as he had explained to her with an over-generous wealth of detail. The young lady had looked very pointedly at the communication cord and then removed herself from the compartment in a dudgeon so high as to have snow on it. Dover took the corner seat without batting an eyelid. For the rest of the journey, when he wasn't sound asleep and snoring with his mouth open, he regaled MacGregor and the rest of his fellow passengers with a twinge-by-twinge account of his latest bout of sick leave. By the time they reached their destination, MacGregor wasn't feeling too good himself.

At the County Police Headquarters they had had a very curt and frigid interview with the Chief Constable. Without actually putting it into words he had made his attitude quite clear. He tossed a bulky police file across the desk in the general direction of MacGregor, told them that if they didn't hurry they'd miss the last bus to Thornwich, and wished them a firm goodbye. Dover and MacGregor shuffle unhappily out. The Chief Inspector hadn't even had time to work up steam and blow his top. He usually managed to have a blazing row with every chief constable he'd ever been sent to assist, and he felt unfulfilled as he and MacGregor huddled together in the pouring rain waiting for their bus. However, there is no point in keeping a sergeant if you can't bark at him, so Dover relieved the tedium by bawling MacGregor out.

'Well,' said the bus conductor suddenly in a voice of complete indiffe ence, 'this is Thornwich. A e you getting off or not?

The two detectives got off. The bus departed in a flur y of black smoke.

'Where,' demanded Dover with suppressed fury, 'the hell are we?'

He did well to ask. Not many people will have heard of Thornwich. It was a nasty little village clinging, without apparent rhyme or reason, to the lee side of a hill and separated from civilization by seven miles of bleak moors on one side and nine on the other. Why anybody should have ever settled in Thornwich in the first place is a puzzle lost in the mists of time. Why anybody should live there now is an even greater enigma. It was one of Thornwic 's numerous misfortunes to have a busy main road running slap bang through the middle of it. Heavy traffi roared through the village day and night in both directions, belching diesel fumes and shedding dirty oily rags in its wake. The e was some respite in the depths of winter when the snows came and the moors were impassable. In these grim periods the villagers sought some compensation for the deathly quiet which descended in fleecing the unfortunate truck-drivers who could proceed no farther. Prices in Thornwich showed a distressing tendency to fluctuate with the depth of sn w.

Dover and MacGregor were, of course, unaware of these minor points of rural economy as they stumbled around in the dark of a Saturday night looking for The Jolly Sailor, the village's only hostelry, where they were destined to stay during the course of their investigations. It was still raining and bitterly cold. Thornwich was on the lee side of its formidable hill only when the wind blew from the west. When it blew from the east, and it always did during the winter, the village caught it full blast. The e seemed to be nobody about – apart from the lorries grinding their way uphill from the direction of Bearle or hurtling downhill on dubious brakes from the direction of Cumberly.

After being thoroughly cursed by Dover for his inefficienc in not immediately locating their lodging, MacGregor found a front door and knocked on it. This was no mean achievement, as the alternation of pitch-darkness and glaring headlights made seeing anything at all extremely difficul

The Jolly Sailor, it appeared, was right opposite on the other side of the road. The large man in shirt-sleeves who had responded to MacGregor's inquiry leaned speculatively in his open doorway, not only wondering who the tall dark handsome stranger was, but whether he'd make it safely across the road or not. It was damned cold away from the fi e, but it'd be pity to miss anything. Some of them blighters came down the hill on nothing but their sidelights.

MacGregor picked up the suitcases, waited his opportunity and made a dash for it. Dover, encumbered only by his own weight, charged across in his wake.

Saturday night it might be, but one would never have guessed it from the interior of The Jolly Sailor. Things were very quiet. Dead, you might say. The e were only two men in the public, one with a whippet dog on a piece of string. The saloon bar didn't even have a light on.

The two men and the whippet stared with interest as Dover and MacGregor, cold and breathless, came crashing in.

'Bert!' shouted the man with the whippet. 'The 're here!' He grinned a toothless welcome at the detectives. 'Come on in out of the cold, lads, and make yourselves at home. Bert's just coming.'

Not even the warmth of his smile could cheer up the public bar of The Jolly Sailor. It was dingy, dirty and flybl wn. The only source of heat, a one-bar electric fi e, was safely tucked away behind the counter where its effo ts were restricted to bringing comfort and solace to the legs of the landlord.

Bert Quince, when he appeared (and he wasn't the man to hurry himself for anybody), assumed a strategic position behind the bar and let the warmth of his fi e play on the back of his calves. He regarded his new customers with an equanimity bordering on total indiffe ence.

'You'll be the policemen from London,' he observed.

'Tha 's right, landlord,' said MacGregor with a winning smile. 'I believe you've got a couple of rooms for us.'

Bert Quince's eyebrows rose slightly at the 'landlord' bit but he made no comment. If this young fellow-me-lad thought he was going to patronize the inhabitants of Thornwich with his lah-di-dah ways and his lah-di-dah voice, he'd got another think coming. He'd soon learn, probably with somebody's boot up his backside. They ere a ruggedly independent lot in Thornwich

'I hope they told you,' said Bert Quince, still warmly ensconced behind his bar counter, 'that we're only putting you up to oblige. We don't let rooms in winter. Only in summer. To cyclists and suchlike. Still, you're welcome to what we've got' – his voice didn't ring with anything approaching sincerity – 'just as long as you bear it in mind that we're only doing it to oblige. I reckon' – this came out with grim relish – 'I reckon you'll fin us a sight more rough than you're used to up in London.' He pushed two keys across the counter. 'Up them stairs and you'll find your rooms just at the top. Numbers one and two. You can't miss 'em.'

'We would like some supper,' said MacGregor, producing another friendly smile.

'Supper?' Bert Quince scratched his head. 'I dunno about that. The old woman's out playing bingo. She always plays bingo on a Saturday night.'

'But we've had nothing to eat,' protested MacGregor, and Dover's stomach rumbled loudly in support.

'Charlie!' Bert Quince turned ponderously to address the old man with the whippet. 'How about popping across to Freda's and bringing back a couple of plates of dinner? I reckon these gentlemen'll think it's worth the price of a pint.'

Charlie shot to his feet with that frantic spryness which, when it suits them, only the elderly and fragile can achieve. 'Hot pie, chips and beans, do you?' he asked, and was gone in the twinkling of an eye.

'Well, that's very kind,' said MacGregor helplessly as the door banged to behind Charlie.

'It's across the road,' explained Mr Quince. 'It's less dangerous for him. He's used to it.'

'Oh,' said MacGregor. 'Well, perhaps we should go up to our rooms and have a wash – shall we, sir?'

Dover, who had not so far opened his mouth in the confines of The Jolly Sailor, gave a disparaging and ominous sniff and headed for the stairs. Meekly MacGregor toted up the suitcases and followed him. He already had an uncomfortable premonition that this was going to be a typical Dover case. The signs were all pointing implacably in that direction.

Chapter Two

When Dover and MacGregor came back into the bar twenty minutes later their dinner was congealing on the counter. Bert Quince obliged by opening up the musty saloon bar and finding some cutlery. In solemn state the two detectives settled down to their pie, beans and chips followed by a couple of apple tarts in little cardboard boxes.

'We can't stay here!' snarled Dover, spraying beans and chips in several directions.

Unhappily, MacGregor nodded his agreement. It wasn't often he and the Chief Inspector saw eye to eye on anything but on this occasion there was no dissension in either mind. The Jolly Sailor just didn't come up to scratch. Visiting detectives had every right to expect the taxpayer to provide them with something several stars better than this. The beds were hard, narrow and damp. Each miserable room was furnished with a bowl and ewer the like of which MacGregor had never seen outside a junk shop, and it looked highly unlikely that anfbody would ever oblige with hot water for shaving. Both rooms faced the front and got the full benefit of the morning sun and the endless heavy traffi tearing past on the main road. With commendable selfishness the Quinces had commandeered the back rooms for themselves. And the toilet! In spite of the fact that the electric light bulb had expired, enough could be seen to make the strongest stomach heave. The e was a wad of newspaper hanging on a nail, and MacGregor didn't see how the piece of hairy string which served as a chain could long withstand the tugs of a man like Dover.

'I don't think there is anywhere else, sir', said MacGregor, examining the inside of his meat pie with some distress. 'The e's nowhere nearer than Bearle and that's seven miles off. And I do 't suppose those buses run more than once in a blue moon.'

Dover glared at him. Wet-blanket MacGregor sounding off again! 'Well, you'll just have to find somewhere, won't you, laddie?'

'But where, sir?'

'Don't ask me!' snapped Dover crossly. 'Use your initiative!' He unwrapped his apple pie. ''Strewth! It's got whiskers on it. They damned well want prosecuting, selling muck like this.'

Things, however, took an unexpected turn for the better. After supper MacGregor announced that, with the Chief Inspector's permission, he would retire to his room and study the file on the case. Dover, not at his brightest and best, gave a ready consent – he was always glad to see the back of his sergeant – but no sooner had MacGregor gone than he realized that he had been left all alone in a public house with nobody to buy him a drink. He was just about to haul MacGregor downstairs again at the double, when one of the men who'd been patiently sitting in the public bar since the detectives first arrived nobly stepped into the breach.

'I wonder if you would permit me to buy you a drink, Chief Inspector? Just to welcome you to Thornwich and wish you every success.'

No sooner asked than accepted, and Dover found himself clutching a glass of whisky and beaming quite happily at the donor as he joined him and the old man who had fetched the suppers. Introductions were soon made. The old man was called Charlie Chettle and Dover's new-found friend was called Arthur Tompkins. The whippet answered to the name of Jack. It was not quite the sort of company with which Dover would mix from choice but, as the jolly sailors say, any port in a storm.

'Enjoy your supper?' asked Charlie Chettle, who was still waiting for his pint.

Dover grunted.

'She does a good pie, Freda does. I'd have put you some tomato ketchup on it, if I'd thought. Always tastier with a bit of tomato ketchup, if you ask me.'

Dover grunted again.

'You'll be all right tomorrow,' said Mr Tompkins reassuringly. 'They can say what they like about Elsie Quince, but she can cook. Her steak and kidney puddings are out of this world, you'll see.'

'She were trained up at the big house,' said Charlie Chettle. 'Tha's where they learned her. Up at the big house.'

'Really?' said Dover with massive indiffe ence.

Charlie Chettle didn't mind. At his age he was happy to have any kind of audience. It didn't have to be a listening one. ''Course, it's gone now,' he went on. They pulled it down years ago. 'The 're going to build one of these housing estates on it, you know. I'll bet the old squire's spinning round in his grave. He wouldn't let 'em chop down not a single one of his trees while he was alive, never mind build a lot of blooming houses on his land. Mind you, all this was before the war. I used to know the bailiff in the old days. And he was a queer old cuss, too. He used to…'

'Well, I don't think the Chief Inspector's interested in that sort of thing, Charlie,' said Mr Tompkins with an indulgent smile. 'It's modern Thornwich ou'll be dissecting, isn't it?'

Dover indicated that this was so, managing to embrace his empty glass in his nod. Reinforcements were ordered immediately.

'Well, I reckon you'll have a pretty tight job on your hands,' said Charlie Chettle, affectionately screwing up his dog's ears. 'The local police didn't get very far and it wasn't for want of trying. They came and asked me if they could look around me cottage. "Typewriter?" I says, "You won't find more than a ninepenny ballpoint pen that I use for me pools, but you're welcome to come and look."'

'They searched every house in the village,' Mr Tompkins explained eagerly. 'They were looking for the typewriter and the notepaper. You didn't have to let them look through your house, of course, but nobody refused.'

'The 'd have been putting the noose round their necks if they had,' said Charlie Chettle with a chuckle. 'Some of them women are in such a state, they wouldn't think twice about a lynching party.'

'Tha's very true,' Mr Tompkins assured Dover earnestly. 'Feelings are running very high, very high indeed. Mrs Tompkins has always been what I call a very nervous woman – very sensitive, you know – but you should see her now. Trembles like a leaf every time she hears letters drop through the box. Shocking, it is, the way this business has pulled her right down. It wasn't so bad at the beginning when it was only one or two, but it's been going on and on for weeks now. Do you know she's had sixteen of the dratted things? I don't know how much longer she'll be able to stand it.'

'It's a crying shame,' agreed Charlie Chettle.

'And it's not knowing who's writing them that makes it ten times worse,' said Mr Tompkins, waxing indignant.

'They do say a couple of women came to blows at the Christian Fellowship t'other night,' said Charlie Chettle, smacking his lips.

Dover felt it was time he got in on the act. After all it was his case, even if he did know considerably less about it than his two companions. 'Who's the favourite candidate?' he asked.

Charlie Chettle gave a bitter laugh. 'You name him,' he said, 'we've got him. Do you know' – he leaned across the table and tapped Dover's arm in a friendly way – 'some of them old bosoms even suggested that my daughter was at the back of it! Ruddy sauce! I soon gave 'em a piece of my mind, I can tell you. Just because she was about the only lass in the whole perishing village who hadn't had one of them letters.'

'Go on!' said Dover with some surprise. 'I thought everybody'd had at least one.'

'Well, my Doris hadn't. Tha's why they picked on her, see? Because she hadn't had one.'

Dover leaned back in his chair and, encouraged by the whisky, prepared to pontificate. 'In my experience,' he announced, 'these poison-pen cases are all much of a muchness. 'Frinstance, the person who writes them always writes some to herself. She thinks' – Dover gave a pitying laugh – 'she thinks it'll put us off the scent. So you see, Mr Chettle, if your daughter hasn't had any letters that automatically crosses her off the list '

'Oh, but nobody really thought it was Doris,' protested Mr Tompkins. 'She's much too nice a person. But, Mr Dover, you can't seriously be suggesting that it's a woman writing these letters?'

'Thousand to one it is' said Dover grandly.

'Oh, no! Surely not? I mean – the language! Well, I've knocked around a bit in my time and I flatter myself I'm pretty broadminded, but some of the filth in those letters to my wife – well, they made my hair curl, I can tell you!'

'It'll be a woman.' Dover's speech lacked its usual clarity of diction but he made his point firmly enough. 'It always is. Whoever heard of a man writing poison-pen letters? No, if a man goes off the rails in that sort of way, he starts flashing. Men don't write anonymous letters.'

'Flashing?' Charlie Chettle asked. 'And what's that when it's at home?'

'Indecent exposure of the person with intent to insult,' explained Dover, 'in a public place.'

'Oh,' said Charlie Chettle. 'Well, you live and learn, don't you?'

'But, surely, Mr Dover' – Arthur Tompkins shook his head in bewilderment – 'a woman – well, not one who lives in Thornwich – a woman just wouldn't know the words, would she? Some of them were pretty strong, you know. I'd never seen one or two of them written down before myself.'

'Any your wife didn't understand?' asked Dover dryly. 'Of course there weren't! Same with every other woman in the village. They all look as though butter wouldn't melt in their mouths and

Lord knows where they pick it all up, but pick it up they do. Talk about fishwi es – you ought to hear what some of these well-born, posh young ladies can come out with when they've had a few. Filth? You wouldn't believe it!'

'But, we *know* all the women in Thornwich' wailed Mr Tompkins. 'The 're not like that!'

'They are, sonnie!' Dover was very patronizing. 'You can take my word for it. Besides, who says it's a Thornwich woman, anyhow?'

'Oh, there's no doubt about that, seemingly.' Charlie Chettle resumed the conversation after a short break for reordering. Dover's shrewd eye noted that Mr Tompkins was doing all the treating. Charlie Chettle had made a half-hearted offer at one point to stand his round but Mr Tompkins had said kindly that he'd never taken a drink from an old age pensioner in his life and he'd no intention of starting now. Dover, in a very relaxed and benign mood, thought this was a charming sentiment though not, as it happens, one to which he subscribed.

'No, there's no doubt about it,' said Charlie Chettle, letting Jack lick the froth off his beer. 'It's somebody local. The 're all sure about that. Who else could it be, anyhow?'

'He's quite right, Mr Dover, even the local police were certain it's a local man – woman. Most of the letters aren't what you might call decent, straightforward filth. The e's a good few sly cracks in them as well. Old things, scandal that's been kicked around in Thornwich for donkey's years. Nothing that anybody in the village wouldn't know all about, but I can't see how any stranger could have got hold of it. He – she – might have picked up a bit of gossip here and there, but they'd have taken years to collect all of it. Besides, apart from a few trippers in the summer, and the lorry drivers who pull up at Freda's, we don't have any strangers hanging around the place.'

'Hm,' said Dover, wrinkling his nose in a way he hoped indicated deep and productive thought. 'Where were the letters posted?'

'All in the village, as far as I know,' said Mr Tompkins promptly. 'We've got two boxes, one outside the post offic – well, it's a sub really – and one up at the top just beyond the vicarage. The old squire – that was Dame Alice's father-in-law, I expect you've heard about her – he had it installed, oh, fifty years or more ago. He said he didn't want his footman coming right down here to post the letters and then popping into The Jolly Sailor for a quick one. He was a character, the old squire was.'

'So's his daughter-in-law,' said Charlie Chettle sourly. 'Interfering old busybody! Told me I ought to be in a Home and then when me daughter come back to look after me she tried to get her to go up to the Lodge and do some charring for her. Blooming cheek! If she comes poking around in my affairs again shell get the rough edge of my tongue and no mistake about it. I don't know what she stays on in Thornwich for at all. It's a pity she doesn't clear off and land herself on some of her swanky friends and leave decent people alone.'

'Oh, come off it, Charlie! he's not as bad as all that.'

'Oh, isn't she? Well, I've heard you call her a name or two in your time, young Arthur. What about when she had the inspectors in that time she said you were giving short weight, eh?'

'Oh, that was just a stupid mistake,' said Mr Tompkins with an embarrassed sideways glance at Dover. 'I know she's inclined to be a bit bossy but she's not a bad trout in her way.'

'Thinks sh 's God Almighty,' muttered Charlie Chettle.

'Well, she got cracking on this poison-pen business, didn't she? She got the whole thing organized almost as soon as it started.'

'What are we talking about?' said Dover who had a nasty suspicion that he was beginning to lose track of the conversation. Mr Tompkins's generosity in the distribution of alcohol was rather overwhelming. No sooner had Dover's eyes focused with some difficult on an empty glass than it turned into a full one. As the evening progressed, these optical illusions were beginning to take their toll.

'Dame Alice Stote-Weedon,' explained Mr Tompkins, surprised at Dover's apparent ignorance. 'You know, the one who fi ed it up for you to be sent down here in the first place. She lives up at the top of the village in a house called Friday Lodge – it used to be part of the big estate, the one they're going to build on. She married the old squire's son. When he died she sort of carried on the family tradition – lady of the manor stuff – though she's only a Stote-Weedon by marriage. She's very interested in welfare work.'

'And telling everybody else how to live their lives,' added Charlie Chettle.

'Oh, her,' said Dover vaguely. 'Has she had some of these poison-pen letters, too?'

'Well, of course she has.' Mr Tompkins eyed Dover doubtfully. The chap didn't seem to know much about the case he had come to investigate. Oh well, it was early days yet. All this bleary-eyed, gaping-mouth business must just be part of the act. Underneath there must be a sharp old brain firing away on all cylinders and detecting like mad. 'Practically every woman in the village has had them, Mr Dover. My wife, Mrs Tompkins, got one of the first. She was very upset about it. I told her to chuck the damned thing in the fi e and forget all about it – only thing to do with muck like that. But, of course, being a woman, she wouldn't. She insisted on taking it to the police. I told her she was making a lot of fuss about nothing, but when she got to the station she found Dame Alice there reporting the same thing. Well, they started comparing letters, and obviously they'd both come from the same source, and Dame Alice began wondering if anybody else had had one. She called at every house in the village and found three or four more of the things. She told everybody what to do if they got one. They were to keep the envelope and take it straight round to the police station in Bearle – that's the nearest one to us. The inspector said she'd been a great help. Then we all had to have our fingerprints taken to see if they could find out who was sending the things. Oh, we had a proper field day in Thornwich, I can tell ou. Not that it did much good.'

'So I heard,' said Dover vaguely.

'They reckon whoever's writing them wears rubber gloves. The e isn't a single print on any of these letters – and there's more than sixty of them now, so I've heard – that can't be accounted for

27

by the people who've handled them. It's a fair old mystery and no mistake, and it's making a very nasty atmosphere in the village, too. You mark my words, Mr Dover, if this strain keeps up we're going to have real trouble on our hands.'

Dover twitched his nose and made a stout effo t to sit upright in his chair. 'Be a'right now I'm here,' he said with bleary confidence and reached out to give Mr Tompkins a friendly pat on the shoulder. He missed.

Charlie Chettle looked at the Chief Inspector with wry amusement, transferred his glance to Mr Tompkins and winked. Mr Tompkins shook his head in mild reproof and ordered one for the road.

'Wa'road?' demanded Dover, staring suspiciously round the bar. He didn't wait for an answer. 'You'll see,' – he addressed Mr Tompkins with touching solemnity – 'now I've arrived, she'll pack it in. They a'ways do.' He tapped the side of his nose with owlish sagacity. 'Never fear, Dover's here!'

'Shall we give you a hand with him upstairs, Bert?' – Charlie Chettle rose to his feet. 'If we don't get him moving now while he's still got a bit of strength in his pins, we'll never shift him. He'll be a fair weight, that one.'

Bert Quince came out from the warmth of his electric fi e and a short tactical conference was held. Eventually it penetrated Dover's befuddled brain that the party was breaking up and they were trying to get rid of him. He protested loudly and tearfully. The whippet started barking. Elsie Quince returned empty-handed and in a bad temper from her bingo session. MacGregor came rushing downstairs to see what all the row was about.

Eventually, by a combined effo t, Dover was hoisted to his feet and swept in a headlong rush to the foot of the stairs with sufficien impetus to carry him up the first three or four steps, after which it was a matter of heaving and pushing up to the top. A mortified acGregor put him on his bed.

By about three o'clock in the morning, however, Dover had made a partial recovery. He was somewhat surprised to find himself lying fully clothed on his bed with only an eiderdown tossed carelessly over him, but he wasn't one to be bothered by little things like that. Making noise enough to waken the dead, never mind the other occupants of The Jolly Sailor, he got up and slaked his raging thirst with the water from his fl wer-bespattered ewer. Then he ventured out to the little room at the end of the corridor and succeeded in breaking the piece of string. Cursing loudly he lumbered back to his room, undressed and collapsed thankfully on to his bed. Next door Sergeant MacGregor lay wide awake, fuming impotently.

Nobody was surprised when, on the following morning, Sunday, Dover indicated that he did not intend to rise early. MacGregor had to cart his breakfast tray up to him since Mrs Quince made it clear that she had no intention of obliging that far.

Dover didn't get up for lunch either, though he was much more lively when MacGregor made his second appearance with sustenance.

'Wath is ith?' he asked as he heaved himself up into a sitting position.

'Roast beef, sir,' said MacGregor, carefully stepping over the pile of clothes which lay where Dover had tossed them, on the floo .

'Oh,' said Dover. 'Well, in math cathe, you'd better fetch me my teeth.'

'Your teeth, sir?'

'Yeth, my teeth, you fool! The 're in that glath over there.'

MacGregor stared in blank disbelief at the Chief Inspector who was already reaching imperturbably for his plate of roast beef. Surely the old fool couldn't …? Oh, no – this was too much! This time he'd really have to put his foot down. But as MacGregor observed Dover's beady eye and toothless scowl, he went meekly over to the washstand and picked up a tumbler. The dentures – a full top and bottom set – gleamed triumphantly at him through the milky water. With eyes averted he carried the glass at arm's length back to the bed.

'For God'th thake!' lisped Dover in outraged disgust. 'Rinthe them out fi th!'

When at last Dover had munched his teeth into position, he waved a fork at MacGregor and gave the wilting young gentleman his orders.

'You push off now! You can bring my tea at four o'clock and I don't want to see your ugly mug before then. Got it?'

'Yes, sir,' said MacGregor faintly.

It may seem an unusual way to conduct a criminal investigation, but Chief Inspector Dover was a very unusual detective. He himself always claimed that he got most of his best ideas in bed, a fact which is not surprising considering how much time he spent there.

When he had had his afternoon tea he accepted one of MacGregor's cigarettes and graciously indicated that he was now prepared to discuss the problem of the poison-pen letters. He had abandoned the idea of explaining to MacGregor that he had been temporarily incapacitated by a bilious attack. He had a faint suspicion that he'd used that excuse before. Besides, even MacGregor wasn't such a fool as he looked. It would be better just to ignore the whole episode.

He dropped a lump of cigarette-ash down the front of his pyjamas. 'Well,' he said, 'how far have we got?'

MacGregor blinked. Sometimes it was a bit difficul to know what the old fool was rambling on about. 'Got, sir?' he asked stupidly.

'With the case, you idiot!' snarled Dover. 'You've gone through the file, ha en't you?'

'Oh, yes, sir,' said MacGregor hastily. 'Well, the local police don't seem to have achieved very much.'

'I know that, you blithering nit!' snapped Dover. 'We wouldn't be here if they'd solved the bloody case, would we?'

'No, sir,' said MacGregor.

'All right, you just give me a brief outline of how things stand at the moment.' Dover settled back on his pillows, closed his eyes and prepared – no doubt – to listen.

'Well, sir,' began MacGregor, rapidly marshalling his facts and translating them into language simple enough for a moronic child of two to understand, 'the anonymous letters started arriving just about a month ago. The 've been coming at irregular intervals ever since. We've now got a total of seventy-two. All the letters have been posted in the village, either at the post offic or in the box at the top of the hill. The e seems to be no pattern.' Dover opened one yellowish eye and looked at MacGregor. MacGregor hastened to explain. 'What I mean is, sir, that if the writer had posted the letters in – say – the post offic on Wednesdays and in the other box on – say – Fridays, it might have given us some sort of a clue as to his movements.'

Dover rolled his eyes towards the ceiling. ''Strewth!' he murmured.

MacGregor took a deep, temper-controlling breath and went on. 'Almost every woman in the village has received a letter – some of them have had a comparatively large number. All the letters are couched in obscene language but contain no spelling or grammatical mistakes. I think that may be not without significance, si .'

Dover didn't bother to open his eyes this time. 'Humph,' he said.

'All the letters were typewritten, sir, on Terdy Bond writing paper, white, post quarto size – that's nine inches by seven, sir, and you can buy it in every stationer's shop in the country. They even sell it in the supermarkets.'

Dover grunted.

'The 've identified the make of typewriter, sir. It's a Pantiles Portable with a ten-point long primer type. These machines were produced three or four years after the end of the war and sold like hot cakes. The e must be thousands kicking around and you can buy them in practically any typewriter shop for about £15 second-hand. The villagers co-operated well with the local police – thanks mainly to this Dame Alice woman from what I can gather – and a house-to-house search was carried out. The e was no sign of the typewriter, though a number of people use the Tendy Bond writing paper – which is only what you'd expect.'

'Humph,' said Dover again, just to show that he was still awake.

'Whoever is typing the letters, sir, is – according to the experts – an efficien two-finger typist. Not a professional touch-typist, but somebody who's done a fair amount of typing in his time. Neat and fairly quick.'

'Very interesting,' mumbled Dover. 'Anything else?'

'No, I don't think so, sir. The writer is being extremely canny about not leaving fingerprints and obviously he's somebody well up in all the local scandal. It looks very much as though it must be somebody actually in the village.'

'Yes,' said Dover and yawned. 'Shouldn't be too difficul to find. It's a woman, of course.'

'I suppose so, sir.'

'No supposing about it!' retorted Dover crossly. 'Typical woman's crime. Always has been. Everybody knows that. Now then, which of these women have had the most letters?'

'Well, up to the present, sir,' – MacGregor hunted amongst his papers and produced a list – 'there are four women who've received more than fifteen each: Mrs Tompkins, Dame Alice Stote-Weedon, Miss Poppy Gullimore and Mrs Crotty – she's the vicar's wife.'

'It'll be one of them.'

MacGregor looked anxiously at his recumbent superior offic . God knows, he ought to be used to the old idiot going off half-cock and jumping to conclusions, but this was going a bit too far, even for Dover. He hadn't read a single one of the poison-pen letters nor even opened the local police file on the case, but he had already narrowed down his list of suspects to one of four women.

Some of MacGregor's astonishment and outraged professional feeling must have communicated itself to Dover. The Chief Inspector opened his eyes, sat up and actually showed signs of getting out of bed.

'These cases are all the same,' he explained offhandedl . 'Some blasted woman goes off her nut and starts writing dirty letters. Form of exhibitionism, really. Naturally – chuck my trousers over, there's a good lad – naturally she writes a good few to herself to avoid suspicion.'

'But would she write so many to herself, sir? I mean, what's the point?'

'Circulation,' said Dover with a grunt as he pulled his stomach in and struggled to fasten the top button of his trousers. 'She wants as many people as possible to read her literary effo ts. Naturally, she doesn't burn *her* letters. No, she carts 'em straight round to the police like an upright and conscientious citizen and has a fine old time watching some sweating young copper plough his way through the muck she's written. Nine times out of ten she even goes so far as to persuade her friends to take their letters to the cops as well. The more people who read 'em, the merrier. 'It's always the same.'

'Yes, sir,' said MacGregor with a marked lack of enthusiasm.

'It's all a question of psychology,' Dover pointed out kindly, in an effo t to blind MacGregor with science. 'You've got to analyse the motives of the criminal and put yourself in his shoes and see what he'd do.'

'Yes, sir,' said MacGregor who hadn't much sense of humour left where Dover was concerned.

'Well, tomorrow morning, we'll start off and have a look at these women. An exploratory interview, you might call it – shove my boots over, laddie – we'll cast our eyes over the field '

MacGregor nodded. What else could he do?

'Of course,' Dover went on, red in the face from the effo t of tying his laces, and anxious not to have any misunderstandings, 'I don't want you to think we're going to clear this up in a couple of shakes of a lamb's tail. No, I reckon we shall have to go very carefully. Softee, softee, catchee monkey,' he added, somewhat to MacGregor's surprise. 'No, this is going to be a long job. It'll probably take us' – a sideways glance at MacGregor – 'several weeks.'

MacGregor nodded again. He understood all right. The departure of Dover's sister-in-law would no doubt coincide with the solution of Thornwic 's poison-pen case if Dover had anything to do with it. And, thought MacGregor with a shudder, Dover, as the senior office in charge of the case, was going to have a great deal to do with it.

'Is there anything else, sir?' he asked, gathering up the file which Dover had contemptuously pushed to one side.

'Just one question, laddie,' chuckled Dover in spanking good humour. 'Are they open yet?'

Chapter Three

Late on Monday morning, Dover set out to make a show, at least, of doing some work. The day was cold and wet and the bitter east wind blowing straight off the moors cut through their clothing as Dover and MacGregor stood and shivered by the bus stop. They were waiting for the 10.28 bus to take them into Bearle. It was 10.45. Normally Dover would have abandoned the whole idea and retreated back into the relative warmth and comfort of The Jolly Sailor, but things were not normal. The e was Dame Alice.

She had telephoned The Jolly Sailor on Sunday evening in a state of some annoyance and pained surprise. She had expected, she informed MacGregor at length, that Chief Inspector Dover would have called ere now at Friday Lodge and presented his compliments. MacGregor, with stout loyalty, told her that the Chief Inspector had been fully occupied with his preliminary studies of the case. Dame Alice retorted that she was glad to hear it. Obviously the intelligence she had received – to wit, that the Chief Inspector had spent the entire day in bed – was erroneous. She couldn't she said in a sour aside, understand why Mrs Quince should lie, but there it was. MacGregor cleared his throat and prepared to tangle the web a bit more, but he was saved the trouble. Dame Alice announced that she would like to see the Chief Inspector up at Friday Lodge as soon as possible. Tonight? MacGregor asked her to hold on while he consulted the Chief

Inspector who, unfortunately, was not able for unspecified reasons to come to the phone himself.

Dame Alice held on with grim determination and tried to interpret the howl which came dimly along the wires.

MacGregor was sorry but tonight was quite impossible. Tomorrow morning? If Dame Alice would just hold the line for a minute.

Long mutterings this time as Dover and MacGregor worked out a new set of excuses.

MacGregor was extremely sorry but tomorrow morning the Chief Inspector was going to Bearle.

'Bearle?' repeated Dame Alice in tones of frank disbelief.

'Yes, Bearle,' said MacGregor miserably. 'He's going to interview Miss Poppy Gullimore. She teaches at a school in Bearle so we understand.'

'But why not wait till she comes home at night and interview her then?' demanded Dame Alice reasonably. 'She's back by fi e o'clock.'

'I'm afraid that wouldn't quite fit in with Chief Inspector Dover's plans,' explained MacGregor.

'Well, what time are you going to be back in Thornwich?'

MacGregor couldn't say.

Dame Alice breathed heavy dissatisfaction down the telephone. MacGregor couldn't blame her. He listened sympathetically while she enumerated her pressing obligations and appointments for the next week. Yes he could quite see that Dame Alice was a very busy woman. Perhaps it would be better if Chief Inspector Dover rang *her*. MacGregor knew he was most anxious to see her. Dame Alice indicated that she didn't think this was a very good idea. She would be sorry to think that the Chief Inspector was trying to avoid her.

It was ten minutes before MacGregor was able to rejoin Dover in the public bar.

'She's going to ring you again tomorrow night, sir,' he told Dover.

Dover was not pleased. He said so loudly. Mr Quince listened sympathetically as he polished the glasses.

'Well,' concluded Dover, 'when she does ring, you can damned well tell her to take a running jump at herself. I'll see her when I'm good and ready, and not before. She may have the Chief Constable and the Assistant Commissioner in her pocket, but she hasn't got me, and the sooner she realizes it the better. You can tell her that when you answer the phone. Now, you're in the chair, laddie. Mine's a pint.'

They had spent a quiet evening. Mr Tompkins, Dover's new-found and generous friend, did not turn up. Charlie Chettle, who stood alternate rounds with MacGregor, explained why.

'It's his missus,' he said, sharing a packet of potato crisps with his dog. 'She doesn't like him having a drink at the best of times, but Sunday evenings she really puts her foot down, doesn't she, Bert?'

Bert Quince nodded agreement and turned away to serve a couple of lorry drivers who'd come in to break their journey.

'You don't have to look far to see who wears the trousers in that household,' Charlie Chettle went on, giving Dover a broad wink. 'Hen-pecked, that's what Arthur Tompkins is.'

'More fool him,' observed Dover who prided himself on not having any nonsense like that in his house.

'Ah, but you don't know Winifred! She was a right bossy little madam when she was nothing but a nipper and she's not changed much. Of course, her health's not good,' – Charlie Chettle grinned slyly at Dover – 'being crossed upsets her. She's led Arthur Tompkins a fair old dance in her time, I can tell you. Every time she doesn't get her own way she has a heart attack or something. Mind you, Arthur's a right old mutton-head or he'd have packed it in years ago, especially when he got the money.'

Dover obliged. After all, the dreary old codger had bought him a drink. 'What money?' he asked.

Charlie Chettle's grin widened and he leaned forward, his watery old eyes sparkling. 'Do you mean you don't know? He won the pools, Arthur did, about fi e years ago.' Charlie Chettle lowered his voice and spoke with suitable awe. 'One hundred and seventy thousand quid!'

'One hundred and seventy thousand quid!' yelped Dover. 'And he still lives in a dump like this? He must be barmy!'

'Oh, Arthur'd be off to the Riviera if he got half a chance,' said Charlie Chettle. 'It's Winifred as won't budge. She was born and bred here, you see. When they got the money she made Arthur buy that grocer's shop and, as far as she's concerned, they'll stay here for the rest of their lives. One hundred and seventy thousand quid! 'Swelp me!' He shook his head in honest, if senile, bewilderment. 'Crikey, if I had half that, you wouldn't see me for dust! I'd be off to the bright lights and the pretty girls and blue the blinking lot!'

'Me, too,' said Dover with a deep sigh.

MacGregor was quite disgusted. A couple of revolting, dirty old men, that's what they were. Bright lights and pretty girls at their age, it was enough to make you throw up. A pair of slippers and the telly, that's what they ought to be dreaming about. 'Perhaps the Tompkinses have children,' he suggested severely. 'Maybe they're saving the money for them instead of squandering it.' MacGregor didn't approve of idle gossip and had quite made up his mind not to join in the conversation, but occasionally one set of principles had to be permitted to overcome another.

Charlie Chettle shook his head. 'No, no kids. She can't have any. Not, if you ask me that she's tried very hard. Or' – he sniggered into his tankard and winked yet again at Dover – 'allowed Arthur to, which is more to the point, eh? I did hear as how they were thinking of adopting one but they seemed to have dropped the idea. Arthur wasn't keen, not that what he thinks cuts much ice with her.'

As he stood waiting for the bus to Bearle, Dover pondered enviously over Arthur Tompkins and his hundred and seventy thousand pounds. Some people have all the luck! The Tompkins's shop was right opposite the bus stop and The Jolly Sailor. Dover stared moodily at it as the heavy lorries thundered past. It was a dingy place with a window full of faded cardboard boxes and piles of dusty tins. They couldn't be making their fortunes with a shop like that. But then, as he reminded himself gloomily, they didn't have to. The 'd already made it. A hundred and seventy thousand pounds! 'Strewth!

'The bus is coming, sir.' MacGregor's voice broke into Dover's esoteric dreams and he returned to the world of public transport, Dame Alice Stote-Weedon and poison-pen letters. With a scowl he climbed aboard.

The headmaster of the Violet Stote-Weedon County (Mixed) Secondary Modern School was surprised to find a couple of stalwart detectives from Scotland Yard invading his offic and demanding to interview a member of his staff

'Miss Gullimore?' he asked, distractedly tugging down a brown, hand-knitted pullover in a vain attempt to get it to make contact with the top of his trousers. 'What on earth has she been doing now? If she's been sitting down again, she'll have to go. I've warned her. The School Governors just won't stand for it – and neither will the Office I don't care how good a cause it is, having members of the staff arrested and flung into jail is bad for the school's reputation.'

Dover sat down uninvited in what looked like (but wasn't) a comfortable armchair, and let MacGregor get on with the explanations. The headmaster was even more horrified to find that Miss Gullimore was wanted by the police for something else besides sitting down.

'Poison-pen letters? You don't mean to tell me she's been writing poison-pen letters?'

'No, sir,' said MacGregor patiently. 'We just want her to help us in our inquiries, that's all.'

The headmaster clutched his head. 'You just want her to help you with your inquiries? Tha 's what you always say, isn't it? And the next minute they're being marched off in handcuffs. Now, look, Chief Inspector, I must ask you to be discreet, circumspect, even prudent. Miss Gullimore is not exactly popular with the children, but then neither are the police. If they're given the choice, I think they'll be on her side rather than yours. And don't make the mistake of underestimating them. Some of my senior boys are hefty, tough young thugs, though if it comes to the crunch, it's the girls I'd look out for, if I were you.'

'Really, sir,' said MacGregor, smiling indulgently, 'I do assure you, there's not going to be anything like that at all.'

'Oh, isn't there?' The headmaster looked offended. 'Well, permit me, Sergeant, to point out that I do happen to know what I'm talking about. I've not been headmaster here for twenty years for nothing. And if you think Miss Gullimore is going to go quietly, you've got another think coming. She's a militant, you know. Civil disobedience is right up her street.'

In the end MacGregor found it simpler to assure the headmaster that, if it proved necessary to drag Miss Gullimore bodily from the school, the manúuvre would be performed either when the childen were devouring their dinners or after they had repaired to their classrooms for afternoon school.

The headmaster, still not entirely satisfied, went off to find Miss Gullimore.

Dover shook his head. ''Strewth, anybody'd think we were the ruddy Gestapo, wouldn't they?'

When Miss Gullimore arrived she proved a bit of a shock. She looked about sixteen, though MacGregor, who took an interest in these things, worked it out that she must be at least six or seven years older. Whatever her age, she made a striking impression. She had a thin, sallow face liberally bedaubed with what looked like the entire cosmetics stock of a large shop: lipstick, rouge, dead-white face powder, eye shadow, eyebrow pencil, false eyelashes and several other bits and pieces which mere men like Dover and MacGregor failed to identify. This action-painter's palette effect was draped with lank, shoulder-length, jet black hair, chewed rather than cut into an elongated page-boy style. Pale blue eyes, made interesting by the faintest squint, flicked with interest from MacGregor to Dover, and then rapidly back to MacGregor again.

Miss Gullimore's bosom, decorated not with one but with two CND badges, provocatively placed, heaved seductively.

'Won't you sit down, Miss Gullimore?' said Dover who had moved into the headmaster's chair behind the desk.

Even the Chief Inspector felt a twinge of anxiety as she accepted his invitation. The tight, imitation leopard-skin skirt creaked as it took the strain, but it held fast. It rose alarmingly over Miss Gullimore's knees and revealed her red-nylon-sheathed legs. MacGregor began to lose interest. Miss Gullimore's legs were fat.

Dover had lost interest long ago – and not only in Miss Gullimore. He sighed deeply, helped himself to a cigarette from the box on the desk and started asking Miss Gullimore some pretty pointless questions.

Miss Gullimore, far from being antagonistic to the forces of law and order, almost fell over herself in her eagerness to answer.

Yes, she had received sixteen of these terrible letters and they'd upset her absolutely awfully, though, of course, she wasn't exactly an innocent little virgin, having spent her last three summer holidays hitch-hiking on the Continent. Actually, out of school, she went around with a pretty advanced crowd – they were all way-out, you know. Poets and artists and things like that. Satirists, too. She just daren't tell a policeman some of the things they got up to, she really daren't!

'In Thornwich?' asked   over with weary scepticism:

'Holy cats, no!' squeaked Miss Gullimore, flinging up her hands in mock horror. 'Thornwich is embalmed, mummified. The e's no life there, not what I call life. No,' – she tried a come-hither glance in MacGregor's direction and hitched up her skirt another couple of inches or so – 'I'm talking about London. I often go down for the weekend.'

Dover sighed. Cripes! The people you had to mix with in his profession. It shouldn't happen to a dog.

'How long have you lived in Thornwich, miss?'

'Well, I've *existed* there for about two years. I'm in digs with Mrs Leatherbarrow. It's cheaper than Bearle and not quite so provincial, if you see what I mean. Besides, Mrs Leatherbarrow doesn't interfere. She lets me paint and play records and – well – generally express myself. I think that's vital, don't you? I mean, I've got Bach at the moment and I just have to play him all day long.'

'Quite,' said Dover.

'Of course, Mrs Leatherbarrow is frightfully understanding for a landlady.'

'She must be,' said Dover.

'When I had puppets she used to help me with the clothes – just the sewing, of course. I did all the designs, naturally. Mind you, she's a terrible old gossip.' Miss Gullimore ran her tongue thoughtfully along her top lip. 'She knows absolutely everything that goes on in that village. I did wonder if she was maybe writing those letters. The ones I got were absolutely potty, of course, but – well – some of the details were bang on.'

'Really?' said Dover.

Miss Gullimore shrugged her shoulders extravagantly and crossed her legs. The e was another quick glance at MacGregor to see if he was registering anything. He wasn't. 'Of course, whatever you can say about Mrs Leatherbarrow, she's not *sick*,' said Miss Gullimore fairly. 'And, I mean, whoever's writing these letters must be sick, mustn't they? Sexually repressed, I should think,' said Miss Gullimore, offering her contribution with great nonchalance. After all, she had had to read several books on psychology to get her diploma in education. 'Tha 's why the letters to me were so bitchy. Sheer green jealousy! If you catch her, will there be a trial? Will you want me to give evidence?'

Miss Gullimore's eyes snapped with excitement and Dover regarded her sourly.

'We may be able to spare you that ordeal, miss,' he said drily.

'Oh, I don't mind,' said Miss Gullimore, tossing a couple of yards of dank hair over her shoulder. 'It'd be quite exciting, really.'

Dover scowled at her. 'You ever done any typing, miss?'

Far from being offended at the implication, Poppy Gullimore appeared to be delighted. She could, she revealed coyly, actually type quite well. At one stage in her short career she had seriously considered taking up secretarial work but had changed her mind with shrewd appreciation that teaching offe ed shorter hours, longer holidays and less competition. 'Besides,' she added candidly, 'I couldn't stick the shorthand business. Terribly drab! I'd have probably had to go on living at home, too, and that would have been the end! My stepfather keeps trying to seduce me and I'm terrified my mother will find out. Tha 's why I never go home.'

'Very wise, miss,' said Dover placidly and reached for his bowler hat. 'Come on, MacGregor!'

'Is that *all*?' asked Miss Gullimore, highly disconsolate at losing her audience.

'For the moment, miss,' said Dover. 'We may want to see you later on. I suppose,' he gazed at her thoughtfully, 'I suppose you've no pet theories of your own as to who's writing these letters?'

'How about Dame Alice?' suggested the girl sulkily. 'She's always had a down on me. I suppose it's because I'm young and I won't kowtow to her like the rest of them do. She's one of the governors of this school, and about once a term she invites me to dinner at Friday Lodge to pump me about what goes on here.'

'And do you tell her anything?' asked Dover.

'Well, of course I do!' Miss Gullimore looked surprised. 'It's every man for himself, isn't it? The 'd tell tales about me if they got half a chance, so why shouldn't I do the same about them?'

'That was a funny girl,' said Dover some three hours later when he and MacGregor were trundling along in the bus back to Thornwich

'Very odd, sir,' agreed MacGregor, glad to see that they were once more on speaking terms. Buses ran very infrequently between Bearle and Thornwich and the long wait, hanging around an exceedingly dull little town after the pubs had closed, had placed a severe strain on Dover's good humour, never a very hardy plant at the best of times.

'They must be damned short of teachers to employ her,' observed Dover, watching the mist settling down on the moors. He sniffed. 'I should think a young lady like her would get very bored up here, wouldn't you?'

'I should think so, sir,' said MacGregor.

'The poison-pen writer could be bored,' said Dover ponderously. 'Might be somebody who wants to stir the old fuddy duddies up and have a good giggle.'

'Would she know enough about Thornwic 's scandals though, sir?' asked MacGregor doubtfully.

'The landlady might have told her. It's amazing how much gossip you can pick up, just casually like, if you put your mind to it.'

'Miss Gullimore is a touch-typist, sir,' MacGregor pointed out. 'Those letter ere typed by somebody who only uses two fingers '

'She's probably bright enough to know we can check that sort of thing,' said Dover gloomily, 'and changed her style accordingly.' He yawned. 'I wonder if that school's got any typewriters.'

'Oh, it's bound to have, sir,' said MacGregor, rather impressed as he saw the line that Dover's reflections were taking. 'The school secretary definitely had one, but it wasn't a portable. But I believe these schools sometimes teach the girls commercial subjects. They probably have typewriters for that.'

'I don't suppose anybody's bothered to check, have they?' said Dover, yawning again.

'No, sir.' MacGregor was getting very alert and efficient They were really getting somewhere now. It wasn't often the Chief Inspector had any bright ideas. It made them all the more welcome when he did.

'Well, in that case,' said Dover, happy to be able to drop it right in Smart-Alec MacGregor's lap, 'you'd better get cracking and do it yourself, hadn't you? Check all the typewriters in that school and find out if any members of the staff own typewriters. It's just possible that our Miss Gullimore borrowed a typewriter from one of her colleagues. She may even have written those letters in the school itself. It'd be a damned sight safer than doing it in her lodgings. This landlady woman might have heard her or seen her. You know what nosy old devils most of 'em are.'

'Yes, sir,' said MacGregor. 'I'll get on to it first thing in the morning.'

'You'll get on to it tonight, laddie,' said Dover heavily. 'You can catch the next bus back into Bearle.'

'But it's nearly four o'clock now, sir,' protested MacGregor, his spirits understandably flagging at the thought of yet another tedious, chilly bus ride. 'The school'll be closed by the time I get back and ...'

'The e'll be a caretaker, laddie,' said Dover unsympathetically. Unfortunately for MacGregor there was a bus due in the return direction just ten minutes after he and Dover were deposited at The olly Sailor.

'Hardly worth your bothering to come in,' said Dover. 'I'll tell 'em to keep your dinner for you if you're back late.' He walked happily into the pub and left MacGregor shivering at the bus stop.

Mrs Quince provided a substantial afternoon tea and Dover consumed it in solitary state, congratulating himself with every mouthful – not, of course, on having solved the identity of Thornwic 's poison-pen writer, but on having got young MacGregor out of his hair and from under his feet for a few hours. Dover didn't think for one minute that Poppy Gullimore was the woman he was after, but she and the school typewriters were as good an excuse as any for achieving a bit of peace and quiet. As a matter of fact Dover had already selected his candidate for the anonymous letter stakes, but it was far too early yet to start solving the case. His sister-in-law never visited for less than a week and could be relied on to stay longer given half a chance. The unmasking of the scourge of Thornwich was going to be a very delicate matter of timing, not too soon and not too late. The trouble with MacGregor was that he always wanted to rush things. Usually Dover did, too, but on this occasion he was in no hurry. The Jolly Sailor might not exactly be the Ritz, but at the moment it was a damned sight better than Dover's semi-detached in Benbow Close.

Dover finished off his last cup of tea and ambled out into the kitchen to find Mrs   uince.

'I'll have my dinner at half-past seven,' he informed her. 'Sergeant MacGregor probably won't be back by then so you can shove his in the oven and he can get it when he comes in.'

'It'll be all dried up,' said Mrs Quince.

'Well, that'll be his funeral,' said Dover who couldn't have cared less if it had been shrivelled to a cinder. 'I'm going up to my room now, just to have a quiet think, and sort the case out in my mind.' He looked Mrs Quince straight in the eye as he said this. Mrs Quince nodded sceptically. 'And I don't want to be disturbed on any account until dinner-time.'

'What about Dame Alice?' asked Mrs Quince. 'She's likely to phone, isn't she?'

'Dame Alice can …' Dover put the brakes on in time. The e was no point in getting Dame Alice's back up more than he had to. Things might not work out the way he was hoping and Dame Alice had a bit too much influence in certain quarters for Dover's peace of mind. Better to be diplomatic at this stage. 'You'd better tell Dame Alice I'm engaged.'

'She'll not believe me,' said Mrs Quince unhelpfully.

'Well, tell her I'm out!' snapped Dover, beginning to find Mrs Quince somewhat obstructive in her attitude.

'That' said Mrs Quince flatl , 'would be a lie.'

'Look,' – Dover was turning nasty – 'I don't care how you do it but, if I'm disturbed before half-past seven, there'll be trouble. I should have thought that somebody in your position would have been only too pleased to keep on the right side of the police. Considering some of the things I've seen in this establishment,' he added meaningly.

'Dame Alice is on the Licensing Committee,' said Mrs Quince. 'I can't affo d to put her back up.'

'You can't affo d to put my back up either!' stormed Dover. 'Just tell the old faggot I'm out.'

Mrs Quince shrugged her shoulders and said unconvincingly that she would do her best. Dover snorted and went upstairs to his own room. Within fi e minutes he was giving his subconscious full rein to solve the problem of who was writing Thornwic 's-poison-pen letters.

Just after seven o'clock, his meditations were rudely interrupted by a violent hammering on his door. Only half awake he groped for the bedside light as the eiderdown slid to the floo .

'What is it?' he bawled. Then he remembered there was no bedside light in this cyclist's haven of rest. He clambered out of bed to get to the switch by the door. Mrs Quince beat him to it.

Dover charged back to the bed for his eiderdown.

'You shouldn't come barging into people's rooms without knocking,' he protested, draping the eiderdown modestly over his long underpants.

'I did knock,' retorted Mrs Quince.

'If it's Dame Alice I'm not in. I told you that before.'

'It's not Dame Alice,' said Mrs Quince with a certain amount of malicious satisfaction. 'It's Poppy Gullimore, the young schoolteacher girl. She's just killed herself!'

Chapter Four

The next fifteen minutes passed quickly as Dover behaved as he usually did when confronted with any kind of crisis. His firs reaction was one of blinding fury at the inconsiderateness of fate and other people. His second was to shout for MacGregor. On this occasion the thwarting of the second reaction merely added fuel to the first, and Dover vented his surging ill-temper on Mrs Quince.

Mrs Quince retreated to the other side of the bedroom door while Dover dragged on those articles of his clothing which he had removed to assist his meditative powers.

'How do you know she's croaked herself?' yelled Dover.

'Miss Tilley rang me!' shouted Mrs Quince.

'And who the hell's Miss Tilley?'

'She runs the sub post offic '

'Well, what the devil's it got to do with her?'

'She heard them phoning for the ambulance.'

'Who was phoning for the ambulance?'

'I don't know,' said Mrs Quince crossly, 'but whoever it was she heard them. She always listens in to the telephone calls. It's the only excitement she gets, poor thing, what with her mother and everything.'

Dover emerged from his room, his bowler hat crowning a black and scowling face. 'Where is it?' he roared.

'Where's what?' asked Mrs Quince, very sensibly retreating as Dover advanced.

'The house!

'What house?' Mrs Quince had now been forced into descending the stairs backwards. It was awkward, but preferable to taking her eyes off the menacing fig e of Dover.

'The house where this blasted girl's killed herself!' screamed Dover.

'It's half-way up the hill on the other side of the road. Mrs Leatherbarrow's place. The 've got gardens at the front. Hers is one from the top just before you get to the Parish Rooms.'

'Hasn't it got a confounded number?'

'I think it's called "The Ferns",' said Mrs Quince, making a sudden dash for her kitchen and locking the door behind her.

Dover set off up the hill in pouring rain. Thornwich appeared to possess only two street lamps, neither of which was any help at all. Every now and again a lorry went swishing past, spraying passers-by with water and dazzling them with its headlights. Dover wasn't much of a one for physical exercise and by the time he'd groped and fumbled his way to 'The Ferns' he fervently hoped that Miss Gullimore was being made to suffer for it all, wherever she was.

The front door of 'The Ferns' stood open. Dover, panting with temper and his exertions, staggered up the crippling flight of steps and entered the narrow hall. He leaned against a mahogany hall-stand while he got his breath back.

Somebody was coming slowly down the stairs. Dover gulped air into his deprived lungs and raised his head. Gradually the figu e came into view. First a pair of carefully moving feet in brown carpet slippers, then a pair of shaky legs. The final vision was of a very old gentleman with a tartan travelling rug wrapped round his shoulders. He gave a nervous little start when he caught sight of Dover.

'All right!' said Dover in a tone that indicated he wasn't going to stand any nonsense from anybody. 'Where's the body?'

The old man regarded him doubtfully and then gingerly negotiated the last two stairs to reach the hall.

'The 've taken her away,' he said in a thin, wavering voice. 'Only a couple of minutes ago,' he added helpfully. 'You've only just missed her.'

Dover took a deep, deep breath.

'I'm Dr Hawnt,' said the old man, pulling his rug tighter round his shoulders. 'They sent for me. As usual. I keep telling them but you might as well talk to a brick wall. They don't take any notice.'

'Why did you move the body?' demanded Dover in a roar that bounced menacingly off the walls and nearly blasted Dr Hawnt back to the foot of the stairs.

'I'm eighty-four,' said Dr Hawnt, 'and don't tell me I don't look it. I do, every day of it and more. Do you realize' – he peered at Dover through his glasses – 'I qualified as a doctor in 1904? And I can assure you without fear of contradiction I've hardly opened a textbook since.' He paused and frowned. 'What body?'

'Miss Gullimore's, you old fool!' rasped Dover, who didn't have much patience for the elderly and decrepit.

'Oh, yes, that's her name, isn't it? Oh, I sent her off to hospital. I may not be much of a doctor but I flatter myself I've got some sense of responsibility. It's what I always do. They keep calling me in and I keep coming and the first thing I say is "Send for the ambulance!" Well,' he appealed to Dover, 'what would you do?' He came nearer to Dover and clutched at him. 'Suppose you were lying out in a field with a broken leg and they brought me along, would you so much as let me touch you? Because, by all that's holy, I wouldn't! Look at these hands!' He held up a pair of nobbled claws in front of Dover's nose. 'See that tremble? How'd you like an emergency appendix operation done with a pair of wobblers like that? And on a kitchen table with no anaesthetic. Makes the blood run cold, doesn't it, just to think about it?' He paused for breath but, before Dover could get a word in edgeways, old Dr Hawnt was off again. ' he's not dead, you know.'

'Who isn't?' Dover had taken about as much as he could stand.

Dr Hawnt jerked his head in the direction of the stairs. 'Her. The one upstairs. You know. She's not dead.' He scratched his head. 'At least, I don't think she is. Tha 's why I sent for the ambulance. My eyesight isn't what it used to be. Don't hear so well, either. I'm cracking up, you know. Senile, that's what I am. They ought to put me in a Home, that's what they ought to do.' He sat down suddenly on the chair next to the mahogany hall-stand.

Dover shook himself, stalked down the hall and slammed the front door shut. Then he came back and plonked himself squarely in front of Dr Hawnt. The old ma 's eyes were closed.

Dover spoke loudly. 'I am a police offic .'

Dr Hawnt's eyes crawled open. 'Oh yes,' he said politely. 'How very interesting.'

'I want to know,' enunciated Dover through clenched teeth, 'what the hell's going on here.'

'Well, nothing, really,' said Dr Hawnt, taking a pill box out of his pocket and dosing himself thoughtfully. 'Mrs What's-her-name who lives here came in and found Miss What's-her-name unconscious on the floor of her room. Naturally she came rushing round to me. They always do. One of these days' – he cocked a rheumy eye at Dover – 'I'll be had up for murder. Of course, they'll cover it up by calling it professional incompetence and strike me off, but if I ve killed somebody, I've killed somebody – haven't I?'

'Miss Gullimore!' shouted Dover.

'Eh? Oh, that's her name, is it? The memory's going, too. I'll be forgetting my own name one of these days.'

'What had she done?' screamed Dover.

'Who?'

'Miss Gullimore!'

'Oh, yes. Well, when I got here she was unconscious. In a coma, we call it – at least, I think we do. The e was a bottle of aspirins on the rug beside her. Oh, and there was a glass as well.'

'She'd taken an overdose of aspirins?' Dover tried a short cut.

'How should I know?' Dr Hawnt blinked reproachfully at Dover. 'Your guess is as good as mine. Better, probably. It looked to me as though that's what happened but I'm not one to force my opinions down anybody else's throat. Silly girl! She was a school-teacher, wasn't she? You'd have thought she'd have known better. Aspirins! Good heavens, even I know you can't commit suicide with aspirins. Well,' – he glared belligerently at Dover who hadn't said a word – 'have you ever heard of anybody really killing themselves with aspirins? No, I thought not. And why not? Because it can't be done, that's why not.'

'Oh?' said Dover.

'I can't remember who it was who told me,' mused Dr Hawnt, 'but he was a very good chap, a fine specialist in his line, whatever it was. I did think he'd offer me a partnership at one time, but he said he'd got his patients to consider. I could quite see his point, mind you. I was never much good, even in my prime. The e was something about me, don't you know, that seemed to frighten people who probably weren't feeling too chirpy in the first place '

'The aspirins!' bellowed Dover, nobly restraining a powerful desire to grab Dr Hawnt by his tartan rug and shake him till he rattled.

'Eh? Oh, yes. Well, you've got to take a terrific number of 'em before they get anywhere near killing you. I forget how many exactly but let's say a couple of hundred for the sake of argument. Now, apart from the fact that you'd be gagging long before you got a quarter of that lot down your gullet, you'd be unconscious, too, wouldn't you? You'd pass out before you'd time to finish 'em '

'Are you sure of this?' asked Dover.

'Of course I'm sure,' said Dr Hawnt, somewhat offended. 'Well, something like that, anyhow. Typical of the younger generation. No sticking powers. Slip-shod. If a job's worth doing, it's worth doing properly, that's what I always say. Anyhow,' he added with a sudden spitefulness, 'that Miss What's-her-name's not succeeded in taking the easy way out. She'll be as right as rain in the morning if I'm any judge. Which I'm not, but the ambulance-man said the same thing and they all have certificates for first-aid, don't you know. I sometimes wish I did. Oh, yes, she'll have to answer for all the trouble she's caused, she will! And I don't just mean getting me away from a warm fi e on a night like this. I suppose they told you about the letter she left?'

Dover shook his head wearily.

'Oh,' said Dr Hawnt, 'they ought to have told you about that. Yes, they certainly ought to have told you about that.'

'What did the letter say?' asked Dover automatically. He'd long got past the stage of caring.

'She's the one who's been writing all these sexy letters, you know,' said Dr Hawnt, smacking his dry lips. 'It was a long letter addressed to the coroner but it wasn't stuck down so I had a look at it. I thought it might help me with my diagnosis,' he added primly.

'She confessed to writing the anonymous letters?' said Dover, feeling that things were getting too much for him.

Dr Hawnt pulled his pocket watch out. 'Dear me, I've wasted enough time here. I'll be toddling along now. Good night to you, my dear fellow, and do try to stop 'em calling me in. The e's a perfectly good doctor over at Bearle.' Dr Hawnt got to his feet with some difficul . He looked round vacantly. 'Now, which way's the front door, eh?'

Dover pushed his bowler hat to the back of his head and watched Dr Hawnt let himself out of the house. They ought to shoot 'em when they get like that, he thought to himself, it'd be a kindness really.

He went upstairs and located Miss Gullimore's room. It was not too difficul a feat for a trained and experienced detective because only one door had her name on it. Inside he found a fat, comfortable-looking woman seated on the edge of the bed. She was just finishing off the last page of what could only be Poppy Gullimore's suicide note.

'Well,' she said as Dover poked his head round the door, 'you took your time about getting here, I must say! I was going to phone you half an hour ago, but Miss Tilley said Mrs Quince told

Dame Alice you'd already left. What happened? Couldn't you find the house?'

'I've been talking to Dr Hawnt downstairs!' snapped Dover. 'And, if that's the note she left, you can hand it over! You've no right to be reading it, anyhow.'

'Don't you speak to me like that!' said Mrs Leatherbarrow. 'If I haven't got the right to read her last words, I don't know who has. I've been like a mother to that girl. Two pounds ten a week inclusive, a front-door key and keep her own room tidy.'

'Do you call this tidy?' scoffed Dover, looking with distaste at the litter in which Miss Gullimore had wallowed. The e were at least half a dozen table lamps made out of old chianti bottles, interspersed with misshapen woolly toys and the leftovers of innumerable hobbies. Miss Gullimore had been (and probably still was) a person of wide interests: hand weaving, book binding, painting by numbers – she'd tried the lot.

'She was always talking about expressing herself,' said Mrs Leatherbarrow defensively. 'Besides, how was I to know what she was up to? She was a funny sort of girl, I grant you, but I always put that down to her being educated. I never thought she was at the back of anything like this.' She waved the letter at Dover. 'She's the one who's been writing these anonymous letters, you know. It's all down here. A full confession.'

Dover grabbed at the sheets of paper but Mrs Leatherbarrow whipped them smartly out of his reach.

'You can have it in a minute,' she said generously. 'I just want to phone Dame Alice first and ead a few bits out to her.'

'That letter is evidence!' shouted Dover. 'It's mine! Hand it over!'

This time he was quicker and managed to get one podgy hand on the untidy sheets of paper. With a yelp of triumph, he pulled. Mrs Leatherbarrow held firm. The letter parted quite neatly down the middle.

'Now look what you've done!' they said in unison, each clutching a handful of evidence.

'The e is such a thing,' snorted Dover furiously, 'as hindering the police in the execution of their duty. If you don't give me the rest of that letter ...'

With a resigned sigh Mrs Leatherbarrow handed it over. After all she could remember enough to give a pretty accurate summary to Dame Alice.

'And now,' said Dover, sitting down resolutely in the armchair, 'I should be obliged if you would answer a few questions.' He fished around in his pockets and produced an old envelope. Mrs Leatherbarrow, impressed in spite of herself, found him a pencil in one of Miss Gullimore's drawers.

'Right!' said Dover, licking the pencil to make the scene look more official.   ull name?'

'Emily Leatherbarrow,' said Mrs Leatherbarrow and watched Dover solemnly write it down.

'Married?'

'Widow. I buried Mr Leatherbarrow ten years ago next Tuesday.' Touched by the nearness of this sad anniversary Mrs Leatherbarrow dabbed at her eyes with a handkerchief.

'Age?' said Dover, removing the kid gloves and getting really nasty.

Mrs Leatherbarrow bridled. 'I don't see what you want all this for. I haven't done anything wrong.'

'Just routine, madam,' leered Dover happily. 'Age?'

For a moment Mrs Leatherbarrow hesitated. 'Forty-nine,' she said quickly.

Dover examined her slowly. He twitched his nose. 'Fifty-fi e if you're a day,' he announced flatl .

'I'm fifty-fou , if you must know,' said Mrs Leatherbarrow with great indignation. 'And you've no cause to go spreading that round the village, either. It is a lady's privilege, after all.'

'Well,' said Dover, shoving his envelope back in his pocket, 'now we've got those little formalities out of the way we can get down to the real business. What happened this evening?'

Mrs Leatherbarrow had had all the stuffin knocked out of her. She was more than willing to co-operate. 'Well, I came back from the whist drive on the 5.30 bus from Cumberley. That got me back in here at about half past six, I suppose. I took my hat off and changed my frock and then I put the kettle on to make myself a cup of tea. Well, just before the kettle boiled, I called upstairs to Poppy. She didn't answer me and I thought it was a bit odd because I knew she was in. Her scooter was in the front garden same as usual. I called her again and she still didn't answer, so I came upstairs to see if anything was the matter. I opened the door and there she was – all sprawled out in that very armchair you're sitting in. I gave her a bit of a shake and then I saw the bottle and the glass on the floor and this letter addressed to the coroner propped up on the dressing-table. I didn't know what to do so I rushed off to get Dr Hawnt. He only lives a couple of doors away and I thought he'd be better than nothing.'

'She hadn't locked this door, then?' said Dover.

'Oh no, it was just closed, that's all.'

'Hm,' said Dover. 'What time does Miss Gullimore get back from work?'

'Well, she's usually in by a quarter to fi e at the latest. She comes on her scooter and that's much quicker than waiting for the bus.'

'Did she know what time you'd be in this evening?'

Mrs Leatherbarrow looked surprised. 'Well, of course she did! The e's a whist drive every Monday afternoon in Cumberley. I haven't missed it in donkey's years.'

'And you always come back at the same time?'

'I haven't much choice, have I? If I miss that 5.30 bus, there isn't another until after seven. The whist drive's always over just before fi e so I've nice time to catch the bus at half past. Sometimes it's a bit late, of course, but never more than fi e minutes or so.'

'And do you always invite Miss Gullimore down for a cup of tea when you get back?'

'Always,' said Mrs Leatherbarrow firml . 'The e's nothing wrong with that, is there? I tell you, I've been like a mother to that girl. She used to like to come down and see what I'd won.'

'But you can't have won every week,' objected Dover.

'Oh, can't I?' Mrs Leatherbarrow preened herself on the bed. 'Let me tell you, it's a bad week when I come home empty-handed. Ask anybody round bere. It's my hobby, you see,' she explained, 'that and bingo.'

'It sounds more like a profession,' grumbled Dover who never won anything.

'Oh, there's plenty that have called it a sight more than that,' said Mrs Leatherbarrow tossing her head. 'I've had some very catty things said about it in my time. Still, sticks and stones may break my bones but names will never hurt me. Tha 's what I used to say to Poppy when these nasty old letters started coming.'

'Oh,' said Dover, 'you've had some, too, have you?'

'I'll say I have, though not as many as Poppy did. She was always getting them, poor girl. Dear me, whatever am I saying!' Mrs Leatherbarrow went off into a sudden screech of girlish laughter which was most inappropriate to a woman of her years and weight. 'Of course it was Poppy writing those dreadful things herself, wasn't it?'

'Did you ever suspect her?' asked Dover with massive indiffe ence. He'd found out all he wanted to know long ago but the room was warm, the chair comfortable and Mrs Leatherbarrow seemed a hospitable sort of woman. Dover concentrated hard on looking as though a cup of tea and a bit of her vaunted mothering wouldn't come amiss.

'Of course not!' said Mrs Leatherbarrow. 'She was only a kid. She tried to make out that she was no end of a woman of the world, but it didn't fool me. Here – is that the time? I must be off! The e's a programme I want to see on the telly and I've got to give Dame Alice a ring first. You can let yourself out, can't you, dearie?'

Dover poked around for a few minutes after Mrs Leatherbarrow had gone. The e was no sign of a typewriter and no sign of any white Tendy Bond notepaper. He knew there wouldn't be. Still, you'd got to go through the motions, hadn't you? He looked disconsolately at the two halves of the suicide note which he was still clutching in his hand. A few chance phrases, hugely scrawled in pencil, caught his eye. *One of my problems has been that there's nobody I can communicate with ... I feel my presence is of no value or interest to anyone ...*

He sighed. Five ruddy foolscap pages of self-pity! Well, MacGregor could plough through them. Dover let himself out of the bedroom and made his way downstairs. He followed the sound of a studio audience roaring its head off with spontaneous laughter and found Mrs Leatherbarrow's sitting-room. Mrs Leatherbarrow was already comfortably installed in front of her set. Her feet were resting on an over-stuffed pouffe and she had a large box of chocolates on the arm of her chair. She heard Dover open the door but didn't turn her head.

'What is it, dearie?'

'Do you know what subjects Miss Gullimore taught at school?' said Dover loudly over another shriek of laughter.

'English and Art, I think,' shouted Mrs Leatherbarrow. 'Don't forget to shut the door behind you when you go out.'

Dover made a rude gesture at the back of Mrs Leatherbarrow's head which gave him some small satisfaction. Out once more he plodded into the cold, driving rain and fumbled his way back to The Jolly Sailor. He arrived there all in one piece, owing to a miscalculation on the part of a driver of an articulated truck, who had left his final, murderous burst of acceleration a fraction of a second too late. Dover had leapt desperately for the kerb and found himself in the embracing arms of MacGregor.

''Strewth!' said Dover. 'I thought he'd got me that time.'

'Some of these drivers want reporting,' agreed MacGregor who had taken in the whole incident with his usual quickness. For a moment his hopes had soared but he accepted Dover's survival philosophically. He was too cold and hungry to do anything else. 'Did you get his number, sir?'

Dover released himself and stood on his own feet instead of MacGregor's. 'Don't be a bloody fool!' he snarled. 'What do you think I've got – X-ray eyes? And where the hell have you been?' He didn't give MacGregor a chance to answer. 'Trust you to be missing when something happens! I don't know how you do it. You must have a bloody sixth sense or something.'

'What has happened, sir?' asked MacGregor, who knew from long and bitter experience that the Chief Inspector loathed explanations and excuses, especially when they were genuine.

'The dratted girl, Poppy Gullimore, has just tried to kill herself. Left a note confessing to writing the poison-pen letters.'

'Oh,' said MacGregor.

'Now, you get straight off to the hospital, and stop there till she comes round. Get a statement from her as soon as she's fit to make one and find out what she took and how much. All the usual rubbish. Oh, and I want to know what her underwear's like.'

'But I haven't had any dinner yet, sir!' protested MacGregor.

'Neither,' said Dover pompously, 'have I.'

And with that he marched quickly into The Jolly Sailor to remedy the omission. MacGregor stared hopelessly after him. Only when the Chief Inspector's portly figu e had disappeared from sight did he realize that he had no idea which hospital Poppy Gullimore had been taken to. And what was all that about her underclothes? He shivered and pulled his overcoat collar up round his ears. Perhaps the old fool had developed a fetish about young ladies' underwear. It wouldn't surprise MacGregor if he had.

Chapter Five

The Jolly Sailor hadn't had a night like it for years. Bert Quince was so overwhelmed by the sight of so many paying customers that he had actually brought another electric fi e down from his bedroom and plugged it in near the fi eplace. He and his wife were rushed off their feet serving drinks but they had enough sense to recognize and cherish a golden goose when they saw one.

'The e's the Chief Inspector now!' Bert Quince hissed to his wife. 'You go and get him his dinner right away. I can manage in here. I'll get Charlie to give me a hand.'

The excitement mounted as Mrs Quince and Dover attended to the wants of the inner man. Half the male population of Thornwich had crowded into the public bar and there were several women there as well. The mystery of the poison-pen letters had never really sparked much interest amongst the men folk, but a young girl's suicide – well, that was something more like it, wasn't it? It was by now general knowledge that this fat policeman chap from London liked his liquor and was certain to be fairly talkative once he'd wet his whistle a couple of times. All in all, with a bit of luck, it looked like being an interesting session.

Dover had been fed – and very well fed, too – in the kitchen. Mrs Quince had apologized, but it was warmer and he had a bit of privacy there, didn't he? Dover had been delighted and paid a delicate, if unconscious compliment to Mrs Quince by wolfing down everything edible in sight. No need to worry about saving anything for Sergeant MacGregor, he assured her, he'd be sure to get a meal out somewhere.

When the Chief Inspector finally entered the public bar he was greeted by a hushed and respectful silence. Those who had not seen him before were a little taken aback but, sensing the prevailing mood, they kept any opinions they might have had to themselves and joined in almost universal offers to stand the great man a drink.

To say that Dover was surprised at this reception would be an understatement. He was flabbergasted. During his chequered career there had been relatively few occasions when he had been the object of popular acclaim. Of course, he was used to other people standing him drinks. He would be an enforced teetotaller if they didn't, but such eagerness was unusual. He beamed happily at the assembled company and selected the lucky man. In many ways Chief Inspector Dover was no fool and no one could accuse him of lack of foresight where his own comfort and convenience were concerned. Nor was he ungrateful for or unmindful of past favours – not when they came from a man with one hundred and seventy thousand smackers tucked away under his mattress.

'Good evening, Mr Tompkins,' he said graciously and walked across to sit down beside his friend.

Mr Tompkins was delighted. The drinks arrived as if by magic. Mr Tompkins didn't smoke – it was one of his few faults in Dover's eyes – but he was one of nature's gentlemen and had brought a packet of Dover's favourite brand from the shelves of his own shop. He laid it shyly on the table and suggested that Dover should help himself. Dover did.

When Mr Tompkins had lit the cigarette, he and Dover settled down to an intimate conversation. Those standing close around their table listened intently and passed each tit-bit back to the less fortunate ones stuck over by the wall.

'Well, you're a fast worker, Mr Dover,' said Mr Tompkins admiringly and acting as spokesman for the assembled company.

'You've only been here a couple of days and you've got the whole case cleared up. Tha's Scotland Yard for you, eh? I think it's marvellous! How did you pick on her? Why, bless me, she's the only one you've interviewed and there you go – hitting the jackpot first time!

'Oh, come, come!' said Dover with a modest smirk. 'I think you're jumping to a few too many conclusions, Mr Tompkins. This case isn't over and done with by any means. Though we're making progress,' he added quickly.

'But, I don't understand, Mr Dover. I mean, why should Poppy Gullimore try to kill herself if she didn't write those letters?' Mr Tompkins's bewilderment was shared by a number of flushed, sweaty faces which moved in closer to catch Dover's answer.

'Well now, in the first place,' said Dover, 'Miss Gullimore didn't try to commit suicide.'

'But ...' Mr Tompkins's eyes popped. 'You don't mean it was attempted murder, do you?'

'Good God, no!' said Dover with a rich chuckle at such naivety. 'Murder in Thornwich? You'll have to watch that imagination of yours, Mr Tompkins! No, she took the aspirins or whatever it was herself all right, but it wasn't a serious attempt at suicide.'

Mr Tompkins frowned. 'But, how can you tell?'

Dover settled back comfortably in his chair and prepared to enlighten the ignorant. 'Experience, mostly,' he said. 'When you've been in the game as long as I have, it takes a bit more than a chit of a girl to pull the wool over your eyes. Now, just let me tell you how somebody who really wants to commit suicide goes about it. They don't muck about with bottles of aspirins. If they're going to do it that way they get hold of something really lethal and take a massive overdose of the stuff – ten or twenty times the amount you'd need to knock off a whole regiment. Or else they shoot themselves – stick the muzzle in your mouth and pull the trigger and you blow the back of your head off. The e's no shilly-shallying about that, is there? Nobody's going to arrive in the nick of time and bring you round after that, are they?'

The e was a general murmur of agreement from Dover's audience.

'But what does this Gullimore girl do?' asked Dover contemptuously. 'Gets hold of a few lousy aspirins and swallows 'em. Any doctor'll tell you it's well-nigh impossible to kill yourself with an overdose of aspirins. No, if she'd wanted to finish it all off seriously she'd have thrown herself under an express train or tried crossing this murderous road of yours out here when it's dark.' This local reference got an appreciative round of titters. 'And then look at her timing! She does it when she knows Mrs Leatherbarrow'll be coming'home, regular as clockwork, and fin her in plenty of time. No,' – Dover flicked the ash off his cigarette down the trousers of a man who'd approached a bit too near – 'Poppy Gullimore was just trying to make people think she was going to kill herself.'

'But, maybe she didn't know aspirins were no good,' suggested Mr Tompkins, 'and perhaps she was so upset she forgot about Mrs Leatherbarrow coming home.'

Dover eyed him with mild contempt. 'Come now, Mr Tompkins, give me credit for a bit of common sense! The e are other things, too, you know. Take this suicide note – so-called.' Dover produced the rather tattered remains and waved them in front of Mr Tompkins's face. 'Five blooming pages of it! Mostly about herself and dripping in self-pity! Now then, would it surprise you to learn that genuine suicides practically never leave a note? And when they do, it's usually a couple of lines scrawled on a bit of paper – not a blooming thesis like this. It's the phonies who write reams and reams of stuff because they want people to feel sorry for them and give 'em bags of sympathy' – Dover waggled a fat, admonitory finger – when *they're brought round*. Real suicides don't give a damn what people think. Why should they? The 're not going to be there to find out, a e they?'

'Gosh!' said Mr Tompkins in a hushed voice.

'The e are a few other points, too,' said Dover nonchalantly, 'which I'm expecting my sergeant to confirm any minute now.

Not that there's any doubt about it. Besides, why should Poppy Gullimore commit suicide?'

'Well, she thought you were going to arrest her for writing those poison-pen letters,' said Mr Tompkins. 'I suppose she couldn't stand the idea of all the disgrace and shame of it.'

'Aha!' trumpeted Dover. 'But Poppy Gullimore *didn't* write the poison-pen letters!'

Sensation! A couple of men slipped unobtrusively out of the bar to get this startling revelation on the village grapevine without delay. Ben Quince popped into the kitchen and told his wife she'd better leave the washing-up and come and listen.

Mr Tompkins opened and shut his mouth several times. 'You're having us on!' he croaked, but his protest lacked conviction. Chief Inspector Dover didn't look the type to indulge in merry practical jokes. 'But, I thought she confessed to everything in that letter you're holding? Look, Mr Dover, I know I'm not very bright but really, you've got me all confused.' A few heads nodded in sympathy and agreement. 'You say Poppy Gullimore hasn't tried to commit suicide and that she didn't write the poison-pen letters, although she wrote a letter before she tried to kill herself saying she did. Tha's right – er – isn't it?'

'Search me!' said Dover. 'I don't know what the blazes you're talking about. Look, it's dead simple. The Gullimore girl is just trying to get in on the act. She no more wrote those poison-pen letters than I did. I've searched her room. No Tendy Bond notepaper, no typewriter. My sergeant's been checking at the school. He won't have found anything there either, or I'm a Dutchman. No, there's no doubt about it. She couldn't possibly have written them.' Mr Tompkins looked as though he was about to pick several very relevant holes in this bit of argument so Dover, flushed with best bitter and success, hurried on to get his trump card down on the table. 'Besides,' he said, 'there's the spelling.'

'The spelling?' repeated Mr Tompkins, still dutifully playing Watson to Dover's Holmes.

'The spelling!' said Dover and took a long pull at his beer to let the excitement build up. When he finally came up for air, he wiped the back of his hand across his mouth, belched slightly and prepared to carry on. 'Whoever is writing these poison-pen letters is a good speller. Miss Gullimore isn't. It's as simple as that.'

'But she's a school-teacher!' protested a voice from the back of the crowd. Mr Tompkins was justifiably annoyed. That was his line.

'I don't care if she's a blinking astronaut,' retorted Dover, 'she can't spell for toffee. You've only got to read this so-called suicide note.' Several hands reached forward in answer to the implied invitation, but Dover crossly pushed the letter back in his pocket. The cheek of some people! Fancy thinking he was going to hand round an officia document as though it was a bag of chips or something!

Chips! Now that was an idea. 'Any chance of getting a bite to eat?' he asked Mr Tompkins. 'All this talking's making me a bit peckish. And a bit dry too, too,' he added quickly with a deprecating laugh. You might as well kill two birds with one stone while you were at it.

Charlie Chettle, who must have suffe ed from a subconscious death wish, was dispatched across the road to Freda's Café and another pint of beer was transferred from hand to willing hand.

'Well now,' said Mr Tompkins when things had settled down again, 'I must say, speaking on behalf of all of us, what a great privilege it's been, Mr Dover, and how interesting to hear all about this – er – unfortunate business straight from what you might call the horse's mouth.' The e was a shy spatter of applause. Mr Tompkins cleared his throat. 'The e's just one last question I would like to ask – if you don't mind.' Dover inclined his head graciously. 'Why did Poppy Gullimore do all this? I mean, why did she confess to writing the poison-pen letters and why did she pretend to commit suicide?'

'Ah, Mr Tompkins,' said Dover blandly, 'I'm afraid you're asking me to delve into the mysteries of the human mind. Of course, I could expound on all the psychological ramifications of Miss Gullimore's motives and her general mental state, but I hardly think this is either the time or the place for discussions of such profundities. On the other hand, I could perhaps express it more simply in terms that a layman could understand. To put it briefl , she's a nut-case.'

'Ah!' said Mr Tompkins as though one of his own more adventurous theories had been confirmed

'As nutty as a fruit cake,' said Dover, expanding his theme with typical originality of phrase. 'We see millions of 'em up at the Yard. They come along in their hundreds and confess to any old crime we have on our books – the more sordid the better. Exhibitionists, that's what we call 'em. They just want somebody to pay a bit of attention to them. The 'll do anything to get in the limelight. Your Miss Gullimore's typical. I thought so as soon as I first clapped eyes on her. "You'll have to watch out for this one, Wilf," I told myself. "She'll be rushing up to make her free and voluntary before you can say Jack Robinson, if I know anything about it." And, of course,' said Dover, modestly casting his eyes down, 'I was right.'

Mr Quince passed a message from behind the counter. The Chief Inspector was wanted on the telephone. Dover made his way to the back of the bar, turning this simple movement into a triumphant procession. Everybody fell silent and listened hard, but they could only catch a high-pitched squawking coming from the other end. Thornwich had to wait until the following morning to get from the ever vigilant Miss Tilley a verbatim account of what Sergeant MacGregor said. Dover restricted his part in the conversation to a series of knowing grunts.

He put the receiver down and returned to his table, revelling in the knowledge that all eyes were focused upon him.

'Just a final bit of confirmation from my sergeant,' he announced. 'I sent him to the hospital to make some inquiries. Your Miss Gullimore had only swallowed about thirty aspirins – hardly what you might call trying. And,' tantalizingly Dover saved his titbit till the last – 'her underwear was grubby, distinctly grubby! Well, you see what that means, don't you?'

'Well, no, Mr Dover,' confessed Mr Tompkins unhappily, 'I don't.'

'Genuine suicides,' said Dover, a trifle impatiently, 'realize that somebody's going to examine their bodies when they're dead and they're usually most particular about being clean and tidy underneath. Phony suicides never think about things like that because they know damned well they're not going to be laid out on a marble slab.' He was getting fed up with Miss Gullimore, in spite of the fact that she'd provided him with an excellent excuse for showing off in front of the yokels. 'It's one of the ways in which we policemen tell the diffe ence between a real attempt and a fake one.'

The timely arrival of Charlie Chettle with a selection of Freda's hot meat-pies allowed Dover to drop the now tedious subject of Miss Poppy Gullimore's suicide, and for the rest of the evening he regaled the company with stories of his past detective exploits. He went into great detail about a surprising number of cases which would have remained for ever unsolved in the files of Scotland Yard had it not been for Dover's keen eye and agile brain. These stories were highly effecti e and mostly culled from the memoirs of senior officer who had retired from the Yard in a blaze of popular glory. Dover, a masochist if there ever was one, assiduously read all the books they wrote. He had ideas of writing a book himself one day, if he could find enough material to hold the hard covers apart.

Mr Quince called time promptly at 10.30 in deference to the forces of law and order which were sheltering under his roof but although even Dover got to bed at a reasonable hour, nobody in Thornwich was surprised to learn that the Chief Inspector was taking it easy on the following day. It was generally agreed that, in view of his expert handling of the Gullimore business, he'd earned it. It was a view which Dover whole-heartedly shared. He was surprised and annoyed to find that MacGregor was still bouncing around like an excited sheep dog, eager for action.

'What's your sweat?' asked Dover, peevishly putting the final touches to his appearance before venturing out. He scraped his cut-throat razor slowly down one jowl, cutting a broad swathe through the soap.

'Well, we've been here two full days now, sir, and we haven't got anywhere really, have we?'

'Haven't got anywhere?' squeaked Dover, nearly slicing off half his moustache. 'Wadderyemean, not got anywhere? I solved this Gullimore business, didn't I? I spotted straight away that it was just a try on. Plenty of people'd have spent weeks chasing a red herring like that. 'Swelp me,' he said bitterly, wielding his razor with increasing abandon, 'what do you want, jam on it?'

With a great deal of tact, MacGregor pointed out that brilliant though the Chief Inspector's handling of Poppy Gullimore's suicide had been, it had not advanced by one whit the case which had been assigned to them.

Dover peered disconsolately at his face in the mirror. 'I don't see what we can do,' he grumbled. 'Nobody's been able to find the flipping typewriter, and we haven't a snowball's chance in hell of tracing the notepaper. You know that as well as I do. Where are we supposed to go from here? Our one hope is that this poison-pen joker will slip up and leave a fingerprint som where.'

'We could perhaps keep a watch on the post boxes, sir,' suggested MacGregor diffident . The Chief Inspector did not as a rule take kindly to reasonable suggestions from subordinates, particularly when they looked as though they might involve him in some work.

'Oh, very original!' sneered Dover, and wiped his razor on one of The Jolly Sailor's towels. 'I can see that producing a lot of results. Two policemen sat on folding chairs by the post boxes for the next two or three weeks! For God's sake, MacGregor, we aren't dealing with a cretin! If we were we'd have caught her before now. Whoever's writing these letters is smart – a damned sight smarter than you by the sound of it. She's worked out a pretty watertight little scheme, and she's not going to be nabbed red-handed posting a batch of letters by a great lumbering copper breathing down her neck. No,' – Dover sat down wearily on the edge of the bed – 'if you ask me, I don't think we're ever going to catch her. Not unless she does something absolutely bloody silly. As I see it, we shall just have to hang on here and go through the motions for a bit and then tell 'em we aren't getting anywhere and chuck the whole thing up.'

MacGregor looked shocked.

'Well, it's not as though it's what you might call a serious crime, now, is it?' asked Dover. 'Frankly I wouldn't have touched it with a barge-pole if it hadn't been for the wife's sister. I'm not one to stand on my rank but I don't mind telling you, I think they've got a bit of a cheek sending a man of my experience and seniority on a job like this.'

'Actually, sir, I'm inclined to agree with you,' said MacGregor, deciding to play it subtle. 'It doesn't look as though we're ever going to solve this case unless we get a real bit of luck.' And you can say that again, he thought. 'But I do think, in view of the rather peculiar circumstances surrounding this business, that we ought to – well, you expressed it so aptly yourself, sir – I think we ought to go through the motions a bit more realistically, shall we say? After all, sir' – Macgregor introduced the subject carefully – 'Dame Alice Stote-Weedon has got the ear of the Assistant Commissioner and she is very anxious that this whole business should be cleared up as soon as possible.' Dover's brow blackened ominously. 'I think it would be diplomatic, sir,' concluded MacGregor lamely, 'if we could give the impression of *trying* to solve the case.'

Dover sniffed unpleasantly and twitched his nose. The e was a lot in what MacGregor said, though the Chief Inspector would fight tooth and nail before he admitted it. He sighed. It was all go. From morning till night. Drive, drive, drive! Outsiders – they just didn't understand the *strain* of the job. The long hours, the endless questionings, the danger. Do some of 'em good, it would, to try it themselves for a few days. The 'd soon be laughing on the other side of their silly faces.

'As a matter of fact, Dame Alice phoned again this morning, sir,' said MacGregor, breaking into what was proving to be a lengthy silence.

Dover sighed again. He got slowly to his feet, heaved his stomach in, and with an effo t fastened the top button on his trousers. MacGregor recognized the signs of impending action and hastened to help the old fool on with his jacket and overcoat. Dover, with every indication that he considered he was being put upon, accepted his bowler hat from MacGregor's outstretched hand.

'She said she'd like to see us this morning, sir,' said the sergeant, feeling he'd handled things rather well. 'Might be a good idea just to pop in and keep the old dear happy, eh, sir?'

Dover stared sourly at him.

Popping in to see Dame Alice had been a slight, but understandable, understatement on MacGregor's part. Dover, in tacitly agreeing to call on the lady, had not realized exactly where she lived.

'Here,' he protested indignantly to MacGregor when they had passed a row of slate-grey cottages and reached the Baptist Chapel, 'how much farther is it?'

'Just at the top of the hill, sir,' explained MacGregor brightly. 'Opposite the church.'

''Strewth!' grumbled Dover. 'If I'd known it was going to be a blooming marathon I damned well wouldn't have come. My feet are killing me! Why the hell didn't you order a taxi?'

'It can't be more than half a mile, sir.'

'Oh, can't it?' snapped Dover, gingerly placing one boot down after the other. 'I'd have you remember, young fellow my lad, that I'm still supposed to be on light duties. Being out in all this cold's not doing my stomach one bit of good. Here,' – Dover stopped abruptly in his tracks – 'you walk next to the kerb for a change. These damned lorries keep splashing water all ver me.'

After ten minutes' laborious uphill progress, Dover and MacGregor turned into the drive of Friday Lodge. The house was a pleasant, late Victorian building, set in its own grounds and much the most impressive residence in the village. Opinions diffe ed as to why Dame Alice, whose interests and commitments ranged so wide, continued to live in a cultural backwater like Thornwich. It was true, of course, that a small village gave her genius for officiousnes full play, and what she didn't know about the private and public lives of the villagers was just not worth knowing. Then again, her marriage to a Stote-Weedon gave her an unassailable social position which might not, elsewhere, have been yielded to her with such passive resignation.

In the old days the Stote-Weedons *were* Thornwich. They had owned the big house and, like previous brides, Dame Alice had been initiated into the rites of rigorous social service by her mother-in-law, whose soup had been known and feared by every poor cottager for a radius of fi e miles. Comparatively early widowhood had left Dame Alice free to develop her humanitarian instincts, and her DBE had been won for welfare work on a county and, at times, even on a national scale. The villagers had for years expected, and hoped, that she would move to some more congenial part of the country, but she appeared to like Thornwich. It wasn't what it had been in her young days, of course, but she was comfortable there and saw no good reason for moving. The villagers shrugged their shoulders and accepted the fact that she would be with them for ever: either bossing them from the crumbling splendours of Friday Lodge, or reproaching them for their past lack of co-operation from the family vault in the parish church. The village would miss her when she was gone and almost everybody was eagerly looking forward to the deprivation.

MacGregor mounted the steps to the front door and rang the bell as Dover lumbered up behind him. The peals had hardly died away, when an enormous dog, black, hairy and of uncertain breeding, came bounding out from round the back of the house. It leapt about at the foot of the steps, barking and revealing its teeth aggressively. Dover, in spite of his bad feet and ailing stomach, sprinted so as to position MacGregor between himself and the ravaging animal. When the door was opened the Chief Inspector was across the threshold in a flash, and slammed the door so quickly behind him that MacGregor was nearly shut outside.

A tall woman with straight, iron-grey hair regarded this undignified manoeuvring with undisguised disdain

'The e's no need to be afraid,' she announced calmly. 'Bonzo is quite harmless. He wouldn't hurt a fl .'

'When I start worrying about flies' snarled Dover, 'I'll tell you. You ought to keep that brute chained up. Or have him destroyed.'

'Good heavens,' – the woman laughed unpleasantly – 'I never realized that policemen were afraid of poor little dogs! No wonder the number of crimes with violence is rising steadily every year.'

Dover snorted and changed the conversation. 'You're Dame Alice, I suppose,' he said in a voice which implied that his worst suspicions had been realized.

'No, I'm not,' said the woman smugly pleased at being able to contradict him. 'I am Dame Alice's companion and secretary. My name is Thickett, ary Thickett. *Miss* Mary Thickett'

'Ah, an unplucked rose!' countered Dover smoothly. 'Well, where is Dame Alice?'

'She is waiting for you in the sitting-room,' said Miss Thickett frigidly. 'If you will kindly let me have your coats and hats, I will take you in to her. I suppose,' – she smiled sweetly and stared pointedly at Dover's bowler – 'you *do* remove your hat when you are in a private residence?'

'Only,' rejoined Dover with a wittiness which made MacGregor cringe, 'when I'm in the presence of a lady!'

Miss Thickett took the hats and coats and tossed them contemptuously over a chair.

'By the way,' said Dover, who sometimes just didn't know when to stop, 'speaking of poison, I suppose you've had some of these anonymous letters, too, have you?'

'No,' said Miss Thickett, looking down her nose, 'as a matter of fact, I have not. I have been spared that particular humiliation.'

'Oh,' said Dover. 'Tha 's a bit funny, isn't it?'

'Not to me,' said Miss Thickett severely. 'We clearly have widely differing senses of humour.' She walked stiffl across to a small table by the front door and picked up a cardboard tray and a tin collecting box. With the air of one delivering the *coup-de-grâce* to a detested enemy, she proffe ed the tray to Dover and rattled the collecting box under his nose. 'Perhaps you would care to purchase your poppy from me,' she said with a faint smile. 'I see you're not wearing one.'

MacGregor fumbled sheepishly in his pocket for half a crown, while Dover backed away like a nervous horse from this blatant attempt to extort money from him.

'You're a bit early, aren't you?' he asked suspiciously.

'Remembrance Day is a week on Sunday, my dear Chief Inspector. Now, come along, I'm sure we can rely on you to give generously.' This was hitting well below the belt, and Miss Thickett knew it.

But Dover was not one to be caught napping. With a flourish he turned back the lapel of his jacket and revealed a wide, if tattered selection of paper flags and emblems. He picked out a moth-eaten-looking poppy which had given him sterling service for the past six years and stuck it defiantly in his buttonhole

'Thank ou,' he said, 'but I already have mine.'

Chapter Six

Not surprisingly after such a beginning, Dover's visit to Dame Alice was neither enjoyable nor pleasant. It didn't even have the merit of being brief. Dame Alice was an experienced committee woman and never used one word if ten would do. She had found that one could bore one's colleagues into submission just as effecti ely as brow-beating them there.

She invited Dover and MacGregor to sit down and then spent several minutes weighing up the opposition. What she saw neither impressed nor inspired her. She was surprised, though. She had met many policemen in her time and had found them a respectful body of men on the whole, worthy if not over-blessed with brains. This bad-tempered, overweight hulk scowling from the depths of a chintz-covered armchair was a new experience for her. And those boots on her Persian prayer-rug! Oh well, it was her own fault. She should have interviewed them out in the hall, although she had not expected that a senior detective from Scotland Yard would have been quite so gross. The young one looked quite a decent boy. He could even be a gentleman if he weren't quite so well-dressed. But this Dover man! She shuddered.

Dover stared truculently back. He was going to have trouble with this old cow or he'd eat his hat.

MacGregor sat quietly, wondering what they were waiting for.

'Well,' said Dame Alice at last, 'I am glad that we have finally met, Chief Inspector. I was beginning to think that you were trying to avoid me.'

Dover grunted.

Dame Alice didn't really look like a man-eater. She wasn't very tall, short enough to have most men towering over her and feeling masterful. She was on the plump side, though her legs and ankles were slim. Her face was motherly in a vague way, but people rarely got around to noticing her features. Their eyes tended to linger on the rimless spectacles on the bridge of her nose, and the untidy mass of soft grey hair which surrounded her face.

'You probably know,' Dame Alice went on placidly, 'that I was largely instrumental in having you brought here. Our local police were somewhat difficul to convince that Thornwich is facing a very nasty and potentially dangerous situation. I am referring, of course, to these poison-pen letters with which the women in this village are being bombarded day after day. I myself have received yet another of these disgusting communications this morning. You may as well take charge of it.'

She picked up a white typewritten envelope from a small occasional table and handed it to Dover. Dover, not even bothering to glance at it, handed it to MacGregor. The Chief Inspector had so far not examined any of the poison-pen letters and he saw no reason to start now. He'd get around to it in his own good time.

'Now, I realize,' Dame Alice resumed her monologue, 'that the police do not take things like this outbreak of poison-pen letters very seriously. No doubt their time is fully occupied with harassing motorists and checking on dog licences.' Dover raised his eyebrows but offe ed no comment. 'But I happen to live in Thornwich and, as I think anyone who knows me will confirm, I don't go around with my eyes closed. Thornwich women are rapidly reaching breaking-point. Theyhave suffe ed this disgusting form of persecution for a month now and, you can take my word for it, they are not in any condition to stand much more. Apart from the unpleasantness of actually receiving, one or more of these missives, there is inevitable speculation as to who is writing them. Nerves are being torn to shreds as the finger of suspicion points this way and that, as the gossip grows, as the…'

'I can't say I've noticed much hysteria about the place,' said Dover suddenly. 'If you ask me, I'd say people were taking it remarkably calmly.'

Dame Alice blinked behind her glasses. 'I find that a very odd remark, Chief Inspector,' she commented. 'To the best of my knowledge you have so far interviewed only one person in this village, and she tried to kill herself immediately afterwards. No doubt that is evidence of the remarkable calm which you claim to have found in Thornwich'

'It wasn't a real attempt at suicide,' protested Dover.

'Maybe not,' agreed Dame Alice, 'but it is indicative of a very disturbed state of mind. And Poppy Gullimore is not alone in feeling that some form of violent action is the only way out of this dreadful predicament in which we have all been so shamefully placed. Well now,' – Dame Alice sat more upright in her chair – 'just what have your investigations, or whatever you call them, achieved so far?'

Dover slumped deeper in his chair and stared resentfully into the coal fi e which was burning cheerfully in the hearth. 'I'm afraid I'm not at liberty to reveal information like that to you, madam. It's confidential'

'Tommyrot!' exploded Dame Alice. 'You appear to have no scruples about discussing the case freely in the bar-parlour of The Jolly Sailor. From what I am told you apparently consider that the culprit is a woman, an inhabitant of this village, and one who has herself received some of these poison-pen letters.'

'Tha's right,' admitted Dover sulkily.

'Well,' – Dame-Alice nodded her head with approbation – 'so far I am inclined to agree with you. It is, after all, a perfectly logical deduction which would be obvious to anybody. Now, what are your opinions on the motive?'

'Motive?' repeated Dover stupidly. He was still staring into the fi e and the flickering flames were having a hypnotic effect on him.

'Motive,' said Dame Alice with signs of impatience. 'Have you considered *why* this woman is writing the letters?'

Dover sighed. The room was warm and the chair was comfortable. He yawned and wondered if Dame Alice was going to be good for a cup of tea. 'Well,' – he reluctantly returned to his surroundings – 'I don't reckon motive comes into it much. This woman's barmy. Judging by the tone of the letters she's sexually repressed in some way or another. It's the usual sort of thing. For some reason she's developed a grudge against the other women and this is her cock-eyed way of hitting back at them. I expect there's a motive of some sort but it'll be all twisted up in her imagination. It won't be the kind of thing we can take into account.'

'You think the culprit is a psychological case?'

'Er – yes,' said Dover doubtfully. 'Barmy. Off her rocker. You know.'

'Some poor, distraught, mentally sick woman who doesn't really know what she is doing?'

'Tha's it,' said Dover through another yawn.

'Poppycock!' said Dame Alice firml .

Dover burrowed deeper than ever into his chair and closed his eyes. When a lecture was inevitable, you might as well relax and enjoy it.

Dame Alice swung round slightly so as to include MacGregor in her audience. She had reached the erroneous conclusion that he must be the brains of the partnership. MacGregor contrived to look bright-eyed and intelligent.

'Absolute poppycock!' repeated Dame Alice. 'You have examined the letters. They are carefully typed with no spelling mistakes or grammatical errors. Do you mean to sit there and tell me that they are the work of a candidate for a lunatic asylum? And what about the fingerprints – or, rather, the lack of them? Is that the sort of thing a person with a sick brain would be so cunning about? And there's another point. All those letters have been posted in the village. Well, I dare say that was easy enough at the very beginning, but what do you think it's like now? People look at you as if you were a criminal if you so much as go near a pillar-box in Thornwich. I've nothing to be ashamed of but, I don't mind telling you, I post practically all my letters in Cumberley or in Bearle these days. Now then, does it stand to reason that a neurotic woman, one who must be practically insane, has enough gumption to take the necessary precautions to post those letters completely unobserved? Everybody is watching everybody else like a hawk. Only a very shrewd, calculating person could get away with it.'

Dame Alice paused, either for breath or to let her arguments sink in. MacGregor nodded understandingly and something – it might have been a grunt or a snore – came from Dover.

'Well, Chief Inspector,' demanded Dame Alice loudly, 'what do you think?'

Dover opened his eyes and looked vacantly at Dame Alice. 'Oh, very interesting,' he said. 'Yes, you've got a point there.' He gave himself a little shake and opened his eyes very wide. His feet were giving him hell. He bent down and undid the laces. ''Strewth!' he murmured. 'Tha's better.'

Dame Alice watched him with an expressionless face. Really, this man was the absolute end! 'I don't believe you've heard a word I've been saying!' she said.

'Oh yes, I have!' protested Dover indignantly. 'It's just that I always concentrate better with my eyes closed. Tha's right, isn't it, Sergeant?'

'Oh, never mind!' said Dame Alice, who prided herself on an instinctive immunity to red herrings. 'The point I was endeavouring to make is that we are dealing with a person of intelligence – cold, calculating intelligence. I cannot accept your theory that we are looking for a kind of female village idiot.'

'Even crackpots can show a fair bit of cunning from time to time,' Dover pointed out. He looked at the ornate china clock on Dame Alice's mantelpiece. Far too late for elevenses. Maybe the old cow would lash out with a drop of sherry before lunch.

'In my opinion,' said Dame Alice, showing remarkable stamina for one of her age, 'the poison-pen letters are being written with a definite aim in vi w.'

'Oh yes?' said Dover politely.

'Somebody is trying to drive me out of Thornwich!

And good luck to 'em, whoever they may be, thought Dover. He scratched his head. The usual shower of dandruff fell gently on his shoulders.

'Do you find the idea fanciful, Chief nspector?'

'Oh no,' murmured Dover, 'not at all. Have you' – he dragged his eyes away from the fi e and tried to concentrate – 'have you any idea as to whom it might be?'

'If I had,' said Dame Alice reasonably, 'I should not have wasted public time and money by having you and your assistant sent down here. No, though I have naturally given the problem a considerable amount of thought. The e are several people in the village whose attitude towards me is what I can only describe as antagonistic. I propose to give you a brief outline of their relationship to me so that you can pursue your inquiries along more fruitful lines.'

'Now, just a minute …' Dover put in quickly. He was wide awake now and scenting danger on all sides. If he didn't choke her off good and quick she'd have them there all day. 'If you are the sole object of attack why have the letters been sent to everybody else as well?'

'I should have thought that was obvious,' sniffed Dame Alice. 'The other letters are just a blind. We already know that our culprit is a woman of the utmost cunning. This is merely another example of it. If I alone had been singled out, her real motive for writing the letters would have been crystal clear from the very beginning. As things are, she has succeeded in clouding the issue for a full month and in masking her plans even from such an experienced and astute detective as yourself.'

Dover, sensing that Dame Alice was taking the mickey, gave her a good hard look, but she took no notice. She had got the bit well between her teeth now and nothing short of a swift toot from the last trump was going to stop her.

For the next three-quarters of an hour, Dame Alice held forth with that fluent gift of the gab for which she was known and loathed from one end of the country to the other. Dover's stomach rumbled audibly but unheeded. He concentrated as hard as he could, but closed eyelids were no barrier against Dame Alice's remorseless tirade. The bright, attentive look on MacGregor's face grew fi ed and stiff. With a great show of efficienc he got out his notebook and doodled furiously. He produced a quite creditable sketch of a woman being burned alive at the stake, which filled the whole of one page. Dame Alice dropped, and blackened, quite a few names which Dover had heard before.

The e was Mrs Tompkins, for instance. She was nursing a grudge over that baby business. 'As if it was my fault,' complained Dame Alice. 'I told her right from the beginning that I couldn't pull any strings for her, though, of course, I have a large number of contacts in that particular field. I warned her that adoption wasn't easy in this day and age and I tried to point out that she and her husband were hardly the ideal couple. In spite of having all that money, they are living in conditions at the back of that shop which are, really, from an adoption society's point of view, quite unacceptable. I endeavoured to stop Mrs Tompkins from letting her hopes rise too high and, naturally, I warned her that Mr Tompkins's marked lack of enthusiasm wasn't going to help, but of course, when three societies in a row turned her down she blamed it all on me.'

'It's getting late, Dame Alice,' said Dover half rising hopefully to his feet. 'We don't want to keep you from your lunch. The Sergeant and I'll come back later.'

'I never eat lunch,' said Dame Alice, frowning at the interruption. 'Where was I?'

Both Dover and MacGregor were scrupulously careful not to tell her, but it didn't make any diffe ence.

The e was Mrs Crotty. She was jealous. 'Nobody,' proclaimed Dame Alice, 'could hold the Church in deeper respect than I do.

I consider it plays a most important part in our social life, and everybody who knows me would confirm that the last thing I would do is slight, by word or deed, any aspect of the Church or the people connected with it. It is hardly my fault if our local Chapter of the Christian Mothers' and Wives' Work and Prayer Group wished to re-elect me as President for the tenth year in succession. "I am well aware," I told her, not mincing my words, "that all the other presidents of the local chapters are the wives of the incumbents. If this is not the case in Thornwich, I suggest that you know the reason better than I." She had no answer, of course. One would have thought that she would have been grateful but I'm afraid gratitude is entirely alien to Mrs Crotty's nature, "Most vicars' wives," I told her, "would be glad to have somebody who took an active interest in the parish and relieved them of some of their duties." And then there was that business of the altar fl wers. You've never heard such a fuss and palaver just because I ...'

'Do you mind if I have a cigarette?' said Dover.

MacGregor, well trained, had the case half out of his pocket when Dame Alice's reply cracked across the room like a cat-o'-nine-tails in the hands of a sadistic master at arms.

'I certainly do mind! It is a filthy habit and I am surprised that a man of your standing and position should be a slave to it. It is nothing more than a breast substitute, you know. You can't have been weaned properly as a child.'

Dover's jaw dropped in blank astonishment. Before he could rally, she was off again

Then there was Mrs Leatherbarrow, Poppy Gullimore's landlady. She had already threatened Dame Alice with court action so there were no doubts about her attitude. 'Mind you,' said Dame Alice, 'it's all been smoothed over now. We're on very amicable terms, on the surface. But I fancy my perfectly innocent remarks were a little nearer to the bone than Mrs Leatherbarrow cared to admit. She's always letting rooms to these young, rather forward girls, you know. That Poppy Gullimore person is one of the most respectable-looking she's had, so you can imagine what the rest were like. I did happen to mention, in a conversation I considered entirely private and confidential, that Mrs Leatherbarrow's young ladies seemed blessed with an inexhaustible supply of gentlemen friends and, of course, the next thing you know is that she's around here, hammering on my door and accusing me of accusing her of running a brothel. Absolute nonsense, of course. I've been in public life long enough to keep a guard on my tongue. Naturally I explained that I had said nothing of the sort and eventually she seemed satisfied, but I've never been really sure, you know, that it's all forgotten and forgiven. In fact, Mrs Leatherbarrow was *so* upset that I have been keeping a discreet eye on her establishment – just in case. If there is anything nasty going on there you can rest assured it won't escape my eagle eye, and I shan't have any scruples about reporting the facts to the proper authorities, either.'

Dover tried again. He had lost all hope of defeating the enemy and could only resort to guerilla tactics designed to confuse and lower morale.

'I want to go to the lavatory,' he said in a loud clear voice. 'Where is it?'

Dame Alice, wincing at such crudity, informed him that there was a downstairs cloakroom just outside in the hall.

Dover dragged himself up out of his chair and headed in the prescribed direction.

'Well, really!' exclaimed Dame Alice, and shuddered.

She and MacGregor sat in an embarrassed silence as Dover's footsteps thudded across the hall. A door opened in the distance and closed. The e was silence for the next fi e minutes.

'He's being rather a long time, isn't he?' asked Dame Alice at last in a voice stiff with fury but tinged with a modicum of anxiety.

'He's got a very delicate stomach,' said MacGregor, wishing quite hard that the floor beneath his feet would open. 'Perhaps I should …'

The e was a sound of rushing waters.

'I shouldn't bother,' said Dame Alice faintly. 'I think he's coming.'

A few moments later Dover lumbered back into the room. 'Tha's better,' he grunted as he collapsed back into his chair. He turned imperturbably to Dame Alice. 'You were saying?'

Then there was Freda Gomersall. Dame Alice had tried to get her café closed down on the grounds of hygiene. Freda had appeared to resent this interference with her sole means of livelihood and was reputed to have threatened to punch Dame Alice up the hooter. 'Such a common woman,' Dame Alice said. 'And her café is frequented by a most undesirable type of man. Not the kind of people we want hanging around Thornwich at all hours of the day and night.'

Then there was Miss Tilley at the post office Dame Alice had not only suggested that she tampered with the mail but had also offe ed the near expert opinion that old Mrs Tilley, bed-ridden these many years, would be better off in an old people's home. Miss Tilley had reacted with surprising venom against these remarks.

Then there was Mrs Quince, landlady of The Jolly Sailor. Some trouble there about selling drinks to minors. It all turned out to be a storm in a tea-cup but Mrs Quince was reputed to have a jumbo-sized memory.

Then the e was Mrs Belper, the butcher's wife.

Then there was Mrs Poltensky, abandoned spouse of one of our gallant war-time Polish allies.

Then there was ... The list was well-nigh endless. No detail was too trivial and no reference too obscure for Dame Alice. She spared neither herself nor her unwilling audience.

The church clock was striking three when at last Dover was in a position to direct an ill-tempered kick at Dame Alice's hairy dog, but his heart wasn't in it and he missed.

He spoke from the bottom of his soul as he hobbled down the drive and began the long limp home. ''Strewth!' he said. 'The things I do for England!'

'Yes, sir,' agreed MacGregor, trying to keep it on a jocular note. 'A policeman's lot is not a happy one.'

Dover scowled crossly. He couldn't stand people who always had to cap one Shakespearian quotation with another.

The dog gave a final snap – from a safe distance – at Dover's heels and retreated, barking furiously, back to its lair behind the house.

'Mind you,' said Dover who found the going considerably easier downhill, 'if you look at it one way, it was all very interesting.'

'Was it, sir?' said MacGregor, feeling that a new Dover was about to be revealed to him.

'Yes,' said Dover and indulged himself in a most unpleasant smirk. 'The old cow was so busy telling us how many enemies she'd got, she didn't seem to cotton on to what else she was telling us.'

'No, sir,' said MacGregor whose ability to follow a logical analysis had been somewhat impaired by the experiences of the last few hours.

'They may hate her,' said Dover, 'but what about her feelings towards them, eh? She loathes their guts! She thinks they're persecuting her and trying to run her out of the village. She thinks they're all ganging up on her. She's got a chip on her shoulder the size of Buckingham Palace against damn near every woman in Thornwich'

'Oh,' said MacGregor as the light began to dawn, 'I do see what you mean, sir. You mean she's a son of megalomaniac.'

'Yes,' said Dover vaguely, 'something like that.'

'And you mean,' crowed MacGregor as the penny dropped, 'that she's got a grudge against all the other women. Of courses sir! You're right! You mean ...'

'I wish you'd stop telling me what I mean,' snapped Dover. 'What I mean is that Dame Alice What's-her-name is as good a suspect as we've met yet for writing those poison-pen letters herself. Why, she's tailor-made for it!'

MacGregor executed a smart mental about turn. He knew the Chief Inspector's methods of old, and they were enough to make strong men tremble. The usual pattern consisted of a lengthy initial period of masterly inaction, followed by the taking of a violent dislike to one of the vaguely possible suspects. After that there was no holding him. His detective's instinct, as he liked to call it, told him who the culprit was, and all subsequent evidence which didn't confirm his usually quite unfounded suspicions, was chucked grandly out of the window, or swept surreptitiously under the carpet. It was a system which certainly produced results but not, unfortunately, those which were acceptable to a judge and jury. MacGregor congratulated himself on seeing the precipice of disaster just in time. Never mind all the clever stuff about Dame Alice unconsciously revealing her true self. All that had happened so far was that Dover had taken a dislike – justifiable, no doubt – to Dame Alice and was going to pin the poison-pen letters on her, or blow a blood vessel in the attempt.

'Yes,' said Dover, chuckling gleefully and quite unaware that he had already lost his assistant's support, 'it all fits. Do you remember how keen she was to impress us with the fact that the poison-pen writer was a real smart alec, eh? Now, that sort of bragging's typical! Straight out of a case-book. She's a ruddy psychopath, that's what she is,' said Dover, prepared to chuck psychological jargon around as glibly and ignorantly as the next man. 'She was nearly breaking her neck to tell us how clever she'd been.'

'Yes,' said MacGregor doubtfully.

'Then there was that stuff she said about smoking.' Dover pursed his lips and narrowed his eyes significantl . 'Fancy a lady using language like that in her own drawing-room! Breast substitute! That shows what sort of a woman she is. If my wife came out with words like that in mixed company, she'd get the back of my hand, I can tell you. Must have a mind like a cesspool, that woman – Dame Alice, of course, not my old woman. No wonder she's venting her spite by writing a lot of dirty letters to all and sundry.'

'Oh, steady on, sir!' warned MacGregor hastily and added a nervous laugh to show that his natural caution should be taken in good part. 'We're a long way off being able to say definitely that Dame Alice is the poison-pen letter writer.'

'She's enjoying every minute of it,' said Dover. 'She's patting herself on the back for outwitting the police. She's upsetting all her favourite enemies by writing dirty letters to them. And she's a widow, isn't she?'

'Yes, sir,' said MacGregor.

'Well, there you are!' said Dover with relish. 'Sexually repressed! You can always tell. Oh, it fits her like a glove. I'll bet she can type, too.'

'But, why should she insist on the case being properly investigated, sir?' asked MacGregor, trying to preach caution without getting Dover's goat. 'She was taking a terrible risk, wasn't she?' he added. Well, after all, the Assistant Commissioner might have sent one of his more competent detectives down to Thornwich

'Satisfies her power complex!' Once Dover got his teeth into a theory it took more than MacGregor's cautious bleatings to get them out again. 'Bigger audience to be shocked by the muck she's writing. All adds to the fun. Yes, I think we can relax now and take things easy for a bit, laddie. We've got our woman. Just a question of tying up a few loose ends and making up a neat parcel for the public prosecutor.'

In spite of his aching feet and protesting stomach, Chief Inspector Dover achieved the demeanour of a conquering general as MacGregor held the door open for him to sweep into The Jolly Sailor, his latest case as good as solved.

Chapter Seven

Although he put a brave face on it to impress Sergeant MacGregor, Dover wasn't at all that optimistic about the progress he was making. Nothing would give him greater pleasure than to pin the poison-pen letters fairly and squarely on Dame Alice, but even he realized that there was a formidable gap between the desire and its achievement. He grew more depressed as the evening wore on. The Jolly Sailor wasn't exactly the last word in luxury, and Dover had got past the age, if he'd ever been at it, when he willingly sacrificed his bodily comforts in the chase for glory. His room was cold, damp and noisy. His bed was lumpy. The food on the whole wasn't bad, but Mrs Quince thought more about bingo than she did about the deeds of the inner man. She'd rushed off again to another session and their evening meal had been brought, once more, across the road from Freda's Café by the ever-willing Charlie Chettle. It wasn't really good enough, but any remonstrance flounde ed upon the rock of Mrs Quince's already limited sense of obligation. Even after dinner, things got no better. Mr Tompkins didn't put in an appearance and MacGregor was a remarkably slow drinker, almost as though he wasn't trying.

At half past nine Dover decided that nothing ventured, nothing won. He phoned his home. His sister-in-law answered. As soon as he heard her voice Dover replaced the receiver. The e was no hope from that quarter. He'd just have to stick it out in Thornwich a bit longer. He hoped his wife would have the decency to let him know the instant it was safe for him to return to his own bed and board.

Wednesday morning dawned, bright and sunny for a change. It was still quite a nice day when Dover opened his eyes and wondered how he was going to get through the next twenty-four hours. He could, he supposed grumpily, go out and interview a few more of these dratted women, but the prospect was uninviting. It was all so boring and, besides, what was the point? He'd already unmasked the nigger in the woodpile and it was unlikely that anybody else in the village would be able to give him concrete evidence of Dame Alice's guilt. He turned ponderously over in bed and tried to shut out the sounds of the traffi which was tearing noisily past his window.

'Strewth, thought Dover miserably, what a life! He screwed his eyes up as a sudden ray of sunshine pierced the grubby lace curtains which covered the window. Typical of the blasted place: when it wasn't soaking you with rain it was blinding you with sunshine! He'd have to do something, damn it. Well, he'd have to *look* as though he was doing something. Dame Alice had a set-up in Thornwich which could well be the envy of the OGPU or the Gestapo and until she was safely behind bars or tied up in a strait-jacket – according to the whim of the judge – it would be as well not to provide her with additional ammunition. Dover drifted off on a side speculation as to what the real relationship between Dame Alice and the Assistant Commissioner had been all those years ago. Could they really have …? Mind you, they were younger then. Dover wrinkled his nose thoughtfully. Even so … Oh well, it was probably like female hippopotamuses. Still, it conjured up a pretty revolting picture all the same. Oh, be fair, Dover, who could spend hours on this sort of thing, told himself, there is a Mrs Assistant Commissioner and there was a Mr Stote-Weedon, so …

A scream of brakes and a roar of vulgar abuse from the road outside brought Dover back to reality. He still hadn't got the rest of the day organized. He turned over on his back. He could, perhaps, go and see another poison-pen victim. Mrs Crotty, for example. 'Strewth, no! She lived right at the top of the hill, even higher up than Dame Alice, and he wasn't going to slog up there again for anybody. Who else was there? Mrs Tompkins? She lived right opposite, just across the road. It wouldn't be so far to walk. Oh, to hell with it, thought Dover with sudden inspiration, he could spend the day in his room studying the file. That sounds reasonable enough, doesn't it? Or had he already used that one before? Well, whether he had or he hadn't, he hadn't actually read the blasted file yet and today was as good a day as any. Dover pulled the sheets up over his head with a grunt of satisfaction. The relief at having found an agreeable solution to his problem was so great that he managed to drop off to sleep again for another blissful hour.

Eventually Dover settled down to his studies and Sergeant MacGregor was dispatched into the fresh air with the vague instruction to go and ask some questions and see what he could find out. It wasn't long before Dover discovered, once again, that it is better to travel than to arrive. The Chief Inspector had as healthy an interest in smut as anybody you could name, but these poison-pen letters were a bit too much of a good thing. The e were now nearly a hundred of them on the police file and Dover's initial interest had palled rapidly after he had ploughed through the first ten. They really were amazingly disgusting and, for a moment, his conviction that Dame Alice had typed them was severely shaken. However he gallantly steeled his resolution and his confidence in his ability to spot a wrong 'un and read doggedly on. Compared with Thornwich, Sodom and Gomorrah must have been purer than the driven snow. All the women who had been honoured by this unwanted, one-sided correspondence were accused of a wide range of exotic deviations, the detailing of which left nothing to the imagination. If one-tenth of the accusations were true, the village ought to be a happy hunting ground for students of morbid psychology. It had everything from algolagnia to zoophilism, and a lot of nasty things in between.

Dover was so punch drunk by this battering of obscenity that he had to take a short nap after lunch to get his strength back. Following his nap he had his tea, then he went on desultorily leafing through the file. The notes made by the local police on the various lines they had investigated were totally uninteresting. All the ideas had crumbled into dead ends and even Dover's critical eye, ever ready to spot the faults of others, couldn't pick out anything which ought to have been done which hadn't.

Dover blew fretfully down his nose and scratched his head. He got up from the table and went to look out of the window. The sky had clouded over and it looked as though the rain would start again at any minute. Dover sighed hopelessly. What a life! He watched the stream of lorries thundering by. He had been pursuing his studies in the bar parlour. The e was nobody else about at this time of day, and it was a locale less open to malicious misrepresentation than his bedroom. It was even, fractionally, less depressing. He went on staring through the window. Th shops opposite, Arthur Tompkins's grocery store and a scruff little sweetshop and tobacconist's, had blinds lowered across their windows. Wednesday afternoon. It must be early-closing day. Dover leaned his elbow on the window-sill. The place was like a bloody morgue. He had just started wondering what MacGregor was up to, when he saw a small black saloon car pull up and park on the other side of the road. For want of something better to do, he watched it. The car door opened and Arthur Tompkins, looking quite natty in a swagger overcoat and light-coloured driving gloves, got out and carefully locked the door behind him. As he was turning away from the car, he glanced across the road at The Jolly Sailor and saw the pathetic figu e of Dover standing in the window. Arthur Tompkins waved. Hopefully Dover waved back. Arthur Tompkins crossed the road, having looked carefully in both directions, and a few moments later joined Dover in the bar.

'Hallo, Mr Dover! I wondered if I'd find you in here. I'd heard you were spending the day catching up with your paperwork.'

'We can't affo d to leave any stone unturned,' said Dover. 'Every little detail is important on a job like this.'

'Oh, I'm sure it is,' agreed Mr Tompkins. 'I must say, you make me feel quite guilty. Here you are, stuck indoors, and there I am, gadding off enj ying myself.'

'Where've you been?' asked Dover enviously.

'Oh, well, just into Cumberley, as a matter of fact,' admitted Mr Tompkins, 'doing a bit of shopping. They close early on Saturday so it's quite convenient, really.'

'You didn't take your wife with you?' observed Dover, who had reached the stage when he was grateful for anybody to talk to.

Mr Tompkins frowned. 'No, she wasn't feeling at all herself. She got another of those blessed letters this morning and she seemed really upset about it. I tried to laugh it off but you know what women are like. She seemed to take it really to heart, this one. Even more than the others and, heaven knows, those played enough havoc with her nerves. I was really worried about her this morning and I said I'd stay at home this afternoon, but she wouldn't hear of it. Said she'd have a nap after dinner and that she'd be all right by tea-time. Well, now,' – Mr Tompkins put a brave face on it – 'I mustn't bore you with my troubles. I'll bet you've got enough of your own, eh?'

Dover nodded his head. He had.

'What I really popped across for, Mr Dover,' said Mr Tompkins, lowering his voice, 'was to see if you'd like to come back to the shop with me and have a cup of tea, or maybe something a bit stronger. It'll be nearly an hour before they open up here and, although I'm not claiming our place over there is any palace, it's a damned sight more comfortable – if you'll pardon my French – and warmer.'

'Well, that's very nice of you, my dear fellow,' said Dover, already half-way up the stairs to collect his hat and coat. 'Very nice of you indeed. I shan't be a jiff .'

Solicitously Mr Tompkins piloted Dover across the road. 'We don't want you to get run over and killed do we, Mr Dover?' he joked as they nipped between a couple of lorries.

'Nice little car you've got,' remarked Dover politely as they reached the opposite pavement.

'Oh, that!' Mr Tompkins's tone was contemptuous. 'Nothing but a blooming soap-box on wheels. And about as fast. I'd like one of those nice little Mercedes sports. A white one. Lovely jobs, they are. But' – he fished in his pockets for his keys – 'Mrs Tompkins doesn't like going fast and, of course, an open car's quite out of the question with her neuralgia. Shall I go first, Mr Dover? It's a bit tricky unless you know your way about.'

Dover followed Mr Tompkins into the shop and carefully shut the door behind him. Then he stood and waited while Mr Tompkins walked across to the light switch.

'I'm always meaning to have another switch put in by the front door,' he apologized, 'but somehow I never seem to get around to it.'

Dover had smelled it as soon as he had entered the shop, but amongst the varied aromas coming from packets of detergents and dog biscuits, it had taken him a second or two to identify it. As soon as Mr Tompkins opened the door into the livingquarters at the back there was no mistaking what it was.

'Here, can you smell gas?' asked Dover, sniffing suspicious .

'Gas?' said Mr Tompkins. 'Are you sure? I haven't got a very acute sense of smell myself.' He sniffed too. 'My God, you're right!'

Things started happening quickly and, not surprisingly, Dover got rather out of touch. Mr Tompkins, with a shout of 'Winifred!' flung himself into the corridor. He rushed up to a door on the left-hand side and seized the handle.

'Oh my God!' he shouted frantically. 'It's locked!' He hurled himself at the door, trying to burst it open with his shoulder, but the door was much more stoutly built than Mr Tompkins was. Dover hurried along to help and found Mr Tompkins charging back up the corridor.

'I'll go round through the yard!' shouted Mr Tompkins. 'We'll never break that door down. You go into the kitchen and turn the gas off at the meter!'

They did a panic-stricken jig in the narrow passage as each tried to push past the other. Dover flattened Mr Tompkins against the wall. 'Where's the kitchen?' he bellowed.

'Down there at the bottom of the corridor!'

Mr Tompkins, his hat falling off in the process, belted across the shop. He struggled a moment with the lock before he could get the door open and then he disappeared outside.

Dover headed at a dignified gallop for the kitchen. It took him some moments of feverish searching to locate the gas meter which was concealed in a cupboard under the sink, and then he had to lie down on his stomach before he could find the tap. Panting and groping and cursing he fumbled around in the dark. 'Matches!' he muttered to himself, rolling over on the floor to get to his trouser pocket. ''Strewth, no! Not matches!' He rolled back on his stomach.

By the time he'd actually found the tap and turned it off, a white-faced, sick-looking Mr Tompkins came into the kitchen at a run.

'It's Winifred!' he gasped as Dover picked himself up off the floo, wiping his hands on his overcoat. 'I've got to go back to her. Get a doctor, quick!'

''Strewth!' grumbled Dover again as he hurried in Mr Tomkins's wake out of the kitchen. As he went heavily down the hall he glanced into the room from which waves of stinking, choking gas still seemed to be issuing. He got a vague impression of a sofa with Mr Tompkins bending over it.

Dover pounded back through the shop and reached the pavement outside. His hands were filthy and the front of his overcoat was covered in dust from the floo . His bowler hat had disappeared somewhere in the confusion and his hair sprouted in all directions like a golliwog's. All in all he was not a sight to inspire either confidence or espect.

Naturally there was nobody about. Dover looked disconsolately up the hill. He had a hazy idea that Dr Hawnt lived in the same row of semi-detached houses as Mrs Leatherbarrow. It looked a long way. It would be far better to delegate the somewhat ignominious rôle of messenger-boy and get back inside to comfort and support Mr Tompkins, especially, as Dover realized with a start, since it was now raining.

'Is anything wrong, Mr Dover?'

It was Charlie Chettle calling to him through cupped hands from across the road. Dover nodded his head and waved vigorously. Mr Chettle bided his time and then skipped smartly through the traffic with s y expertise.

Dover welcomed him as though he were manna from heaven. 'Do you know where Dr Hawnt lives?'

Charlie Chettle nodded his head. His exertions in crossing the road had left him speechless. His eyes were watering and his nose was running, but Dover had no time to be bothered with petty details like that.

'Right! Well, you run up there as fast as you can and tell him he's wanted immediately. Mrs Tompkins.'

The old-age pensioner's eyes grew wide and he would doubtless have asked a few pertinent questions if Dover hadn't given him a hefty shove in the back to get him moving. Coughing and choking, Mr Chettle set off up the hill. It was one thing to be able to cross a few yards of main road without getting crushed under the wheels of a lorry, but quite another to tackle the formidable pull up to Dr Hawnt's house. Mr Chettle was more of a sprinter than a long-distance man, but he prided himself on being game for anything. He staggered heroically on, his cloth cap pulled well down over his eyes and his muffler tight ound his scraggy neck.

Dover watched him disappear into the gloom. Couldn't the old fool go any faster than that? 'Get a move on!' he bawled at Mr Chettle's slowly retreating back. 'It's an emergency! Matter of life and death!'

Mr Chettle half-turned and waved. 'Right you are, lad!' he gasped. 'Leave it to me!'

Dover shrugged his shoulders and went back indoors. Mr Tompkins was still in the little sitting-room which contained the sofa and, Dover presumed, the gas fi e. Dover poked his head round the door.

'How's it going?' he asked in a tone which turned out more conversational than he had intended.

Mr Tompkins dropped the hand he had been holding. It belonged to a woman who lay, covered with a hand-knitted shawl, on the sofa.

'I don't think it looks too good, Mr Dover.' Mr Tompkins gulped and shook his head. 'I don't think it looks too good at all.'

'The doctor should be here in a minute,' said Dover, feeling that under the circumstances he should take as optimistic a view as possible. The odds were strongly in favour of Mr Chettle taking a trip through the pearly gates himself long before he got as far as the doctor's house.

Mr Tompkins nodded his head absent-mindedly.

'Anything I can do?' asked Dover, looking idly round the sitting-room which, as yet, he had not entered. It was a tiny room and seemed to be packed with furniture, though Dover realized, on reflection, that it contained nothing more than a sofa, two upright chairs, a television set and a low table. Rather incongruously there was a french window set in the wall opposite the door. It led out into a little backyard stacked with empty packing-cases and mouldering cardboard boxes.

Dover shivered. The e was a howling gale blowing through the room. 'Might be a good idea to shut that french window,' he suggested. 'I reckon you've cleared all the gas out now.'

Meekly Mr Tompkins left the sofa and closed the french window. As an afterthought he drew the curtains. 'Mr Fewkes is a great one for staring in,' he explained.

'What do you think happened?' asked Dover, still lingering uneasily by the door.

'I don't know,' said Mr Tompkins, who suddenly looked very tired. 'She came in here to have a lie down after dinner. I suppose the light on the gas fi e must have blown out somehow and she'd fallen asleep and just didn't notice.'

'Hm,' said Dover. 'Well, it's a very small room, isn't it? It wouldn't take long to fill with gas'

'All this accommodation at the back of the shop is lousy,' said Mr Tompkins with an unexpected burst of anger. 'It's poky and cramped. The e isn't room to swing a cat round. I wouldn't have minded if we'd been forced to live here, but we weren't.'

Dover sighed. 'Did she usually lock the door when she had a nap?' he asked.

Mr Tompkins looked at the Chief Inspector in surprise. 'No,' he said slowly, 'of course she didn't.'

'The door was locked on the inside?

'Yes. I found the key on the hearth-rug when I broke in. That must mean she locked the door herself, from inside the room, mustn't it?'

'Was the french window shut?'

'Oh yes, and locked. I had to break a pane of glass to get my hand through to open it.' Mr Tompkins turned to look curiously at the french window.

'How about the gas fi e,' asked Dover, 'have you ever had any trouble with it blowing out before?'

'No.' Mr Tompkins, like an automaton, transferred his gaze to the gas fi e. 'It's as old as the hills. You've got to use matches to light it, but it's always been perfectly safe.'

Unwillingly Dover advanced into the room and bent down to have a closer look. 'I supposed you turned the gas off?

Mr Tompkins nodded. 'It was the first thing I did, Mr Dover. Naturally. Of course, I knew you were turning it off at the meter but it was still coming through when I got in here.'

Dover tried the tap. It turned easily, neither too stiff nor too slack. He straightened up with a grunt and looked at the face of the woman lying motionless on the sofa. Dead as mutton, if he was any judge.

'What do you think?' asked Mr Tompkins anxiously. 'Do you think it would be a good idea to carry her outside into the fresh air?'

The e was a sound of voices in the shop, and a few moments later a feebly protesting Dr Hawnt was escorted, somewhat energetically, down the corridor by Sergeant MacGregor.

'Trust you!' growled Dover to his assistant as he backed out of the way. 'You're never bloody-well here when you're wanted!'

Dr Hawnt was propelled into the sitting-room and pointed in the direction of his patient. He managed to fling one glance of mute reproach at Dover before collapsing in an involuntary heap by the sofa.

Dover and MacGregor retired to the kitchen while Mr Tompkins, thinking that the doctor would prefer to be left alone, hung miserably in the corridor by the sitting-room door.

'I'm sorry I wasn't here, sir,' said MacGregor as Dover settled himself on a kitchen chair. 'I didn't know anything was wrong until old Mr Chettle asked me if I'd help Dr Hawnt down here. He's a funny old codger, isn't he? He kept shouting, "Tell 'em to fetch a doctor!" all the way down the hill. He gave way completely at the knees a couple of times and I thought I'd finish up by having to carry him.'

'Have you got a fag?' asked Dover.

'In here, sir?' MacGregor sniffed the air doubtfully. 'Do you think it's safe?'

'Well, you go out in the corridor,' said Dover sourly, 'when you strike the match. If we don't get an explosion I'll have a cigarette.'

MacGregor looked at him to see if he was joking. He wasn't. With a resigned shrug of his shoulders MacGregor did as he was told. The e was no explosion.

Dover dragged the cigarette smoke into his lungs and coughed. ''Strewth,' he remarked, 'you aren't half buying some muck these days.'

'What's been going on, sir?' asked MacGregor, restraining an almost overwhelming desire to ram Dover's dentures down his throat.

'Mrs Tompkins has croaked herself,' said Dover in a bored voice. 'Suicide, sir?'

'Looks like it. The door was locked on the inside, and from the look of the tap on the gas fi e it couldn't have been turned on by accident.'

'Oh dear,' said MacGregor, feeling the remark rather inadequate, but what else could you say? 'Has it anything to do with these poison-pen letters, sir?'

Dover wrinkled his nose. 'Might have. Mr Tompkins says she's been getting very upset about them. She got another one this morning. You'd better collect it later on for the file ' He flicke the ash off his cigarette on to the kitchen floo . 'She seems to have been a pretty neurotic type from what I've heard.' He looked round the kitchen with a sniff of disparagement. 'Fancy living in a slum like this with a hundred and seventy thousand quid in the bank!'

It was a long wait before Dr Hawnt came tottering out of the sitting-room. It was Dover who took charge of the proceedings.

'Well, doctor,' he said when they'd got Dr Hawnt balanced on another chair in the kitchen, 'is she dead?'

Dr Hawnt's face expressed a horrified astonishment. 'Gracious heavens!' he squeaked. 'I didn't think there was any doubt about it!' He made a feeble effo t to get to his feet. 'I'd better go and have another look.'

'Oh, sit down!' snapped Dover irately. 'Of course she's dead!'

'Well, *I* thought so,' mumbled Dr Hawnt. 'The e's no pulse and I couldn't see any signs that she was still breathing. Mind you, we're all human and if you'd like to call in a second opinion you won't hurt my feelings in the least. In fact,' Dr Hawnt added with pathetic anxiety, 'I'd prefer it, really I would.'

'How long's she been dead?'

'Oh dear!' Dr Hawnt fidgeted restlessly on his chair. 'I do wish people would realize that I'm just not up to this kind of thing. I don't know how long she's been dead. I've been retired for over twenty years. I haven't got a thermometer these days. And you need the body temperature, I remember that quite clearly. The e's some sort of formula you've got to work out but, of course, I've forgotten that years ago. Why don't you get that chap from Bearle? He'd be much more help to you than I am.'

Dover scowled. 'What did she die of?' he asked.

'How should I know?' retorted Dr Hawnt reasonably. 'You need a doctor to tell you that sort of thing. I suppose it was an overdose of sleeping tablets.'

'An overdose of sleeping tablets?' howled Dover, going quite red in the face.

Dr Hawnt fumbled half-heartedly through his pockets. 'Well, I found this under the body,' he said. 'It fell to the floor when I moved her. Gave me quite a turn, I can tell you. I thought she was coming back to life for one dreadful moment.' Dover almost snatched the little bottle out of his hand. 'You can see for yourself, it says sleeping tablets on the label.'

'Are these hers?' Dover turned furiously on poor Mr Tompkins.

'Oh yes, Mr Dover. Definitel . She's been taking them for some months now. Only one at night, though. The 're very strong and the doctor warned her not to exceed the dose.'

'Do you know how many there were – last night, say?'

'It was a new bottle,' said Mr Tompkins faintly. 'She gets them fifty at a time so there'd be forty-nine left, that's allowing for the one she took last night.'

Dover counted out the pills which were still in the bottle on to the palm of his hand. 'Fifteen,' he announced. 'That means she's taken twenty-four.'

'Er – thirty-four, sir.' MacGregor corrected Dover's arithmetic and got a scowl of black fury for his pains.

Dover relieved his feelings by taking it out on. Dr Hawnt. 'Didn't you even notice she'd been gassed?' he asked in his most bullying manner. 'The oom was full of gas when we found her.'

'Well, it wasn't when I arrived,' snapped Dr Hawnt with a sudden burst of irritability on his own account. 'I'm not a magician, you know! I shouldn't have been sent for in the first place, and well you know it. It's not nice for a man of my age to be confronted with dead bodies just when he's sitting down to his tea. Still,' he added fairly, 'there wasn't any blood splashed about this time, I will grant you that.' He turned to MacGregor as being the most hopeful source of sympathy. 'It's only accidents and things they call me out for,' he explained unhappily. 'When it's just a nice touch of the 'flu in bed, they send for the chap in Bearle. Besides,' he said crossly, 'I don't approve of suicide.'

'Oh,' said Dover with crushing sarcasm, 'you do agree it was suicide, do you?'

'The e's no need to be rude, young man,' said Dr Hawnt haughtily. 'Why else would she leave a note if it wasn't suicide?'

Dover took a deep breath to steady his nerves. 'What note?' he roared.

Dr Hawnt began fumbling in his pockets again while Dover clenched his fists in a praiseworthy effo t to prevent himself tearing the old man apart with his bare hands. The note was found at last, a little crumpled and smelling of peppermints but otherwise just as it was when the doctor had discovered it, tucked under the late Mrs Tompkins's dead body.

'What the hell have you been doing,' snarled Dover, 'dancing the Charleston with her? I should have thought you could have made the sort of examination you do from twelve feet away!'

Dr Hawnt preserved a hurt but dignified silence. Dover read the note: a few words – 'I'm sorry but I just can't go on with this any longer' – scrawled in blue ball-point pen on a torn piece of paper. The final 'r' of the message ended in a long tail as though the pen had jerked uncontrollably in the writer's hand.

Chapter Eight

At this stage in the proceedings Chief Inspector Dover threw up
the sponge without a qualm and hurried back to The Jolly Sailor
for his dinner. With great consideration he took the dazed, but
wealthy, Mr Tompkins with him and left MacGregor behind at the
shop to clear up the mess. It meant that the sergeant would almost
certainly miss his dinner again, but that was an occupational
hazard and if he couldn't take a joke he shouldn't have joined.
Besides, as Dover pointed out, MacGregor's dinner wouldn't be
wasted. The newly bereaved Mr Tompkins could eat it. Dover was
a great believer in the therapeutic powers of food.

Once he'd been relieved of the Chief Inspector's presence,
MacGregor got down to his various tasks with vigour if not good
will. He was used to being Dover's dog's-body but this was passing
the buck a bit too far. The e was old Dr Hawnt to be returned,
alive if possible, to his residence but, after his gruelling experience
at the hands of Dover, he was clearly incapable of tackling that hill
even with MacGregor's sturdy assistance. Luckily Mr Tompkins
had accidentally left his bunch of keys on one of the counters
in the shop and MacGregor found them. He felt that, in the
circumstances, no harm would be done if he drove Dr Hawnt
home in the little black car.

Then there was Charlie Chettle, who'd turned up again out of
the blue, to be got rid of. He seemed to think that there had been

some financial agreement between himself and Dover to cover the fetching of Dr Hawnt. MacGregor grimly pointed out that this was extremely unlikely, but he gave a grinning Charlie Chettle a couple of half-crowns, just in case. Mr Chettle touched his forelock with old-world courtesy and plunged expertly into the traffic on his way to Th olly Sailor.

Then the proper authorities had to be informed and an ambulance summoned to convey Mrs Tompkins's remains to the mortuary. The e would have to be an autopsy, thanks to the unnecessary confusion Dr Hawnt had introduced into the cause of death, and MacGregor spent a long time on the telephone fixing everything up. The telephone was in the sitting-room with Mrs Tompkins's gradually stiffening body and it was, thought MacGregor, typical that nobody had even thought of using it. Everybody, not forgetting Dr Hawnt and Charlie Chettle, would have been saved a lot of trouble if they had.

It must have been well after nine o'clock when MacGregor at last had the shop and the living quarters to himself. After striking endless matches over a gas stove that wouldn't work, he finally thought of the meter and turned the main tap on again and made himself a cup of tea. Alone in the bleak kitchen he smoked a cigarette, drank his tea and thought. When he'd finished thinking he made a tour of all the rooms, opening drawers, poking into cupboards, pulling letters out of old envelopes and reading them. By a nice bit of luck the key ring which Mr Tompkins had accidentally left behind on the counter held all his keys, not only those for the car. MacGregor was able to open all the locks which otherwise might have restricted his search. Not that he was looking for anything in particular. It was just a vague idea that he had in the back of his mind and he thought he might as well indulge his natural curiosity while he had the chance. In any case it was preferable to going back to The Jolly Sailor and spending what remained of the evening in Dover's company.

When Dover heard the discreet tap on his bedroom door at midnight, he'd a pretty good idea who it was and feigned sleep, even adding a few snores to prove it. MacGregor was not fooled. Dover's light was still on and shone, like a good deed in a naughty world, through the cracks of the ill-fitting doo .

'What the hell do you want?' asked Dover crossly. 'Waking me up at this time of night! I'd just dropped off. Well, come on, you damned fool, don't just stand there. Tell me what it is and then push off!'

MacGregor told him and sat down resolutely on the chair by the bed. Dover's eyes popped and MacGregor waited with resignation for the storm to break.

'You must be out of your tiny mind!' said Dover, staring at his assistant with loathing. 'I can't start doing anything like that! Damn it all, man, Mr Tompkins is a friend of mine. I can't start going around asking him questions about where he was and what he was doing. What on earth's he going to think? Besides, it's ridiculous.'

'Yes, I'm sure it is, sir, but we can't just accept everything at its face value, can we? The e'll be plenty said if we don't make a normal investigation. It'd look as though we were trying to hush things up.'

'Rubbish!' said Dover, looking very cross and sulky. 'You don't think anybody else is cracked enough to think Tompkins murdered his wife, do you?'

'The e's bound to be talk, sir, especially in this village. Besides, it's not necessarily a question of Mr Tompkins having killed her. Somebody else might have done.'

'Who, for example?' asked Dover with a sneer.

'I don't know, sir,' explained MacGregor patiently. 'Tha 's what we've got to do a routine investigation for. But two days ago she did draw three hundred pounds in cash out of the bank, and there's no sign of the money anywhere in the house or in the shop.'

'I expect there's a perfectly simple explanation,' said Dover, glaring furiously at his sergeant.

'The e probably is, sir, if you ask Mr Tompkins about it.'

'Besides,' said Dover, switching quickly, 'Tompkins can't have anything to do with it. Damn it, MacGregor, I was there when he found her.'

'He might have set the whole thing up earlier, sir. You know that.'

Dover snorted despairingly. 'What for?' he demanded. 'God damn it, the man's got a hundred and seventy thousand quid! What in hell's name should he want to kill his wife for?'

'I think you should ask him to account for his movements this afternoon, sir, that's all,' said MacGregor, stubbornly determined that, however long it took, he was going to get his own way.

'Can't we wait until after the post-mortem?' asked Dover.

MacGregor shook his head. 'Even if the pm confirms suicide, sir, it still doesn't mean anything. We shall still be expected to make purely routine inquiries.'

Dover clutched at a last straw. 'I don't reckon it's our job at all. It's up to the local police.'

'They won't touch it, sir, I had a chat with them earlier on. They say this business is tied up with the poison-pen letters and the poison-pen letters are our pigeon.'

'What bloody nonsense!' snorted Dover. 'How the hell do they know what it's tied up with? That note Mrs Tompkins left might mean anything.'

'Well, that's why we must do a routine investigation, sir, isn't it? Just to determine if Mrs Tompkins did commit suicide and, if she did, why she did it.'

Put like that MacGregor's proposals sounded eminently reasonable, but that wasn't, from Chief Inspector Dover's point of view, any reason for accepting them. The trouble was, he thought petulantly after the sergeant had at last gone and left him in peace, that you just couldn't talk to a fellow like MacGregor. He was too rigid, too much bound by rules and regulations, didn't realize that a policeman had to use a bit of judgement and discretion. Any fool could see that Mrs Tompkins's suicide was an open and shut business. The e was just no point in trampling around and upsetting her poor bereaved husband. Just because you were a copper it didn't mean that you hadn't got a heart. And where Mr Tompkins was concerned Dover certainly had got a heart, or something.

He had spent the evening with the newly created widower and had chatted about a variety of subjects, just to take the poor chap's mind off things. They had discussed some of Dover's more successful cases, of which Mr Tompkins had received a skilfully edited account, and then, somehow, the conversation had drifted on to capital punishment. At this point Dover had got rather starry-eyed and spoke at length and with nostalgia of the good old days when you could wave the threat of the gallows before a suspect.

'It's not the same now,' he complained. 'You can't scare the living daylights out of a chap with life imprisonment. He knows as well as you do that he'll be out in twelve years or so, as long as he keeps his nose clean and doesn't spit in the governor's eye.'

'Really?' said Mr Tompkins with a very faint, polite smile.

'Ah,' said Dover smacking his lips. 'It was diffe ent in the old days. The pinions, the white cap, the knot under the left ear. They didn't strangle you, you know. The drop broke your neck. Or,' – Dover chuckled lugubriously – 'it was supposed to! The e was many a slip.'

Mr Tompkins gulped but it simply didn't enter Dover's head that anybody would object to his homely 'shop' talk about miscalculated drops, ropes incorrectly adjusted, novice hangmen and nervous performers in the main role.

Mr Tompkins did. He changed the conversation. He asked Dover's advice about his future. He was going to sell the shop and clear out of Thornwich. Now that Mrs Tompkins had gone there was no point in staying on. Maybe he should go abroad? Dover, who'd once gone on a day-trip to Calais, didn't think this was a very good idea. Too many bloody foreigners jabbering away like a parcel of monkeys. Maybe, said Mr Tompkins, he could use his pools money to invest in another sort of business, something a bit more exciting than the grocery trade. He knew Mr Dover would think him silly, but – now, he was quite serious, really – he'd always wanted to be a private detective. Well, of course, he knew it wasn't anything like what you read about in books, but even so ... What did Mr Dover think?

Mr Dover, his brain working with the speed of a computer, didn't think it was such a silly idea as all that. 'The e's a lot of money to be made out of a private detective agency,' he said. 'Of course,' he pointed out slowly, 'you'd need an experienced chap to go into partnership with you.'

Mr Tompkins grinned shyly. 'I've heard that a lot of senior detectives retire from the Yard and go into business on their own account.'

Dover took it even more slowly. 'You need quite a bit of capital for that sort of thing.'

'I've got quite a bit of capital,' said Mr Tompkins.

And there, for the time being, the matter rested. While Dover fully realized that nothing definite had been said he did go to sleep that night, when he'd got rid of MacGregor, musing gently about a nice, comfortably furnished offic with ex-Chief Inspector Dover sitting there. He dropped off before he got much beyond the 'sitting there' stage but, obviously, there would be a staff of hardworking operatives to do the actual labouring. Dover smiled in his sleep. He'd been dreaming about the joys of retirement ever since the first day he sta ted work.

So, although it was all a bit castles-in-Spain and counting unhatched chickens, Dover's attitude to Mr Tompkins on the morning following Mrs Tompkins's tragic death was benevolently neutral. Connoisseurs of the Dover interrogation technique ('don't hit 'em where the marks will show') would have been surprised if they could have seen how delicately, how gently and how considerately the Chief Inspector handled a rather offended Mr Tompkins.

The interview took place in Dover's bedroom. It was the only room both private enough and large enough to hold two policemen and Mr Tompkins at the same time. Mr Tompkins had the easy chair, Dover the hard upright one, and MacGregor perched himself on the bed.

'I'm sure you understand,' Dover began with a scowl for MacGregor and a reassuring beam for Mr Tompkins, 'that in all cases of sudden death we have to ask a few questions, just to get the record straight. The coroner rather expects us to, you know. It's just a question of routine, pure formality.'

Mr Tompkins nodded his head.

'Now,' said Dover, continuing to beam away like a Cheshire cat on full purrs, 'just tell us in your own words what happened yesterday morning. Let's start with breakfast. Did your wife seem all right then, her usual self, you know?'

'Well, yes, I think so,' said Mr Tompkins looking worriedly at MacGregor's pencil poised over his notebook. 'I took her breakfast up to her as usual just on eight o'clock.'

'She was ill then, was she?' asked Dover, pouncing like a hawk on any detail that would strengthen the simple suicide theory.

'Oh, no,' said Mr Tompkins, 'she always had her breakfast in bed.'

Dover looked at Mr Tompkins with some amazement. 'Go on,' he said with a sigh. 'What time did she get up?'

'About a quarter past nine, just before Mrs Poltensky, our daily help, arrived. I went out into the shop and I was in there till about eleven when Winifred – that is, Mrs Tompkins – brought me a cup of coffee. She said she wasn't feeling too good and I said, "Shall I call the doctor?" and she said, "No," and I said, "Well, why not go upstairs and have a hot bath and then have your lunch and have a nice lie-down on the sofa in the afternoon?" Well, she sort of seemed to think this was a good idea – about the bath, I mean. She said something about "Oh, yes, I'd like to feel clean," but I wasn't taking much notice because a customer had just come in and was rattling all the packets of biscuits she could lay her hands on to see if they were broken. The cheek of some people, you just wouldn't believe it!'

'So your wife went off to have her bath?' prompted Dover who could see this going on all morning.

'Tha's right. She came down again about twelve, I suppose, and we had a bite of lunch – Mrs Tompkins didn't eat much, I remember, but, then, she had never much of an appetite. After lunch she went to lie down in the sitting-room. Mrs Poltensky went with her to light the gas fi e' – Mr Tompkins swallowed hard – 'and get her settled on the sofa. I was still in the kitchen. Then Mrs Poltensky came back and said Mrs Tompkins had a touch of indigestion and she wanted a glass of brandy and hot water. My wife is – was – strict TT – never touched a drop except for medicinal purposes. Well, I got the brandy and hot water ready and Mrs Poltensky took it in to her. Then Mrs Poltensky got on with her work and I went upstairs and wrote a couple of letters and got myself changed because, of course, it was early-closing day and I was going out.

'I came downstairs and asked Mrs Poltensky how Mrs Tompkins was and she looked into the sitting-room and said she was nicely off in front of the fi e. I went into the kitchen to get some stamps and check the back door was locked while Mrs Poltensky was putting her coat on. Then we both just left the shop together. And that's all I know, Mr Dover. I didn't go near the place again all afternoon until I met you and we went back together.'

'Well,' said Dover, rubbing his hands happily together, 'that seems very satisfactory. Tha's given us a nice clear picture of what happened, hasn't it, Sergeant? I don't think we need distress Mr Tompkins any longer.'

'The e are just a couple of questions, sir,' said MacGregor tentatively.

'Oh, are, there?' Dover glared sourly at his sergeant. 'Well, get on with it! We don't want to be sitting here all day.'

'Mr Tompkins,' – after Dover's fawning tones, MacGregor's voice rang out hard and crisp – 'I understand your wife received another poison-pen letter yesterday. When did she actually open it?'

'I took it up to her on her breakfast tray. It came in the morning post and naturally I knew what it was. I've seen enough of the dratted things not to make any mistake. I think reading it was what upset her. I used to tell her to chuck the damned things in the fi e without opening them, but she just couldn't bring herself to do it, somehow. Curiosity, I suppose. I used to say to her, "You know what curiosity did," I'd say, "it killed the …"'

Mr Tompkins's voice trailed off as the unfortunate phrasing of his words sunk in.

Unperturbed MacGregor consulted his notes and calmly put his next question. Only when he was half-way through it did he realize that he had unwittingly revealed rather more of police methods than he had intended. Luckily for him, Mr Tompkins didn't seem to think it strange that a comparative stranger should be so intimately informed about the contents of his joint bank account.

'Winifred drew three hundred pounds out in cash?' repeated Mr Tompkins in bewilderment. 'No, I didn't know anything about it. She didn't tell me. What on earth did she want all that money for?'

'Well, we don't quite know at the moment, sir. It may have no bearing at all on Mrs Tompkins's death. Now then sir, to get back to the events of yesterday morning. After your wife went into the sitting-room to lie down after lunch, you yourself didn't actually go into the room, did you?'

'Er – no,' said Mr Tompkins uncomfortably. 'I thought it better not to disturb her.'

'Very right and proper, too!' snapped Dover, who was getting thoroughly fed up with MacGregor. 'Anything else, Sergeant?'

'Just one more question, sir. Mr Tompkins, you left the shop at what time?'

'About half past two.'

'Did you …?'

'Tha's two questions already!' exploded Dover. 'What do you think this is, a bloody inquisition? I'm not having any of this third degree carry-on here, you know!'

'It's all right, Mr Dover,' said Mr Tompkins, hastening to pour oil on waters that looked as though they'd be very troubled in a couple of minutes. 'I don't mind in the least. I've absolutely nothing to hide and I'm only too pleased to be of any help I can.' He drew his puny frame up proudly. 'I hope I know my duty as a responsible citizen.'

'Oh well, get on with it, MacGregor!' growled Dover and stalked over to the window. He stood stubbornly glaring down at the lorries rumbling past. Petulantly he prepared to dissociate himself from the whole unsavoury proceedings.

'Mr Tompkins,' – MacGregor got the little man's attention back from its concentration on Dover's sulky rear elevation – 'after you left the house at half past two with Mrs Poltensky, did you return again before you returned in the company of Chief Inspector Dover and discovered the body?'

In spite of himself Dover swung round from his station by the window. 'I'll say one thing for you, MacGregor,' he snarled, 'you're the most long-winded so and so I've ever come across in my entire bloody career!'

'Mr Tompkins?' MacGregor was having some difficult in keeping his temper. One day, he promised himself, he'd belt the old fool round the ears. But not before witnesses.

'No,' said Mr Tompkins, commendably keeping his head when all around were losing theirs.

'Then' pursued MacGregor, at last achieving his snide supplementary, 'where were you?'

Mr Tompkins went quite white. He swallowed hard and looked in Dover's direction. Dover turned round with a frown.

'Come on, man,' he said impatiently, 'it's not a state secret, for God's sake! Tell him where you were and we'll go and have a drink.'

'I can't,' gasped Mr Tompkins from a dry throat.

Dover's eyes popped. 'Can't or won't?' he demanded, forgetting that the recalcitrant witness was his newest and best friend.

'I won't,' said Mr Tompkins stoutly.

And an hour and a quarter later Dover and MacGregor had to admit, to their great chagrin, that he wouldn't.

Chief Inspector Dover did his nut. Far from speechless with fury he turned in a majesty of wrath on MacGregor, whose fault it all was anyhow. While the two policeman discussed their diffe ences in increasingly lurid language and mounting decibels, Mr Tompkins slipped diffidentl away to the peace and quiet of his own room. Nobody noticed his departure.

Dover was cross, very cross, with Mr Tompkins but he hadn't abandoned him.

'The e's some quite simple explanation,' he bellowed at MacGregor who bowed his head to the storm and mentally composed yet another pithy note tendering his resignation to the Assistant Commissioner for Crime. 'Blast your eyes, MacGregor, why can't you leave well alone? Mountains out of bloody mole-hills, that's what it is! Come on, we'll have to go and interview this charwoman. Maybe she'll be able to clear up your storm in a teacup.'

Mrs Poltensky, born and inbred in Thornwich, showed no surprise when she opened her door and found the two detective fellows from London, both breathing heavily, on the step. She lived little more than a stone's throw from The Jolly Sailor, in a cottage next door but one to Charlie Chettle. The Poltensky-Chettle row of cottages had little gardens in front and were considered vastly superior to those on the other side of the main road which had none. Mrs Poltensky lived at No 3, Willow View and was proud of it.

Mrs Poltensky installed her visitors in her front room. Apart from the kitchen, it was the only room on the ground floo , but all the Willow Viewers referred to it as their front room. She was a plump-faced woman with inquisitive brown eyes and a head full of paper curlers. She sat down opposite her interrogators, spread her knees wide apart and clamped two rough, red hands on them. She wiped her eyes on the edge of her apron and, as soon as this token salute to the recently departed had been made, got smartly down to business.

'I've lost a good job there,' she said, looking accusingly at Dover. 'He won't stay on in Thornwich, you know. Before the fl wers have had time to wither on her grave, he'll be showing us all a clean pair of heels. This post mortem they're all talking about – does that mean they're going to cut her up? Ooh, what a horrible thought! I hope they're going to bring her back here before they bury her. I've lost a good charring job and I don't want to lose the laying out as well. Why, I've laid out practically all her family what have died in the last twenty years, all except her cousin Fred who went under a landslide up at the quarry. That happened in 1947 and they haven't found him yet. Now, just you remind Arthur Tompkins that I'm expecting to lay her out. Be a crying shame to let somebody else get the job after all these years. I knew she'd never make old bones, you know,' she explained quickly as Dover took a deep breath preparatory to stopping the fl w. 'Her sort never do.'

She dabbed her eyes again and Dover leapt in. 'Do you know if anything was worrying her recently?'

'Enough to make her do herself in? No, I shouldn't have thought so. Strong as an ox, you know, she was really. All those headaches and upset stomachs and weak hearts, they were just turned on like a tap to bring young Arthur to heel. She'd have lived to be a hundred as far as her health's concerned.'

'What about the poison-pen letters? Did they upset her?'

Mrs Poltensky looked at Dover in some surprise. 'Not as I ever saw. Why should they? They were only dirty words on bits of paper. I've heard worse coming from The Jolly Sailor on a Saturday night in the old days, I can tell you. I've had two or three of the nasty things myself and, if it hadn't been for her ladyship up on the hill there poking her nose in as usual, I'd have thrown 'em on the back of the fi e and had done with 'em. Mrs Tompkins felt the same way. She said all this fuss Dame Alice was making, and bringing the police in, was just encouraging the loony who was writing them in the first place. And, if you ask me, she was right. It was her husband who wanted 'em preserved. He said the police would never catch whoever was writing the letters without the evidence. I can't say as how you've done much with it now you've got it, to my way of thinking.'

Dover sniffed and indicated that Sergeant MacGregor could go on with the questioning.

'Mrs Poltensky,' said MacGregor, 'you've worked for Mrs Tompkins for some time?'

'Four years,' Mrs Poltensky agreed with no small pride, 'and never a day off and ne er no complaints, either.'

'How did Mr and Mrs Tompkins get on together?'

Mrs Poltensky studied her apron. 'Well, now,' she said thoughtfully, 'that's a bit of a facer, a question like that. Since you're asking me, I'd say it was six of one and half a dozen of the other. You see, to my way of thinking, Winifred Bragg-what-was was one of those women who rightly never should have got wed in the first place. I know there's more to marriage than four naked legs in a bed, if you'll pardon the expression, but I reckon any man worth his salt wants a bit more than a pair of woolly bedsocks on a cold night. All Winifred Tompkins wanted out of marriage was a wedding ring and the right to call herself Mrs. It was when she found out her husband wanted a bit more, that half these illnesses of hers started. Anyhow, that's my opinion.'

'Did Mr Tompkins try looking for consolation elsewhere?' asked MacGregor.

Mrs Poltensky's mouth clamped firmly to. 'I'm not one to gossip,' she said righteously. 'What he did was his own affair and I know nothing about it, and don't want to, either. *She* thought he did, I don't mind telling you that. Tha 's why she started all this baby business, thought it'd give him a bit more interest in staying home at nights. Daft, I call it, and I told her so straight. "Adopting a baby?" I said. "You must be out of your mind! You don't know where it's been nor who's had it." Anyhow, as things turned out, I could have saved my breath because they told her she couldn't have one.'

'Did Mr Tompkins want to adopt a baby?'

'He did not and I can't say as I blame him. Not that he ever came right out and told her so to her face, but I could tell. I wouldn't want to see *his* face when he found out it had started up again!' Mrs Poltensky chuckled reflecti ely to herself.

'When what had started up again?' asked MacGregor.

'Why, getting a baby of course. None of these legal places would help, so Mrs Tompkins got on to the idea of getting hold of some girl who'd got herself in the family way and buying the baby off her. It was all supposed to be very hush-hush – sort of black-market thing, really. And black-market prices, too, from what I heard. She told me a bit about it and swore me to secrecy. Even a worm will turn, and she reckoned if Arthur got wind of it he'd go clean through the roof. Spending a small fortune on buying some tart's fatherless brat and her nagging him every time he bought himself half a pint at The Jolly Sailor and moaning that they'd finish up in the wo khouse!'

'A small fortune?' said MacGregor with a look of great satisfaction on his face. 'You don't happen to know how much, do you?'

Mrs Poltensky shook her head. 'No, I didn't have time to get round to finding that out. It was a tidy sum, that I do know. Eh dear, it's a rum life! Some people'll shell out a fistful of pound notes to get rid of a baby and others'll spend their last farthing trying to get hold of one. It makes you wonder, sometimes, doesn't it?'

Chapter Nine

Mrs Poltensky found that being interviewed, while very enjoyable, was thirsty work. Completely off her own bat she suggested that the three of them might take what she called a natural break while she brewed up a cup of tea. Dover showed immediate signs of returning to life and mentioned that, owing to the nature of their work, detectives were always missing their meals and a bite to eat, if available, would be highly appreciated. Mrs Poltensky smiled approvingly and said she liked a man with a good appetite. Roguishly Dover promised to do his best to earn her affection. Mrs Poltensky giggled and said that he was a one. MacGregor winced and suffe ed for the frivolity of his elders.

Mrs Poltensky provided a sumptuous spread. Most of it, including the cake, had come out of the deep freeze in Mr Tompkins's shop where she was privileged to buy at specially reduced prices.

'I can't see the point,' she said as she poured out another cup of tea all round, 'of wasting time cooking things yourself when you can get 'em ready-made, or almost, in the shops.' She helped herself to another piece of cake. 'They say it's not as good as mother used to make but all I say is, you didn't know my mother!' She laughed comfortably.

MacGregor wiped his fingers daintily on his spare pocket handkerchief and resumed the questioning.

'You don't know where Mrs Tompkins was going to get this baby from, do you, Mrs Poltensky?'

'What baby?'

'The illegitimate ba y she was going to buy.'

'Oh, well, I've got an idea something had gone wrong there, too. Funny how some people never seem to have any luck, isn't it? Mind you, she never said anything to me about it – she was never one to admit she'd made a mistake, Winifred wasn't. It was always somebody else's fault if anything went wrong. Tuesday, me day before she passed on, she'd been very funny. Angry, you know, but keeping it all bottled up inside her. Picking on you for every little thing just to give herself an excuse to blow off steam. Childish, I call it, but I just got on with my work and waited for it to blow over. I don't know what made me think it was connected with that baby business, I just did, that's all.'

Dover finished up a processed cheese sandwich which seemed to have been overlooked. 'What about yesterday?' he asked. 'Mr Tompkins says that after his wife had gone to lie down he himself never went into the sitting-room.'

Mrs Poltensky considered this carefully. 'Tha 's right,' she said at last, 'no more he did. I went in to see she'd got everything she wanted and she said she'd got indigestion and wanted a glass of brandy. I told Mr Tompkins and he gave it to me and I took it back in to her. Then he went upstairs and I got on with what I was doing. When he came downstairs again I took another peep at her. She was fast asleep on the sofa in front of the fi e. Then Mr Tomkins and me, we got our hats and coats on and went out of the shop together.'

'Are you sure Mr Tompkins couldn't have slipped into the room at any time?'

'Of course I'm sure. I was doing the passage. He'd have had to climb over me to get to the sitting-room door. Besides,' – Mrs Poltensky looked puzzled – 'why should he? You're not thinking he did her in, are you?'

'Good heavens, no!' said Dover with total assurance. 'It's just that we've got to make inquiries in a case like this. Some people have nasty minds, Mrs Poltensky.' He glared angrily at MacGregor. 'It's as well to stop a lot of unfounded rumours and stupid suspicions before they start.'

'Well, you won't find anybody in Thornwich looking sideways at Arthur Tompkins,' said Mrs Poltensky rather huffi . 'The e's plenty that thinks he's a bit of a cissy and there's plenty that's jealous of his money, but never a one that I've heard of who'd so much as whisper that he'd been a bad husband. I'm not saying as how it was all cakes and ale but, in their tin-pot way, I reckon they were as happy as most. Maybe things weren't as wonderful as he thought they were going to be when he married her, but that's an experience we've all had, isn't it? And I dare say they didn't see eye to eye over the money they won. But if Winifred had given him his head he'd have frittered away every penny of it – and deep down he knows he would. Expensive cars, a flat in London, a trip round the world – he was always on about something. Somebody had to say no, and Winifred Tompkins said it. With all her faults he could have done a lot worse than marry her. And he thought the world of her, really. The e's many a chap'd have given her a good clip across the jaw for some of the things she did and said, but he never so much as raised his voice to her. He waited on her hand and foot when she was feeling poorly, or said she was. It might have done them both a world of good if he'd stood up to her a bit more and I'm not saying it wouldn't, but we'd probably all be better off if e weren't what we are, wouldn't we?'

'Er – yes,' said Dover rather inadequately. 'I suppose we would.'

He seemed prepared to leave it at that, but MacGregor was determined to press on with his investigation, whatever injury it did to Dover's finer feelings. He'd put up with the idiosyncrasies of the Chief Inspector for some considerable time now and, after much heart searching and simple cold feet at the very idea, he had decided that their uneasy tandem would have to be steered from behind. It was going to be hard work, pedalling Dover's excessive and inert bulk up the hill of success, but MacGregor considered himself equal to the task. So far, he congratulated himself, he hadn't done too badly. At least Dover hadn't flatly refused to let him investigate the circumstances of Mrs Tompkins's death or to pursue the line that, if it wasn't suicide, Mr Tompkins was *ex-officio* the chief suspect. Usually the Chief Inspector's mind worked with childlike simplicity along this very track and, when a woman met an unlawful end, he resolutely refused to look further than her husband for the culprit. Had it not been for the special relationship which existed between Dover and Mr Tompkins, the latter would have had a very rough time of it long before now. The e was nothing Dover enjoyed more than a bout of bullying and Mr Tompkins, timid, self-effacing, anxious not to give trouble, was tailor-made for one of the Chief Inspector's more brutal performances. But even MacGregor was forced to admit that things were looking very white for Mr Tompkins. Still, there was this refusal to account for his whereabouts yesterday afternoon, and all a policeman's worst instincts are aroused when people won't confide in them. They seem to take it personally.

The e was a dreadful screech of brakes from the road outside but MacGregor ignored it and put his question loudly over the distant shouts and curses.

'Mrs Poltensky,' he began, making it all very formal and rather pompous, 'as the Chief Inspector has told you, we are very anxious to clear up any suspicion about the way Mrs Tompkins met her death, especially in connection with her husband. Unfortunately Mr Tompkins refuses to tell us where he was yesterday afternoon. Now, we're sure that there is some perfectly innocent explanation' – you could-practically see the guile dripping – 'but Mr Tompkins's reticence on this point is proving rather embarrassing. I wonder if you could help us?'

Mrs Poltensky regarded MacGregor doubtfully. With a slovenly lay-about like Dover she felt perfectly at home. After all, she'd married one of the same ilk, though being a Pole, he'd had a bit more surface glamour about him. MacGregor – young, pushing, beautifully dressed – was a horse of quite a diffe ent colour. As a little girl Mrs Poltensky had seen innumerable cart-horses struggling with heavy loads up Thornwic 's fiendish hill. She'd never seen a racehorse, except on the telly, and for her money you could keep 'em. Stupid, skinny things they were. Never done an honest day's work in their lives, nor – by the look of him – had young hopeful here either. You'd only got to look at his hands to see that. Mrs Poltensky moved her gaze to Dover's enormous fists. She nodded approvingly. Broken nails, dirt-begrimed, yes – that's what a real man's hands were like!

'Mrs Poltensky?' prompted MacGregor sharply.

Mrs Poltensky had forgotten the question. MacGregor repeated it. Mrs Poltensky scratched her chin.

'Wednesday afternoon?' she said to herself. 'Now what is it he's supposed to be doing Wednesday afternoons? I've given up trying to keep track of him,' she told MacGregor. 'He gets a new enthusiasm like other people get the colic, and it's none of my business anyhow what he does with his spare time. Unless it's like when he started breeding racing-pigeons and I had to do all the clearing up, and bury 'em when they kept dying off because he forgot to feed them. Now, let me think. The e was playing with toy soldiers, but I think that was on a Friday and I'm sure he packed that in weeks ago. Then there was pistol-shooting but he did that out in the shed in the yard. Had it made sound-proof to stop the neighbours complaining. He had to do his own cleaning-up in there because I refused to set foot in the place and so did Mrs Tompkins. Anyhow, that particular hobby was at its height this time last year, so it'll be dead and buried now. You don't happen to know where he'd been, do you? That might jog my memory.'

MacGregor looked questioningly at Dover.

Dover gave a massive yawn. 'Well,' he said, 'I remember be did say something about having been doing some shopping.'

'Ah,' said Mrs Poltensky, 'that'd be Cumberley. Bearle closes Wednesdays, same as we do.'

'Tha 's right,' said Dover, 'it was Cumberley. I remember him saying.'

'But it couldn't have been, sir,' said MacGregor, sitting bolt upright and quivering like a gun dog. 'If he'd come from Cumberley his car would have been pointing towards Bearle, wouldn't it? But it wasn't. It was pointing towards Cumberley, which means he'd come from Bearle or from the direction of Bearle, at any rate. I drove Dr Hawnt home in it last night and I remember quite distinctly. I didn't have to turn round or anything. The car was pointing up the hill towards Dr Hawnt's house *and* towards Cumberley. Now that means ...'

'All right, laddie,' said Dover sourly, 'you've made your point. One of these days you'll cut yourself, you're so bloody sharp.'

'Bearle?' said Mrs Poltensky who'd been pursuing her own line of thought. 'Well now, if it's Bearle, it could be one of a couple of things: Judo or French lessons. No, I'm telling a lie! He gave up Judo when he banged his head that time, and anyhow, that was on Mondays. No, Wednesday afternoon in Bearle, he'll have been to a French lesson.'

'A French lesson?' said Dover. 'What the hell does he want a French lesson for?'

'To learn French, of course,' said Mrs Poltensky, who had more common sense in her little finger than Dover and MacGregor had in their combined bodies. 'The Riviera, that's what he was always dreaming about. He's got a box full of them little coloured pamphlets telling you all about how wonderful it is. A villa on the Mediterranean, that's what he'd set his sights on, when it wasn't a luxury flat in Paris. "You don't want to go all gooey-eyed about a bunch of blooming foreigners," I said. "I know what I'm talking about," I told him, "after all, I married one. You take my word for it, once you get past all that fancy way of talking they're just the same as the rest of us underneath, only more so."'

'Do you know where he went to in Bearle?' asked MacGregor, flourishing pencil and notebook

'No, I do not,' said Mrs Poltensky with a plummy chuckle. 'I'm not likely to start learning French at my age. Anyhow, I only ever heard him mention it casual like. I didn't pay no more notice to it than all the rest of his fads and fancies.'

'But why should he keep it quiet?' asked MacGregor with a puzzled frown. 'Why wouldn't he tell us where he was? The e's nothing to be ashamed of, is there?'

'Ah, but you don't know Thornwich, do you?' said Mrs Poltensky. 'You've got to realize that everything the Tompkinses do is news. Mrs Tompkins was born and bred here. Most of us knew her and her family when she was a girl, and a pretty poor lot they were, too. Her father drank like a fish and her mother was the biggest slut I've ever seen in my born days. Why do you think she came back to Thornwich when she got all that money? Just to rub our noses in it, and she did! Many's the odd plate of left-overs my mother's given to Mrs Bragg and her glad to take it. Now, I'm working – or I was – for Winifred. The 're the richest people in the village, you know – and that's counting Dame Alice who's not badly off herself. Well, naturally, everybody in Thornwic 'd jump for joy if they came a cropper. I wouldn't stop laughing myself for a week and I don't bear them any particular ill-will. Arthur's not much of a fellow – they like 'em rough and tough in Thornwich – and, of course, all the other men make fun of him. What do you think they say when they hear he's bought himself a cowboy outfit to wear when he's shooting his pistols? Oh, Arthur's learned the hard way. The 've pulled his leg unmercifully in The Jolly Sailor about some of the daft things he's taken up. He keeps his mouth shut about them now.'

'Well,' said Dover as he and MacGregor plodded their way back under a sky darkening with cloud to The Jolly Sailor, 'I hope you're satisfied. Brrh! This perishing wind's cold. It's cutting right through me. If it hadn't been for your bloody pig-headedness we could have stopped in the pub and kept warm. Damned waste of time, that's what it's been!'

'Oh, I don't know, sir,' said MacGregor, pulling his hat down over his ears. 'I found Mrs Poltensky's evidence a bit long winded but very valuable. What she had to say about Mrs Tompkins trying to adopt a baby under the counter – that was most interesting, I thought.'

'Did you?' growled Dover.

'Well, don't you see, sir? It explains the missing three hundred pounds – the money Mrs Tompkins drew, in cash, out of the bank the other day. I'll bet that was the money to pay for the baby.'

'Th ee hundred smackers?' yelped Dover derisively. 'You want to grow up, laddie! The e's cheaper ways of getting a baby than shelling out three hundred quid.' He sniggered.

'Not for Mrs Tompkins, sir,' said MacGregor primly, refusing to be drawn into an exchange of bawdy with his superior. 'It was the only way she could get one, and I don't suppose in their financial circumstances she considered it was too high a price. And there's another point, sir. You told me that Mr Tompkins told you that he wanted his wife to burn the poison-pen letters she'd received.'

'Well?' snarled Dover.

'Well, sir, Mrs Poltensky said that it was Mrs Tompkins who wanted to burn the letters and Mr Tompkins who insisted that they should be preserved and handed over to the proper authorities.'

'Good God!' Dover rolled his eyes upwards and searched the grey skies for strength. 'What the blazes are you blethering on about now? Look, laddie, let's keep a sense of proportion, shall we? All we're concerned with is this Tompkins woman's suicide. How she spent her life and what she did with her money and who wanted to burn what is no concern of ours. All right, you go off like a threepenny rocket and say maybe it wasn't suicide and maybe her husband killed her, and I went along with you. I'm not the man to blunt your enthusiasm, you know that – but enough's enough! We've crossed Mr Tompkins off the list of suspects, not that there ever was a list because it's an open and shut, text-book case of simple, straightforward suicide if ever I saw one and it's high time …'

'I beg your pardon, sir,' – MacGregor interrupted earnestly – 'but we certainly haven't crossed Mr Tompkins off the list. Thi business of the French lessons will need checking. The e's a bus into Bearle in about fifteen minutes, if I remember correctly. We've just got time to call in at The Jolly Sailor and get the name and address of his teacher off Mr Tompkins and then catch the bus.'

Dover mounted the two steps leading up to The Jolly Sailor in a grim and moody silence. Some mothers certainly did have 'em! At the top he turned and addressed MacGregor. 'Not *we*, laddie,' he said with that outspokenness which was so integral a part of his character, '*you!*'

The e is a saying about the best laid plans of mice and men. It happened to Dover. Mr Tompkins had gone up to the Vicarage and would not be back for some considerable time as he had been invited to dinner.

'He's talking about putting up a stained-glass window in memory of Mrs Tompkins,' Mrs Quince told Dover as he stood warming his bottom by the gas stove in her kitchen, 'but he's not sure if old Crotty'll stand for it – with her committing suicide, you know. Some vicars won't bury suicides in the churchyard, but, as I said to Bert, if you can't bury 'em proper, what are you supposed to do with 'em? Have 'em stuffed and keep 'em on the mantelpiece? And, Mr Dover, if you want one of them little cakes, I'd be obliged if you'd ask for it. You can have one and welcome, but there's no need to try and pinch one when you think I'm not looking. Oh, and a policeman brought this letter for you. It's the post-mortem report. The police surgeon says all the evidence points to suicide. She must have taken an enormous dose of sleeping tablets first, and then turned the gas on. It was a bit of a race, seemingly, which one would kill her, but the police surgeon is pretty sure it was gas poisoning, and he's put that in his report.' Dover took the envelope and passed it on to MacGregor. The e wasn't much point in bothering to read it. 'Well,' Mrs Quince rambled happily on, 'Winifred Tompkins never was one to do things by halves. I'll say that for her. Once she set her mind on something it'd take more than wild horses to put her off. Oh, and speaking of wild horses, Dame Alice rang up. I told her you were out so she said she'd come down here to see you at half past seven.'

Dover buttoned up his overcoat, a desperate, hunted look coming into his little, close-set, black eyes. 'Come on, MacGregor, we'll be missing that bus.'

'But there's no point in going into Bearle tonight, sir, we haven't got the address.'

'The e's no bloody point in stopping here, either,' snapped Dover. 'We can always ask the police station and if they can't tell us, we'll go to the flicks ' He started to leave the kitchen. MacGregor looked at Mrs Quince and disloyally shrugged his shoulders before following the Chief Inspector.

'Here, what about your dinner?' shouted Mrs Quince. 'I've spent the best part of two hours getting it ready.'

A suggestion was thrown back by a rapidly disappearing Dover which, mercifully, Mrs Quince did not catch.

'I shall have to tell Dame Alice I gave you her message!' she screamed as the outer door slammed shut. With a sigh she wiped her hands on the tea towel, and went into the bar and picked up the telephone.

The Station Sergeant at Bearle police station had a well-earned reputation for being a bit of a wag and he spent a large part of his time, both on and off dut , burnishing this image.

'Scotland Yard, eh?' he rumbled, examining MacGregor's warrant card as though he'd never clapped eyes on one before. 'Oh, yes, we got special instructions sent round about you. Gave my boots an extra shine only this morning, just in case you decided to come slumming, eh?'

'We're looking for somebody in Bearle who gives French lessons,' said MacGregor curtly. Dover was temporarily absent, availing himself of the station's toilet facilities.

'French lessons?' The Station Sergeant's eyes twinkled and he scratched leisurely at his head with his pencil. 'In Bearle? I should have thought you'd have done better in London – a good-looking young spark like you. We don't go in much for foreign languages up here.'

'I don't want to learn it. I want to contact somebody who teaches it.'

'Oh, well now, they might teach it at the local school. Have you tried there, eh?'

'I want somebody who teaches it privately,' said MacGregor.

'Privately, eh?' said the Station Sergeant, fighting to keep a broad grin from spreading right across his face. 'Well, now, if you'd said that to begin with I'd have known what you were talking about, wouldn't I, eh?' He gave MacGregor a knowing wink. 'You're a bit of a fast worker, aren't you, eh? You can't have been up here more than a couple of days and here you are, bold as brass, walking right in here asking for private French lessons. You've got a nerve, some of you young bucks!' He leant matily over the counter. 'Who put you on to it, you dirty dog, you? The Chief Constable, eh?

'We got on to it during the course of our investigations,' said MacGregor, consulting his watch with an impatient flourish

This perfectly normal remark had the Station Sergeant in creases. He rocked merrily on his heels behind his counter, tears of pure bovine mirth filling his e es.

Before MacGregor had the chance to demand an explanation of such peculiar behaviour there was the sound of flushing in the distance and Dover came stumping along the passage.

'Right!' he said, scowling as a matter of principle at the Station Sergeant. 'Have you got it?'

'Not yet, sir,' admitted MacGregor through clenched teeth.

'Well, what's the matter?' Dover swung irately on the portly figu e still rocking easily behind his counter. 'Have I said something funny, Sergeant?'

The tation Sergeant rocked to an unobtrusive halt. 'No, sir.'

'Well, what the hell have you got that stupid grin on your face for? Now, are you going to give me the information I want, or do I have to rout out somebody who will?' Dover scowled pugnaciously.

'I think I can help you, sir.' The eyes stopped twinkling and assumed a surly look.

'I hope so, Sergeant,' said Dover nastily. In his opinion there was only one way to deal with the local police: kick 'em where it did most good before they got the chance to put the boot into you. It didn't produce much in the way of willing co-operation, but Dover was philosophical enough to realize you can't have everything.

The Station Sergeant recognized he was going to get no change out of the fat one and sullenly tore a piece of paper out of his Occurrences Book. Laboriously he wrote down a name and address. In answer to Dover's barked request he gave directions, as complicated and inaccurate as he dared, about how to get there.

'And may I suggest, sir,' he added recklessly, 'that if you lose your way, you should ask a policeman?'

By the time they found the address they had been given Dover had calmed down a little. As he told MacGregor, he wasn't going to stand insolence like that from anyone, never mind a twopence ha'penny, overweight yobbo of a sergeant with hay seeds in his hair.

'We ought to have a national police service,' fumed Dover as he stared at a little hand-written notice pinned to the door. 'It's the only solution. Make some of these peasants out in the wilds pull their socks up. I suppose you *have* rung that bell, MacGregor?'

'Yes, sir,' said MacGregor and stuck his finger on the button again. 'Mademoiselle Louise de Gascoigne. French Lessons. By Appointment Only' was certainly taking her time.

Chapter Ten

A small crowd had gathered before Mademoiselle de Gascoigne opened her door. She hadn't chosen the most select area of Bearle to live in, and the neighbouring row of small, grimy houses gradually disgorged their curious inhabitants. On the whole their mood was antagonistic, Dover and MacGregor having been well and truly recognized for what they were. A ring of evil-eyed, grubby-faced kids edged gradually closer. One or two of the bigger boys had efficient-lookin catapults sticking out of their hip pockets. Some remarks, uncomplimentary to the police, were exchanged and Dover swung round fie cely, ready and willing to clip any ears he could lay his hands on. The crowd retreated out of range. A woman standing in the doorway of a house a little farther up the street pushed the man's cap she wore up off her forehead. 'Disgusting!' she shouted. 'Tha's what it is, disgusting! Men!' She spat accurately into the gutter. 'They make me sick!' She shuffle back into the house and slammed the door.

'Charming neighbourhood, sir,' remarked MacGregor nonchalantly. He was keeping a wary eye on a little girl pushing a battered toy pram containing what looked like a tommy gun. She was staring at MacGregor's legs in a speculative way. MacGregor tensed himself, ready to take evasive action should she charge.

In the nick of time for MacGregor's dignity, and possibly his trousers, the door at which they had been ringing was flung open and a young woman, scantily dressed in a scarlet négligé, appeared on the step. Her face was heavily, even exotically, made-up and she had a huge construction of untidy black hair piled up high on her head. She took one look at the group of eager spectators and advanced a couple of paces, both hands before her flashing with long scarlet fingernails. She curled her lip back in a snarl before screaming,

'Fichez le camp! Allez-vous-en! Sales cochons! Vaches puantes!'

Obviously, Dover and MacGregor had found the French teacher.

Having cleared the decks a little, Mademoiselle de Gascoigne turned her attention to her visitors. She smiled. It made her look a trifle more alluring than when she snarled, but not all that much. She flashed da k, mascara-rimmed eyes at MacGregor.

'Et vous?' she asked in dulcet tones. 'Qu'est-ce que vous voulez, messieurs?'

It was all Greek to Dover. He looked at MacGregor. MacGregor smiled confidently and raised his hat. 'Mademoiselle de Gascoigne?' he asked politely. 'Nous sommes de la police.'

Mademoiselle de Gascoigne's smile lasted for the brief moment it took her to work out what MacGregor was saying. Then it faded and the snarl came back.

'Qu'est-ce que c'est?' she screamed in a voice which could be heard at La Petite Roquette. 'Encore des draupères? Mais j'ai déjà payé!'

'Oh, no,' said MacGregor, floundering on manfully. 'Ce n'est pas comme ça. Nous voulons vous poser ...'

Mademoiselle de Gascoigne wasn't listening. She continued to scream in what was, for MacGregor at any rate, unintelligible French. Occasionally she raised her hands to the heavens and appeared to be calling down horrifying Gallic curses on the heads of the two detectives who stood, somewhat at a loss, in front of her.

'What the hell's she going on about?' Dover hissed irately at MacGregor.

'I'm not quite sure, sir,' said MacGregor unhappily. 'I think there's been a bit of a misunderstanding.'

Dover scowled at him and then dealt in his own inimitable way with Mademoiselle de Gascoigne. He grabbed the flailing hands and held them firmly in his massive fists. 'Shut up!' he bellowed and gave her a shake which loosened one of her false eyelashes.

Louise de Gascoigne shut up. Her mouth stayed open but no sounds came out.

'Tha's better,' said Dover complacently. 'Now then, we are from the police, savez? Mr Mulkerrin, the Chief Constable, has sent us. Savez?'

'Meestair Mulkerrin? But zat ees diffe ent! Vy deed you not say so beefor? But,' – she waggled a finger reprovingly at Dover – 'you naughtee boy, you should 'ave telephoned! Mais cela ne fait rien. Je vous pardonne, cette fois, eh? You vant to come een?' Red lips parted in a fetching smile as Mademoiselle de Gascoigne jerked her head towards the open door. She also waggled her hips.

'Yes,' said Dover.

He and MacGregor started to follow Mademoiselle de Gascoigne into the house when she stopped them in some surprise.

'Tous les deux? Boz of you? Togezair?'

'Oh, yes,' explained MacGregor with a jolly laugh, delighted to find that English was spoken here. 'We always like to have a witness, you know.'

Mademoiselle de Gascoigne raised her eyebrows as far as they would go. She seemed about to say something but changed her mind and shrugged her shoulders with a wealth of expression. Then, with hips swaying to near dislocation point, she led the way up a narrow flight of stairs. 'Ma foi!' she muttered to herself: 'Quelles espèces de sales cochons, ces rosbifs! Ils sont tous de vieux vicelards! Et ces poulets, ils sont encore pire que les autres.'

'What did she say?' Dover asked MacGregor in a low voice. '

I'm afraid I didn't quite catch that either, sir,' admitted MacGregor. 'She seems to have a rather unusual accent.'

'It's probably a French one,' said Dover scathingly, not caring, as usual, how low he had to descend for a laugh. 'Well, you'd better leave the questioning to me since she obviously doesn't understand a word you say.'

Mademoiselle de Gascoigne stood aside for them to enter what must once have been a front bedroom. Apart from the fact that there was a large divan up against the window, the rest of the room was furnished, mostly in black, as a kind of sitting-room. Two feeble-watted standard lamps with yellow shades provided illumination, but there were a number of large mirrors scattered about the room. The e was even one fi ed on the ceiling over the divan which gave quite a continental touch to the décor.

'Shall I take your 'at and coat?' asked Mademoiselle de Gascoigne.

'No, thank you, miss,' said Dover stepping gingerly across the threshold and groping towards the most comfortable armchair. He plumped down into it and loosened the laces of his boots to ease his aching feet. With a sigh he surveyed the room. 'Strewth, black carpet! He'd never seen that before. He looked up to find Louise de Gascoigne staring curiously at him. Her négligé had slipped somewhat round the top but this didn't seem to be bothering her.

'You keep your 'at on, and you take your shoes off?' she asked in evident bewilderment.

'Oh no,' said Dover with an understanding chuckle. 'I'm just easing the laces a bit. I shan't be taking my boots off, never you fear!'

'Tonnerre de Dieu!' breathed Mademoiselle de Gascoigne. She rolled her eyes alarmingly and flung herself full length on the black divan. Her scarlet négligé slipped a little more and half of Mademoiselle's ample bosom glowed milkily in the subdued light. MacGregor wondered if he should, perhaps, tell her about it, but the Chief Inspector was already clearing his throat preparatory to starting the interview. MacGregor surreptitiously wiped the palms of his hands on his handkerchief, and pulled out his notebook and pencil.

Mademoiselle de Gascoigne's eyes opened wide. 'You are going to draw peektures?' she asked.

'Mais non!' MacGregor reassured her with easy fluenc . 'Je prendrai des notes.'

'Pourquoi?'

'Pour aider ma mémoire,' said MacGregor proudly. 'Il faut reporter tout à mes supérieurs.'

'Mon Dieu!' said Mademoiselle de Gascoigne. It was more a prayer for help than a simple explanation.

'Now then, miss,' said Dover firml , 'we just want you to answer a few questions.'

'Questions?' A half realization that she might have been jumping to hasty conclusions dawned slowly on Mademoiselle de Gascoigne's face. Her eyebrows clamped down and the line of her mouth hardened. She gathered her négligé modestly around her. 'You are making an inquiry, hein?'

'Tha 's right, miss,' agreed Dover placidly. 'We're making an investigation into these anonymous letters in Thornwich '

Mademoiselle de Gascoigne's face was blank.

'Des lettres anonymes à Thorawich ' translated MacGregor helpfully.

Mademoiselle de Gascoigne's face became blanker. 'Vous ne voulez pas me filer un coup de baguette?' she asked, looking from one to the other in disappointed bewilderment. 'Vous ne voulez pas prendre un ticket?'

MacGregor smiled. It was the only contribution he could make.

With what was obviously a very powerful curse Mademoiselle de Gascoigne made up her mind. She leapt to her feet and rushed out of the room. In a second or two she was back again, cocooned from head to toe in a thick brown dressing-gown. She sat down in a most business-like manner on an upright chair and folded her arms.

'Allons!' she snapped. 'Ask your questions and be queek about eet! For me, time ees money, hein?'

Dover blinked, but queer customers had ceased to bother him a long time ago. 'Do you know a man called Arthur Tompkins?'

'And eef I do?'

'When did you last see him?'

'Yestairday.'

'Wednesday? Can you remember what time he arrived?'

Mademoiselle de Gascoigne shrugged her shoulders. 'Th ee o'clock. 'Ee ees always vairy punctual. You can regulate your watch by 'eem.'

'And what time did he leave?'

Mademoiselle de Gascoigne's eyes narrowed. "Ee 'as keeled somebody, hein?' she asked hopefully. 'You weel 'ang 'eem?'

'What time did he leave?'

'At 'alf past four. Exactement. Othairwise 'ee 'as to pay for anothair 'alf 'our.'

'Now, you're quite sure about this?' pressed Dover. 'Arthur Tompkins was here with you in this room yesterday afternoon for an hour and a half from three to four thirty?'

Mademoiselle de Gascoigne nodded her head. 'Eet seemed longair,' she commented sourly.

'Well, miss,' said Dover, looking triumphantly at MacGregor, 'I think that's all we want to know. Thank you very much for your co-operation.'

He rose majestically to his feet and all the lights went out.

For a moment or two nothing much happened. Dover sat thankfully down again, Mademoiselle de Gascoigne squeaked and MacGregor groped in his pocket for his lighter. Then they heard somebody calling from the bottom of the stairs.

'Louise, have you got a shilling, love? This blinking meter's run out again!'

The e was the sound of footsteps coming slowly up the stairs, the door opened and a waft of cheap perfume entered the room slightly ahead of the owner of the voice.

'Are you there, Louise? I can't see a bloody thing. Whoops! Ooh, my apologies, I'm sure. I didn't know you'd got a friend in. A gentleman friend, too.' She giggled. 'Pardon me!'

'Tha 's quite all right,' said MacGregor, trying – not very energetically – to disentangle himself from the unseen body which was snuggling up to him in a very friendly way. 'If I can just reach my pocket, I think I've got a … Oh, I do beg your pardon!'

The e was a peal of girlish and delighted laughter. 'Ooh, you saucy thing, you! If you do that again you'll have to marry me! Here, you just hold still, gorgeous, and I'll look for the money. Is it in your trousers pocket?'

'Oh, please! No, never mind, thank you!' gasped MacGregor quickly, grateful for the darkness which concealed his blushes. 'I've got it now, thank you so much.' He unclamped the hand which was crawling seductively up round his neck and pressed a couple of shillings firmly into it

'Oh?' The voice sounded disappointed. 'Well, ta very much, love. Sorry if I've interrupted anything, I'm sure.'

They heard her leave the room and patter, still laughing, down the stairs. Then the lights came on again

Dover blinked and scowled through screwed-up eyes at MacGregor who grinned sheepishly back and scrubbed his face with his handkerchief.

'Zat was my friend, Eleanor,' explained Mademoiselle de Gascoigne since nobody else appeared to be going to say anything.

'She seems a very jolly girl,' said MacGregor hoarsely. 'Very gay.'

'Ah,' said Mademoiselle de Gascoigne sadly, 'you vould not say zat eef you knew 'er. She 'as just lost 'er baby.'

'Oh dear' said MacGregor inadequately. 'Poor thing.'

'She was going to sell eet for feefty pounds,' responded Mademoiselle de Gascoigne, blossoming in the warmth of MacGregor's handsome sympathy. 'She was going to get reed of eet but zees woman, she says, no you can sell eet for feefty pounds! Pauvre Eleanor, all zees time and now she 'as lost zee baby and zee feefty pounds. C'est un vrai dommage!'

'Oh, oui,' said MacGregor, and then did a quick double-take. 'Wait a minute! Did you say she was going to *sell* the baby, and then it died?' He could hardly contain his excitement. He looked anxiously at Dover to make sure that the significance of all this had penetrated that solid skull. He towered over Mademoiselle. 'Who was she going to sell the baby to?'

Mademoiselle de Gascoigne cowered away from MacGregor who was a good deal more intimidating than he realized.

'Oh, come on, woman!' barked MacGregor, showing that long association with a natural bully like Dover leaves its mark on the best of men. 'Le bébé,' he repeated in what he fondly hoped was Mademoiselle de Gascoigne's native language. 'Qui est la femme qui veut acheter le bébé d'Eleanor?'

Mademoiselle de Gascoigne flung her arms up in the air. 'Je ne sais pas!' she protested. 'Why don't you ask 'er?'

Abandoning the pouting and now near tearful teacher of the French language without more ado, MacGregor led a rapid descent down the stairs to tackle the fair Eleanor in her lair.

Eleanor was a glittering blonde whose eyes lit up like searchlights when MacGregor entered the kitchen where she was just making herself a cup of tea. It is only fair to record that a marked reduction in her enthusiasm took place when she spotted Dover for the first time.

'Oh, my Gawd!' she complained in deep disgust. 'Coppers!'

Dover pushed his way into the kitchen and looked, as was his wont, for somewhere to sit down. The only chair was already being occupied by Eleanor and she didn't look as though she was going to vacate it in Dover's favour. With a disconsolate pout Dover perched himself uncomfortably on the edge of the kitchen table, his intention that this part of the investigations was going to be short and sharp, and strongly reinforced. He was beginning to get a little perturbed by MacGregor's attitude. The lad was tearing into things like a bull at a gate. Dover had no objection to his underlings shouldering nine-tenths of the work, but it needed to be done with tact and to the greater glory of their Chief Inspector. Being dragged along in MacGregor's wake was not a pleasant experience, nor was it one that Dover intended to repeat or to endure much longer. They had been rushing around from pillar to post like a couple of scalded cats and Dover was in grave danger of losing his bearings. First it had been Arthur Tompkins murdering his wife, and now it was black-market babies. What all this had to do with Thornwic's poison-pen letters, Dover was blowed if he knew, but the whole affair had generated its own momentum and it was difficul to find an appropriate place at which to bawl halt. They hadn't, thought Dover scowling resentfully at Eleanor, even had their dinner yet. It wasn't right, not for a man in his state of health. Light duties, that was all he was supposed to be on. Even the doctor had said that and, God knows, that licensed butcher wasn't one to err on the side of humanitarianism.

MacGregor had noted the protruding bottom lip and the lowering eyebrows. They were danger signs he had learnt not to ignore. 'Will you ask the questions, sir,' he asked tactfully, 'or shall I?'

The e were times when Dover really hated MacGregor. If he'd been at all sure of why they were invading this Eleanor girl's kitchen he would have started shooting off some well-directed questions long before this, but the fact was that Dover's powers of concentration were never at their best when he was hungry. And he was damned hungry now.

MacGregor was still waiting for an answer. Dover gave a deep, bad-tempered grunt and left him to make what he could of it.

'Here,' said Eleanor, 'are you two going to be sitting here all night?'

'We shan't keep you more than a minute,' said MacGregor with a shining smile which might have devastated Eleanor fi e minutes ago but produced no softening of her attitude now. 'We understand that you were going to have a baby some time ago and that you decided to let somebody else have it.'

'So?' said Eleanor.

'We would like to know a few more details about the – er – transaction.'

'Ooh, hark at him!' said Eleanor.

'For instance,' MacGregor went on, still keeping his smile, 'to whom were you going to sell the baby?'

'What baby?' said Eleanor.

'Your baby.'

'I ain't got no baby. You must be thinking about somebody else.'

'But you were going to have a baby,' persisted MacGregor.

'Is that a crime?' demanded Eleanor. 'First I ever heard of it, if it is.'

'For God's sake!' snarled Dover. 'We shall be here all night at this rate! Now, listen you,' – he directed his scowl at Eleanor – 'I'm a very busy man and I don't intend to sit here taking lip from a cheap little tart like you. Now, you can either answer the questions here and get it over with, or you can come down to the nick and answer them there. Suit yourself, but you're going to answer 'em somewhere. And if you start trying to make things difficul for me, my girl, I'll make things so hot for you that you'll regret the day you were born. If I want to turn nasty, I can turn very nasty indeed!'

'Yes,' said Eleanor with a last flicker of insubordination, 'I'll bet you can. All right, all right!' she added hastily as Dover showed signs of getting to his feet. 'You win. Here, I shan't get into trouble over this, shall I?'

'Not if you co-operate,' said Dover. 'We're not concerned with any minor misdemeanours which may lie outside the scope of our investigations. In other words, get on with it!'

Once she had decided to sing, Eleanor sang clearly and fluentl . She had had, so she said, a gentleman friend who, taking advantage of her innocence and with seemingly sincere promises of future marriage, had got her in the family way. 'And then,' said Eleanor succinctly, 'the slimy bastard scarpered!'

Looking at Eleanor in the unflattering light of a naked electric light bulb, Dover couldn't find it in his heart to blame the absconding putative father, but it was, he thanked God, no concern of his. 'Never mind the sob stuff' he snapped, 'get to the point! You decided to get rid of the baby.'

'Well, natch,' said Eleanor. 'What else could I do? I didn't want it and I was damned sure nobody else did.'

'So you found somebody who'd get rid of it for you?' said Dover impatiently. It was the old, old story and, after listening to it with variations all these years, he found it just boring.

'Well, yes,' admitted Eleanor. 'I asked around a bit, and somebody give me the name of this woman. Well, I went off to see her, to have a look at the set up, like, because some of 'em are dirty devils and I didn't want to finish up on no marble slab. And I wanted to know how much the damage was going to be because I wasn't exactly rolling in the stuff at the time. Well, I went to see this woman and I was quite surprised, really, because she seemed quite decent – not a bit like the creepy old witch down Benion Street I went to … Well, we got talking and she said how would I feel about having the kid and then flogging it. And I said, how much, because to tell you the honest I wasn't looking forward to going through all that business again. And she said, fifty quid, plus a pound a week in advance to cover all the extra expenses. Well, it didn't sound so dusty to me because I reckoned I could go on working for quite a bit and most likely fiddle a few quid out of the Welfare or one of these societies as well. So I said, yes. After all, what had I got to lose? It'd have set me back ten or fifteen quid to get rid of it '

Dover sighed and wriggled about on his table and tried to find a more comfortable spot. 'Strewth, how they went on! You asked 'em a perfectly simple question and off they went, yack, yack, yack for hours. It poured out like a blooming great dam bursting its walls. It got a chap down in time, listening to nothing else but people talking. They swamped you with words and half the time they never told you what you wanted to know. Just look at this one! Mouth opening and shutting like a speeded up goldfish. Fair made you sick!

Dover scowled and sighed and grunted. Indiffe ent to the suffering she was causing, Eleanor happily continued to reveal all. She conducted her two listeners steadily through the nine uneventful months of her pregnancy.

'And then I went in this Home, see? Quite the little heroine, I was, because all these other girls that'd got caught just wanted to get their babies adopted and have done with it. But me, I told the old dears I wanted to keep mine and they thought I was a blooming marvel. It wasn't half a giggle! Well, then my time came and that wiped the grin off my face. Fifty quid? The 'll have to give me fi e hundred before I'll go through that again! The first pains started coming, see, about six o'clock and ...'

'You can spare us the details,' said Dover wearily. 'I suppose the baby was born dead, was it?'

'No, it wasn't,' said Eleanor, rather disgruntled at having the thread of her narrative chopped callously in twain. 'It lived for about a week, see. Then something went wrong and they put it in an oxygen tent, but it didn't do any good and then it died. A little boy, it was ... I was ever so upset.'

'I'll bet you were,' said Dover unkindly. 'What did you do then?'

'Well. I rang this woman up and told her. Gawd was she mad! She nearly went through the roof. Called me every dirty name under the sun, the old bitch, as if it was my fault. It seems she'd been paying this pound a week to me out of her own pocket because the woman who was going to take the baby wouldn't cough up till she actually got it. To be fair, I can't say I blame her, but it made things very awkward for this other woman with the baby dying. 'It's no use yelling your head off at me,' I told her. 'I haven't got no money and you can't get blood out of a stone.' Well, she huffed and puffed a bit longer and said she couldn't affo d to chuck nearly forty quid down the drain and I said "bloody hard luck" and she rang off and that's the last I've heard of her.'

A blessed silence invaded the kitchen as Eleanor finished her story and MacGregor waited for Dover to ask the vital question. But Dover, still staring glassily at Eleanor who was now lighting a cigarette, had switched off long ago. MacGregor cleared his throat. Dover blinked, heaved a deep sigh and looked round as though wondering where he was.

MacGregor ground his teeth with impatience and then plunged recklessly in. 'Who was this woman?'

'Which woman?' said Eleanor who had already written MacGregor off as the light- eight in the partnership.

'This woman who was going to sell the ba y for you?'

'Ooh!' said Eleanor coyly. 'I don't know as how I can tell you that. It's very confidential, like. I swore I wouldn't tell a living soul.'

'Here,' said Dover, now staring fi edly at the ceiling, 'or down at the nick. Take your choice.'

'It was a woman called Gomersall, Freda Gomersall,' said Eleanor quickly. Her mother had habitually threatened to fetch a policeman when she was naughty and young Eleanor had always thought this was a load of old cod. Looking at the mean, flab y face of Chief Inspector Dover she wasn't so sure now.

'Freda Gomersall?' said MacGregor, trying hard to remember where he'd heard the name before.

'She runs Freda's Café in Thornwich' said Dover, at last relieving his aching buttocks by transferring his weight to his aching feet. 'You want to train your memory, laddie. It'll let you down badly one of these days. And now, young woman,' – he swung ponderously round on Eleanor – 'what is your surname anyhow? Smith? 'Strewth! Well, Miss Smith, I think that's about all we shall want from you for the moment. Unless, of course, you actually know the name of the woman who was going to adopt the baby?'

Eleanor shook her head. 'No, I never knew who it was. Freda never told me.'

'Well, no,' said Dover, stifling an enormous yawn, 'she wouldn't, would she? Not if she'd any sense.'

Chapter Eleven

'I'm sorry, sir, but I do think we ought to go and see this Gomersall woman tonight, before she gets wind of the fact that we're on to her.'

Dover's nostrils fla ed as he breathed heavily down his nose. Young Charles Edward had been asking for it for some time and, by God, if this went on much longer he'd bloody well get it! It had been nothing but argey-bargey ever since they had left Eleanor Smith. The e had been a fundamental clash of opinions, and not for the firs time. MacGregor wanted to get on with solving their case. Dover just wanted his dinner. The Chief Inspector found himself placed at a most unfair disadvantage: he could hardly be as frank and open about his motives for holding back as MacGregor could be about his for pressing on. The rain dripped off Dover's bowler as he tried to persuade MacGregor to see reason. The streets of Bearle were dark and deserted. Anybody with any sense was indoors watching the telly or enjoying a convivial drink in a nice warm pub.

'What you've got to consider,' Dover pointed out fretfully as he stumped along, 'is that we need a pause at this stage, just to review our findings and plan the next step we're going to take. What's the hurry, anyhow?'

'I should have thought that was obvious, sir. We've got to get hold of Freda Gomersall tonight before this Smith girl gets a chance to warn her.'

'Chance to warn her? What the hell makes you think she'll do that? She doesn't give two hoots what happens to Gomersall. I should have thought *that* was obvious, even to you.'

'She could easily pick up the phone and let her know we've been asking questions,' said MacGregor obstinately.

'Well, in that case she could have done it already,' snorted Dover. 'If she's going to warn the Gomersall woman she's got bags of time to do it before we get back to Thornwich, has 't she?'

'I suppose so, sir,' said MacGregor and let himself be steered towards a dubious-looking Chinese restaurant which was the only place in Bearle where you could get a meal after six o'clock.

Dover spurned the exotic dishes of the East and ordered fish and chips. MacGregor, however, felt it incumbent upon him to look as though he knew his way around and, in consultation with the little Chinese waiter who laughed heartily at everything which was said, was finally served with about ten tiny bowls of smoking and unidentifiable food

Dover eyed MacGregor's plate sceptically. 'What does it taste like?' he asked.

'Oh, all right,' said MacGregor, manfully swallowing a spoonful of fried cornflakes. Very nice, really.'

Dover sniffed. 'Well, rather you than me, mate! See that?' he poked a fork at one of the bowls. 'Cat food, that's what that is! I wish I'd got a stomach as strong as yours. Must be wonderful to be able to eat anything.'

MacGregor started to talk about the case again. 'The way I see it, sir, is this. It's just possible that Mrs Tompkins's suicide wasn't suicide at all. I mean, in any case of sudden death we've got to be on our guard, haven't we?'

'Arthur Tompkins didn't do it,' said Dover, resolutely shovelling a forkful of chips into his mouth. 'He's got a complete alibi, unless you think that French floosie was c vering up for him.'

MacGregor shook his head. 'No, Mr Tompkins is in the clear, I agree. But what about this three hundred pounds, sir? Mrs Tompkins desperately wants a baby. Eleanor Smith is going to have a baby she doesn't want. The connection's obvious, especially with Freda Gomersall actually in Thornwich as the go-bet een.'

'That' said Dover, preparing to tackle a dish of prunes and custard, 'is pure, undiluted, unfounded speculation. It's sheer guess-work that Winifred Tompkins was going to buy the Smith baby. Apart from anything else, Mrs Tompkins drew three hundred pounds out of the bank. Miss Smith talked about getting fifty plus a quid a week till the kid was born. What's the other two hundred odd pounds for? Nappies?'

'Freda Gomersall's commission for arranging the deal, sir?'

Dover grunted. He wasn't much of a believer in letting youth have its fling, but since he was MacGregor's guest he was generously prepared to put up with it. 'Any chance of a glass of beer?' he asked the smiling waiter who pattered up with his cheese and biscuits. He gave MacGregor what attention he could spare from his food. 'All you've said so far just strengthens the case for Mrs Tompkins's suicide,' he pointed out. 'She sets her heart on getting this baby, it dies, she can't have it. Bingo! She croaks herself.'

'But the three hundred pounds, sir,' said MacGregor earnestly, moving an imitation Chinese lantern so that he could get a better look at Dover's face. 'That money has disappeared. Now, suppose Mrs Tompkins paid it over after the baby was born, but before it died. When the deal falls through and she learns she can't have the baby, what's the first thing she's going to want? She's going to want her three hundred pounds back. Let's suppose that whoever's got it – Freda Gomersall, if you like – can't or won't hand it over. Mrs Tompkins threatens to kick up a fuss and there's no way to keep her mouth shut except by murdering her.'

''Strewth!' said Dover with good-humoured banter – he was feeling much more at peace with the world. 'With an imagination like that you ought to be writing novels!' Coming from Dover, this was not a compliment. 'Yes, coffee for me, sonny, a large cup. Here you are, measuring up this Freda Gomersall for the drop when there hasn't even been a murder committed. All the evidence points to a straightforward case of suicide. The e was no sign of breaking and entry – you checked that yourself. The door of the sitting-room was locked on the inside.' Dover ticked off the points on his fat, stubby fingers. 'She wasn't in any two minds about what she was doing, either. The overdose of sleeping pills *and* the gas show that. She left a typical suicide note, just a few words scribbled on a bit of paper. She picked the right time when she knew she'd have the place to herself and nobody'd come in and save her at the last minute. And, to cap everything, she even had a bath before she did it so's she'd be all nice and clean for the post-mortem. Gawd, I could go on all night! Everything points to suicide.'

'But what about motive, sir?' asked MacGregor as he sadly watched Dover selecting the largest cigar from a tray presented, unasked, by the cunning Oriental. Not many people smoked cigars in Bearle and the management were glad of the opportunity to shift some of their surplus stock.

'Motive?' said Dover, puffin away. 'You can take your pick. Maybe the poison-pen letters drove her to it. Maybe it was not getting this baby. Maybe it was her health. Maybe it was any one of a dozen things we've never even heard about and never will. Half the time in these suicide cases you never know what finally pushed 'em over the edge. D'you think that Chink'd fetch us a drop of brandy? My stomach's feeling a bit queer again. A drop of brandy might just settle it.'

'I'm sorry, sir,' said MacGregor, looking at his watch and getting the only satisfaction he'd had from the whole meal, 'we haven't time. If we don't go now we shall miss the last bus back to Thornwich'

On the long cold bus journey MacGregor tried to restart the argument, but Dover wouldn't budge. He didn't object to calling on Freda Gomersall and seeing what she'd got to say for herself – it was as good a way of passing the time as any – but not tonight. Tomorrow morning, maybe, if he felt up to it – or tomorrow afternoon. Having said this firmly three times he propped his head on MacGregor's shoulder and fell asleep.

It was about ten o'clock when the bus disgorged them at the bottom of the hill in Thornwich. They were both stiff, tired and bad-tempered.

'We might just have time for a quick drink before we go to bed,' remarked Dover as they waited for a gap in the traffi before venturing on the mad dash across the road. 'Damned soft place to leave a car!' he snorted, staring at a little blue mini parked outside The olly Sailor.

'Oh, Lord!' said MacGregor. 'I think it's Dame Alice's. She must be waiting for us.'

Dover didn't hesitate. At times he had a remarkable capacity for taking quick decisions. He stepped back from the edge of the pavement, did a quick right turn and strode off in the direction of Freda's Café which stood some fifty yards away in the middle of a vast, muddy lorry park. Freda's Café was open twenty-four hours a day, dispensing cheer and tomato ketchup to the modern knights of the road.

'Come on,' he said to MacGregor, 'we might as well go and get it over with.'

But Freda, unless she had changed her sex and grown a big ginger moustache, was not in the café.

MacGregor bought a couple of cups of coffee and he and Dover sat down at a linoleum-covered table to survey the scene.

'I told you it was a waste of time,' said Dover, stirring his coffee crossly with a spoon which looked as though it had been found on the battlefield after Waterloo. 'If we ask for her it'll only make her suspicious. We've been spotted already.'

A sullen silence had fallen over the large wooden hut in which Freda's Café was situated. The e were only some six or seven other customers, big burly men with dirty faces and thick lumber jackets. They all stared suspiciously at the newcomers. One youngish man in a pair of tight jeans swaggered across to a battered juke box and rammed his sixpence into the slot. Under the cover of a raucous, souped-up version of 'Come Into The Garden, Maud' rendered by the latest adolescent idol, wary conversations were resumed.

Eventually the song came to a blessed halt.

"Strewth!' said Dover, speaking from the heart. 'I thought my ruddy ear-drums had gone.'

'What do we do now, sir?' asked MacGregor.

'Search me,' said Dover whose thoughts were now exclusively concentrated on getting back to The olly Sailor and bed.

However, in every successful criminal investigation there comes a moment when Lady Luck smiles upon the detective involved. We should have an even higher rate of unsolved crime than we enjoy today if this were not so. Hard work, shrewd assessments, inspired deductions, the wonders of modern forensic science – these things are all very well in their way but, as Chief Inspector Dover's record shows, they aren't everything. On many of the occasions when he solved a crime he had employed none of these traditional methods. True, the little bit of luck which he enjoyed in Freda's Transport Café didn't exactly permit him to bring his investigation to a glorious and resounding conclusion, but it did enable him to get to bed and, furthermore, provide him with a cast-iron excuse for staying there for the whole of the following morning.

The door of Freda's Café opened and a thin, bald-headed man came in accompanied by a blast of cold, damp air. Several voices invited him to put the wood in the hole.

The man closed the door and returned the homespun banter as he ambled his way up to the counter. 'Cup of tea and two cheese rolls, George,' he said.

Dover and MacGregor, sitting near by, could hear every word clearly.

'Freda not in tonight?' asked the bald man, sorting through a handful of change.

'No,' said George as he pensively watched the tea struggle out of the spout of the tea-pot. 'Why, was you wanting to see her?'

'I wouldn't mind,' admitted the man.

'She'll be in at dinner-time tomorrow.'

'Oh well, I'll call in on my way back then. I should be through here about mid-day if my ruddy brakes hold out. Tell her I was asking, will you? She'll know what it's about.'

George nodded and swept the appropriate coins into the till.

Dover and MacGregor smiled at each other and felt very clever. They now knew when Freda would be in her café and Freda didn't know that they knew. It was all most satisfactory. For the first time for some days they felt like detectives. With a light step MacGregor nipped out and ascertained that Dame Alice had raised the siege. Her car had gone from outside The Jolly Sailor. Dover beamed, even at MacGregor. Pippa was passing.

Dover's good humour lasted right through lunch on the next day which was a Friday. He had slept solidly through the morning with a clear conscience because, as he carefully pointed out to MacGregor, it was useless to pursue any other lines of investigation until they had cleared this baby business out of the way. They couldn't do this until they had interviewed Freda and the best time for doing that would be round about half past two when the lunch-time rush was over and the café would be fairly empty, if not deserted.

Lunch at The Jolly Sailor was quite a gay affai . Mr Tompkins seemed to have recovered from the initial shock of his wife's death and chattered almost gaily about the inquest and the funeral arrangements and the short holiday he was going to take when it was all over. Dover had twitted him about his whereabouts on Wednesday afternoon and Mr Tompkins had blushed a deep red but had taken the clumsy joshing in very good part.

'Every man's entitled to his hobby, Mr Dover,' he had pointed out with some show of embarrassment. It was a remark which had Dover howling with laughter until the tears ran down his flab y cheeks. After taking a second or two to recover from the shock, Mr Tompkins himself produced a shy smirk.

'I hope I can rely on your discretion,' he said to Dover.

'Of course,' roared Dover, guffawing like a fool. 'We won't breathe a word to anyone, will we, MacGregor?'

MacGregor gave one of his stiff little smiles, shook his head and maintained a prim silence. He wished, not for the first time, that he worked with someone who was a little less philistine in his attitudes. After all, what was so flaming funny about a man wanting to learn French?

Freda Gomersall didn't exactly welcome her two new customers with open arms. 'I was wondering when you were going to get around to interviewing me,' she said, standing behind her counter like Boudicca in her chariot.

'Er – two coffees, please,' said MacGregor, hoping to soften her up a bit by a modest contribution to the café's profits. 'And perhaps you'll have one yourself?'

'You're joking, of course,' said Mrs Gomersall, massively unappeased. 'I may sell the muck but I don't have to drink it.'

Feeling that they were in for a sticky time, MacGregor carried the coffees over to a near-by table, and he and Dover waited a little apprehensively for Mrs Gomersall to join them. After a few minutes she waddled across to them, clutching a glass of some pale green liquid.

'What's that?' said Dover as she sat down.

'Cabbage water,' said Mrs Gomersall shortly. 'It purifies the blood.' She examined Dover's pasty complexion. 'Looks as though a pint or two wouldn't do you any harm. Gives you a good clear-out.'

Mrs Gomersall was colossal. She fl wed, unimpeded by any kind of foundation-garment, in all directions. Her arms and legs were enormous and she wore a pair of old carpet-slippers on her feet. She had made the short distance from behind her counter to the table with considerable difficult and much laborious breathing. Like most plump women, though, she had a beautiful skin, but whether she owed this to the consumption of cabbage water Dover neither inquired nor cared. He decided to treat Mrs Gomersall as a hostile witness. The e was nothing personal in this. He didn't dislike Mrs Gomersall any more than the majority of people he came in contact with, but things had been pretty boring lately and, in his line of business, you had to take your fun where you could find it

'So you were expecting a visit from us, were you?' he began aggressively, laying a trap with such dexterity that a two-year-old child would have spotted the gaping jaws.

Mrs Gomersall had at least fifty years' experience of police methods, and prided herself on having eaten better men than this fat slob for breakfast in her time. 'I've been expecting you for the past week,' she said indiffe ently. 'Apart from the fact George told me you were snooping round here last night.'

'Oh, so George warns you when the police come round, does he?' asked Dover, making it all sound as sinister as he could.

'Part of his duties,' said Mrs Gomersall calmly. 'I expect him to report anything that's likely to have an adverse influence on my trade. Like rats running across the tables and dirty old tramps coming for a free night's kip.'

'And what were we supposed to be coming for?' demanded Dover.

'Jesus Christ!' exclaimed Mrs Gomersall piously. 'Don't *you* know? You're supposed to be finding out who wrote these lousy poison-pen letters, aren't you? I know most people think you're just in Thornwich for a free fortnight's holiday, but I told 'em, "You just don't know the cops," I said. "Tha 's just the usual way the lazy bastards" – saving your presence – "work. The 're not having a rest cure," I said. "They just look as though they a e."'

Dover, blowing furiously down his nose, took this as an open declaration of war. And, of course, it was.

'Never mind the poison-pen letters for the moment,' he snarled. 'We want to ask you a few questions about another little bit of business.'

'Oh, yes?' said Mrs Gomersall.

'Do you know a girl called Eleanor Smith – lives in Bearle?'

'No,' said Mrs Gomersall flatl . 'Never heard of her.'

'She knows you,' pressed Dover.

Mrs Gomersall shrugged her ample shoulders.

'She says she knows you very well,' insisted Dover.

Mrs Gomersall looked at her wristlet watch and started to wind it up.

'She says you paid her a pound a week for the best part of nine months,' Dover went on.

Mrs Gomersall laughed scornfully. 'I should co-co!' she chortled.

'And offered her an additional fifty pounds for her baby when it was born.'

Mrs Gomersall looked pityingly at Dover. 'Somebody's been pulling your leg, lad,' she said kindly. 'I shouldn't have thought you were the type to believe everything some empty-headed little tart told you.'

'Oh?' said Dover, seeing his opening. 'And who told you she was an empty-headed little tart?'

A flicker of annoyance crossed Mrs Gomersall's face. I must be getting old, she thought. 'I was just guessing,' she said aloud.

'Very clever!' sneered Dover. 'Well, let's see if you can guess a bit more. This girl, Eleanor Smith, says you were going to buy her baby off her. Now, I think we can assume that you didn't want to adopt it yourself ...'

'You certainly can!' said Mrs Gomersall.

'Right, well all I want to know is, who were you buying it for?'

Mrs Gomersall looked Dover straight in the eye. 'Drop dead!' she said. 'I haven't the faintest idea what you're talking about.'

'It's a criminal offence' blustered Dover. 'You could go to prison for it.'

'Could I?' said Mrs Gomersall, 'You'd have to prove it first, wouldn't you?'

'We've got Eleanor Smith's evidence.'

'Her word against mine. Besides, what's criminal about it? No law against it as far as I know, is there?'

Dover, suspecting – and quite rightly – that Mrs Gomersall might know a good deal more about the law than he did, reverted hastily to an earlier question. 'Who were you acting for?'

'I've told you,' repeated Mrs Gomersall patiently, 'I haven't the least idea what you're talking about. Honest, I haven't. Cross my heart and hope to die.' Her eye glittered amongst the creases of fat.

'Oh well, if you'd sooner we carted you off to the nick and asked you the questions there ...' sighed Dover in the voice of one who'd done his best to be decent, and failed.

'Look, love, you can ask me your questions where you like and how you like, but if I can't answer them, I can't, can I?'

'It was Mrs Tompkins you were buying the baby for, wasn't it?' This was MacGregor putting his oar in where it wasn't wanted. Dover was furious. Young Charles Edward was getting a damned sight too cocky by half.

If Dover's reaction to MacGregor's interference was predictable, Mrs Gomersall's wasn't. For the first time in the entire fencing-match she was taken completely off her guard. Her eyes opened wide and her mouth dropped in sheer astonishment, doubling the number of her chins as it did so.

'Mrs Tompkins?' she repeated hoarsely. 'Do you mean Winifred Tompkins at the grocer's? Winifred Tompkins – the one who's just killed herself?'

'Tha's right,' said Dover, glaring fie cely at MacGregor and daring him to open his mouth again.

'Well, I never!' said Mrs Gomersall, who still hadn't got her breath back.

'She was a friend of yours, was she?' asked Dover.

Mrs Gomersall looked at him in some astonishment. 'Who, Winifred Tompkins? Oh yes, bosom friends we were, I don't think! She's lived practically next door but one to me for fi e years and not so much as a "good morning" have I ever had out of her. Of course I don't go out much these days, but there's nothing to stop her coming in here once in a while and having a bit of a chat, is there? After all, I could put quite a bit of trade their way if I had a mind to but, as I said to George, I'm not going crawling on my knees to a stuck-up piece like her and she needn't expect me to. I can't see that running a café's any worse than keeping a mucky little grocer's shop, either, if it comes to that.'

'So you didn't know she wanted to adopt a baby?'

'Well, come to think of it there was a bit of talk, but that was ages ago. I did hear he wasn't so keen on the idea and I couldn't see her coping with a baby, I can tell you. I didn't pay any attention to it. The e's always so much blooming gossip in this place – turn you dizzy if you tried to keep track of it all.'

MacGregor looked crestfallen. Even he could see that Mrs Gomersall had been genuinely surprised at the mention of Winifred Tompkins's name. He was so disappointed that he forgot about the wrath further intervention would certainly bring down on his head.

'Are you sure you weren't buying that baby for Mrs Tompkins?' he asked.

Mrs Gomersall recovered her poise immediately. 'If I've told you once, I've told you a hundred times,' she said irately, 'I wasn't buying no baby for nobody!'

'We know that Eleanor Smith was going to sell her baby if it hadn't died,' MacGregor pressed on, stubbornly flogging a horse that Dover knew had been dead for some time, 'and we know that Mrs Tompkins was involved in some kind of negotiations to get a baby on the black-market. She drew three hundred pounds in cash out of the bank only a day or so before she died and …'

All the colour drained from Mrs Gomersall's face and she clutched at her heart. Even Dover was a bit worried at the startling change in her appearance. With lips trembling and chest heaving, she struggled to get the words out.

'Th ee hundred pounds?' she moaned pathetically. '*Three hundred pounds?*'

'Tha 's right,' said MacGregor, exchanging an anxious glance with Dover.

A little colour returned to Mrs Gomersall's face. 'Th ee hundred pounds,' she repeated as though fascinated. 'The bitch! The cold, scheming, snivelling bitch!'

'Who?' asked MacGregor. 'Mrs Tompkins?'

Mrs Gomersall didn't seem to have heard him. Panting slightly she got up from the table. 'We'll see about that!' she muttered viciously to herself. She looked at Dover. 'I haven't time to be bothered with you any more. I've answered all your questions. I know nothing about it, see? Nothing! And if you go on from now till Domesday you won't get anything out of me.'

Not that a statement like this stopped Dover trying, but it soon became evident that Mrs Gomersall wasn't entering into the spirit of the thing. She seemed to have something else on her mind. Finally Dover gave it up as a bad job. He jerked his head at MacGregor, and the two of them hurried out of the café, leaving the proprietress gazing blankly at her glass of cabbage water and mouthing silently the words, 'three hundred pounds'.

Chapter Twelve

'Quick!' barked Dover as the door swung to behind them, 'the post office! With his blood well and truly up he raced across the lorry park, clutching his bowler hat to his head. After a moment's hesitation MacGregor raced after him.

Overcoat tails flying Dover reached the edge of the pavement. He didn't bother about any of that look left, look right, look left again nonsense. He plunged straight in. A white-faced driver with a couple of tons of bricks behind him stood on his brakes. A petrol tanker coming at a fair belt down the hill swerved as Dover cleared the gutter in a wild, heart-stopping leap for safety on the other side.

Windows opened hopefully two hundred yards up the road. The e'd been some nasty accidents on that stretch at the bottom of the hill and the villagers didn't want to miss anything. Even Dr Hawnt heard the squeal of brakes and the shouting. He tottered off and locked himself in the lavatory. It took his housekeeper three hours to get him out again.

Dover was impervious to the anguish and turmoil in his wake. Without pausing he flung himself at the door of the sub post offic and dived in. MacGregor, who'd got across the road before the lorry drivers had recovered their wits and remembered their schedules, pounded along on his master's heels.

Inside the shop Miss Tilley was sorting wool. She had a confused impression of a red-faced man charging towards her with outstretched hands. Miss Tilley gave a delighted squeak of terror and then gracefully pretended to faint across a display of frilly aprons. She had decided long ago that, should the occasion arise, she would sell her honour cheaply.

A bell in the little switchboard at the back of the post offic counter rang loudly and one of the numbers clicked tremblingly down.

'Blast the woman!' thundered Dover and clutched Miss Tilley by the hair in an attempt to restore her to her senses.

'The telephone!' bawled Dover, advancing his lips close to Miss Tilley's ear. 'The telephone!

Miss Tilley shivered with excitement. 'To hell with the telephone!' she breathed and, somewhat hampered by the intervening stretch of counter, made a determined effo t to scramble into Dover's arms.

Dover pushed her off.   e was a trifle mo e panic-stricken than he realized, and even he was distressed to see Miss Tilley skid across the polished wood and collapse in a heap on the floo .

'Pick her up!' he shouted at MacGregor who was hovering uncertainly on the edge. 'Pick her up and get her over to that switchboard! Hurry up, man, or we shall miss it!'

When Miss Tilley found strong masculine hands half dragging, half lifting her to her feet, she nearly did swoon from ecstasy, but she was a woman who had had many disappointments in her life, and she realized that this was not the moment she had been longing for.

'I am quite all right, thank you,' she said tartly as MacGregor hauled her into an upright position. 'And I should be obliged,' she addressed Dover who was still hopping around and trumpeting like an elephant on hot bricks, 'if you would keep your voice down. My mother is lying bed-ridden in the next room and I don't want her to get upset. And now,' – she tidied her hair and smoothed her dress down, 'if you will explain quietly what it is you want.'

'We're police officer ' began Dover.

'I am well aware of that,' Miss Tilley reproved him. 'Though from the way you came barging in here, I think I could have been forgiven for imagining you were drunken hooligans.'

Dover swallowed hard and waved a hand feebly at the switch board. The bell was still ringing and the fallen number still flutte ed impatiently. 'Is that a call from Freda's Café?'

Miss Tilley, with great dignity, walked over and picked up her head-set. 'It is,' she said having looked at the board.

'I want to listen in to the conversation.'

With magnificent aplomb, Miss Tilley handed him a spare head-set and plugged it in for him. Then she sat down calmly and accepted the call. It was common knowledge that she listened in to all the calls herself, but to extend this privilege to others, even the police, was an innovation for her. However, Miss Tilley prided herself on being game.

'Number, please?' she trilled.

'Thornwich 21 ' It was Mrs Gomersall.

'Thornwich 21,' repeated Miss Tilley. 'Can't even be bothered to say please,' she pointed out scathingly to Dover as she fiddled with the appropriate plugs and switches. 'I'm ringing it now, Mrs Gomersall.'

'Whose number is it?' hissed Dover.

Miss Tilley gave him a straight look. 'It's Friday Lodge. Dame Alice's.'

'Strewth!' said Dover, a broad grin spreading across his sweaty face.

After a second or two Friday Lodge answered. The line was not a good one, but Dover and Miss Tilley had no difficult in catching every word.

'Hello? Thornwich 21 ' said a voice from the house up the hill.

'Go ahead, caller! You're through,' chanted Miss Tilley and gave one of her switches a loud click. She winked at Dover. 'It makes them think you've cut out,' she whispered conspiratorially.

Dover didn't answer. He was too busy listening to the telephone conversation which began, on Mrs Gomersall's part, without any of the conventional civilities.

'You double-crossing, lying bitch!'

The voice from Friday Lodge was polite and distant. 'I beg your pardon?'

'You'll be begging for mercy when I get my hands on you, you smelly old cow! Th ee hundred quid! You two-faced slimy-snake! And how much was poor old Freda going to get for doing all the work and making all the arrangements and taking all the risks? A lousy hundred and fifty!

'Mrs Gomersall …'

'Don't you Mrs Gomersall me, you treacherous toad! I paid out nearly forty quid to that blasted girl. Forty quid out of my own money!' Mrs Gomersall's voice squealed in anguish. '"How very sad" you said when the kid died. "An occupational hazard," you said. "Just one of the risks we've got to take," you said. *We*'ve got to take? I like that! And what did you say when I asked you, as one lady to another, to split the loss half way?'

'I …'

'You said you hadn't any money!' screamed Mrs Gomersall. 'You strung me a story as long as your arm about how hard up you were. You even had the bloody nerve '– Mrs Gomersall struggled for breath – 'you even had the bloody nerve to try and touch me for a fi er! You despicable rat, you! Well, you're going to meet your Waterloo, you are, because I'm coming to get you and your three hundred nicker!'

'But …'

'Don't try and kid me you haven't got it! I know you have. Turned out nice for you that Winifred Tompkins died, didn't it. All you had to do was keep your trap shut and hang on to the lolly, wasn't it? If you'd played decent with me,' – Mrs Gomersall's voice dropped sadly – 'I'd have played decent with you. But you didn't, did you, you rotten pig?'

'Now, listen …'

'I've listened to you long enough!' roared Mrs Gomersall at full pitch. 'Now I'm coming to collect. Percy's just come in with his lorry and he's going to run me up to that stinking hovel you live in. And if that money, all three hundred pounds of it, isn't ready and waiting for me when I get there, you're going to be in trouble, my sneaky friend, big trouble!'

Mrs Gomersall crashed the phone down at her end.

Miss Tilley turned large brown inquiring eyes on Dover. What excitement! Why, it was even better than when Mother fell downstairs and everybody thought she'd broken her neck. What with poison-pen letters, suicides and now this, one wondered what had come over Thornwich these days, one eally did.

Dover was disentangling his bowler hat and his ears from the head-set. He brushed aside Miss Tilley's questions.

'Come on, MacGregor!' he yelled, charging for the door like a superannuated war-horse at the sound of the bugle. 'If we don't get there first, the e'll be murder done!'

'Oooh!' moaned Miss Tilley, pressing a pile of blank telegram forms to her bosom. 'Murder!'

MacGregor, who was far from clear as to what was going on, set off once again after his lord and master. It was a comparatively easy task to catch up with him. Dover's progress, although accompanied by enough puffin and panting to satisfy a complete field of marathon runners, was not impressive. Thornwic 's hill was taking a terrible toll, but the Chief Inspector, heart pounding, legs trembling, laboured on.

Not unnaturally, MacGregor couldn't get much sense out of him. What little breath Dover had to spare from the vital task of breathing he used for cursing. He soon became an object of great interest as the sweat poured in rivers down his crimson cheeks. People on the pavement stopped to stare. Lorry drivers leaned from their cabs and, addressing him as grandpa, asked jocularly where the fi e was.

Dover struggled on. At last the gates of Friday Lodge were in sight. Dover, now supporting himself with an arm around

MacGregor's neck, made the supreme effo t. His legs had gone, his lungs were near bursting-point. In an ungainly shamble they turned into the drive just as a car came screeching away from the front door. It swooped towards them.

'Help!' said Dover. 'Oh God!'

He dived one way, MacGregor the other. The car swung out into the road, heading at a rate of knots down the hill. From somewhere there came the sound of confused shouting and screaming. A deep car-horn blazed away.

Dover, panting and dishevelled, dragged himself to his feet. Almost without knowing what he was doing, he took a tentative totter forward. A large double-decker van packed with baaing sheep turned into the drive from the main road. Gravel spurted from under its wheels and one of Dame Alice's gateposts took a severe battering. A tense-eyed young maniac dragged at the steering-wheel as Dover plunged, for the second time in as many minutes, for safety.

Mrs Gomersall was leaning out of the cab window, yelling encouragement and imprecations as her Jehu swung his unwieldy vehicle round Dame Alice's semi-circular drive. The wheels cut great gashes in fl wer-beds and immaculate patches of lawn. The sheep bleated louder than ever. Cries of 'After her! After her!' came from Mrs Gomersall as she battered the side of the cab with a pale plump hand. The van went roaring through the second set of gates leaving no more than a scrape of paint on one of the posts, turned back down the hill and disappeared in a clash of gears and a cloud of exhaust.

Like a punch-drunk boxer who doesn't know when he's taken enough, Dover got himself up on his hands and knees. The e was a yelp of innocent canine joy. Dame Alice's dog, which had been cowering terrified at the back of the house, emerged, saw Dover and hurled himself on his adversary with teeth snapping and paws scrabbling.

''Strewth!' groaned Dover as the dog landed on him, square in the small of the back.

It was MacGregor who sorted things out.

Dover sensibly refused to acknowledge anybody or anything until he found himself reclining with his feet up on a settee. The e was a clink of glasses. He opened his eyes and closed them again in horror as he found Dame Alice standing over him, proffering a tumbler of brandy.

'Where am I?' he asked feebly, thinking it better to stick to the conventional script until he found out what the hell was going on. 'What's happened?'

'You might well ask,' said Dame Alice grimly and rammed the glass of brandy between Dover's teeth. 'My companion has absconded, my drive has been ruined and my dog is having hysterics.'

'Mrs Gomersall?' choked Dover as the brandy seared his throat.

'Oh, she's gone chasing after Miss Thickett' said MacGregor, moving into Dover's view. 'I don't think she'll catch her, though, not in that old van.'

'Miss Thickett?' said Dover with a nasty feeling that his dearest hopes were going to be dashed.

'Miss Thickett!' repeated Dame Alice with withering scorn. 'A viper I have nursed in my bosom! After she had received this very peculiar telephone-call about which your sergeant has given me a most incoherent account, she rushed upstairs, packed a suitcase, and left, without so much as by-your-leave or a word of explanation. From what the sergeant here has been telling me, it seems unlikely that she will return. What has been going on, Chief Inspector? I demand an explanation.'

'I don't know,' said Dover crossly. He took another sip of brandy. It wasn't Dame Alice whom Mrs Gomersall had phoned. It wasn't Dame Alice who had been flogging babies at three hundred smackers a go. His lower lip stuck out in a sulky pout. He'd damned near ruptured himself, rushing up that hill. And for what? Not for the pleasure of slipping the bracelets over Miss Thicket's hairy hands, he could tell you that!

'You must know something!' insisted Dame Alice.

Dover scowled ferociously at her. It was on the tip of his tongue to tell her to belt up, but diplomacy and a tender regard for his public image restrained him. 'During my investigations into the circumstances of Mrs Tompkins's suicide,' he began with great dignity, 'my attention was drawn to the fact that she had withdrawn the sum of three hundred pounds in cash from her bank only a few days before her death. We already knew that Mrs Tompkins had earlier been unsuccessful in adopting a baby through the usual channels and when, in the further course of my investigations, I discovered a girl in Bearle who had been preparing to sell her illegitimate and unwanted infant, I naturally put two and two together.'

Dover perked up a bit. Put like that it didn't sound at all bad. Besides, he reflected maliciously, it might be as well to get the authorized version firmly established before MacGregor got a chance to open his great trap.

'I discovered,' he went on, growing more and more pompous, 'that the girl had entered into negotiations with Mrs Freda Gomersall here in Thornwich. Naturally this confirmed my suspicions that there was some connection with Mrs Tompkins, suspicions which up to now had been little more than inspired guesses.

'When interviewed, Mrs Gomersall was evasive, but it was clear from her manner that she knew more than she was prepared to divulge. I therefore,' said Dover, assuming a cunning look, 'informed her, casually as if by accident, that we had reason to suppose that Mrs Tompkins was prepared to pay, and, as far as we knew, actually had paid three hundred pounds for the baby. The effect was electrifying! Clearly Mrs Gomersall did not know either that the prospective purchaser was – or had been – Mrs Tompkins, nor did she know that a sum of the magnitude of three hundred pounds was involved.

'Immediately upon vacating Freda's Café, my assistant and I repaired to the sub post offic on the other side of the road. The e, with the co-operation of Miss Tilley, I overheard a most revealing telephone conversation between Mrs Gomersall and someone in this house. It was obvious that Mrs Gomersall had got in touch with her fellow conspirator. The two women had been working together to sell Mrs Tompkins the baby recently born to Eleanor Smith.'

'Mary Thickett!' spat Dame Alice. 'How dare she! Living under my roof, how dare she! Of course, she knew all about my dealings with Mrs Tompkins over the legal adoption of a baby. I naturally gave her access to the most confidential material. She must have seen her opportunity to make a profit out of the distress of someone else. I wonder how she got in touch with Mrs Gomersall? Miss Thickett has only been in my employ some three or four months and I didn't even know that she'd even so much as spoken to Mrs Gomersall. Of course, I have been keeping my eye on Mrs Gomersall for some time. I suspect that she carries out illegal abortions, but it is very difficul to get adequate proof in cases of that kind. No doubt' – she shivered fastidiously – 'Mary Thickett considered that background an ideal one for her nefarious machinations. Mrs Gomersall could be relied upon to know where to lay her hands on unwanted infants.'

'Well, there it is,' said Dover. 'Mrs Gomersall and Miss Thickett were in partnership, and it was your Miss Thickett who was trying to swindle Mrs Gomersall out of a fair share of the proceeds. She's hopped it with three hundred pounds in cash that she got from Mrs Tompkins, presumably before the baby died, or before Mrs Tompkins realized it had.'

Dame Alice frowned. 'But why should Mrs Tompkins have committed suicide if she was on the point of adopting a baby?'

'She may have already known the baby was dead,' Dover pointed out. 'That in itself might ha e been the last straw.'

'And she went to meet her Maker without getting her three hundred pounds back?' asked Dame Alice incredulously. 'That doesn't sound like Winifred Tompkins, I can assure you!'

'We're not entirely convinced that Mrs Tompkins did commit suicide, Dame Alice.' MacGregor, unasked, joined in the conversation. 'She may have been murdered,' he added importantly and before Dover could stop him.

'And she may not!' snapped the Chief Inspector.

'Murdered?' said Dame Alice. 'It's the first I've heard of it. Who's supposed to have murdered her – her husband?'

'No!' roared Dover. 'He's got a perfectly water-tight alibi and he's no more motive than any married man.'

'In view of this baby business and the three hundred pounds,' said MacGregor, 'Mrs Gomersall and Miss Thickett might have had good reason for getting rid of Mrs Tompkins. They were clearly swindling her over the whole affai , especially so after the baby died.'

'Balderdash!' snorted Dover after having started off with a shorter word in mind. 'Freda Gomersall didn't even know that Mrs Tompkins was the one who was going to buy the baby. She'd have cut this Thickett woman right out of the deal if she had done. And you can see Ma Gomersall pussy-footing around, murdering Mrs Tompkins and making it look like suicide? Because I can't: It's beyond her physically and mentally.'

'Well, what about Miss Thickett?' asked MacGregor hopefully. 'She had the most to gain and the most to lose. With Mrs Tompkins dead she could hang on to the money, and there was no danger that Mrs Tompkins would start cutting up rough and blowing the gaff on the whole deal' He turned to Dame Alice. 'I suppose you don't remember where Miss Thickett was on Wednesday, the day Mrs Tompkins died?'

'I remember very well,' retorted Dame Alice who prided herself, quite unjustifiabl , on having total recall. 'She spent the whole day with me. We were attending a conference on Venereal Diseases, at Branford, and we didn't get back here until well after midnight. She certainly couldn't have had anything to do with Mrs Tompkins's death, unless it was done by means of some form of remote control which, I presume, is highly unlikely.'

'Highly,' agreed MacGregor, looking thwarted.

'Well,' said Dover, gingerly lowering his feet to the floor and assuming an upright position, 'I don't think we're going to achieve anything by messing about here any longer. If I was you, Dame Alice, I'd do an inventory of the family silver. Miss Thickett may have helped herself to a few of your heir-looms while she was at it.'

Dame Alice showed no inclination to detain her guests, nor did she show any signs of being willing to wield the brandy decanter again. Dover decided to cut his losses and get back to the haven of rest which he was trying to create for himself at The olly Sailor.

He took a step forward, slightly more energetically than he had intended, let out a piercing howl, clutched himself and collapsed heavily on Dame Alice's Persian rug.

'My God!' he howled through lips contorted with pain. 'I've broken my ruddy back!'

Chapter Thirteen

He was, of course, exaggerating. Not even Dr Hawnt, the only medical practitioner he would allow near him, could be inveigled into certifying that Dover had broken his back. Dover was indignant at such professional niceties and insisted on calling MacGregor in for a second opinion.

'There!' said Dover triumphantly as his pyjama trousers collapsed into folds round his ankles. 'Look at that!' He hoisted up his vest and surveyed himself over his shoulder in the wardrobe mirror.

MacGregor, who had witnessed many gruelling sights in becoming a policeman, closed his eyes.

'Well?' demanded Dover impatiently. He was standing in his bare feet upon the cold linoleum.

MacGregor opened his eyes. 'It looks very nasty, sir. Most unpleasant.'

Dover looked pleased. 'That's what I thought,' he said. 'That old fool Hawnt kept jabbering on about stiffness resulting from excessive exertion and minor bruising in the lower back. Stupid old cretin! Would you call that minor bruising, laddie?'

MacGregor shook his head.

'No, and neither would I!' snorted Dover. '"Rub a bit of embrocation on," he said. "I've got an impacted vertebra," I told him, but I might as well have been talking to a brick wall.

However,' said Dover, unable to conceal a smirk of satisfaction, 'I did get him to see sense about one thing.'

'He wants you to stay in bed for a few days, sir?'

'Oh?' said Dover. 'He told you, did he?'

'No, sir. I just thought it seemed the most likely course of treatment – in the circumstances.'

Dover was too busy doing a Narcissus to detect any *arrière-pensée* or maybe it should be *double entendre*. 'See that?' he said, poking at one spot which had a faint circular bruise. 'D'you know what that is?'

'No, sir.'

'It's that bloody dog's footprint, where he jumped on me. Somebody ought to get a gun and shoot the brute.'

'Yes, sir,' said MacGregor and bent at his crippled master's behest to haul the pyjama trousers up again.

Dover hobbled back to bed.

It was inevitable that the investigation into Thornwic 's poison-pen case should hang fi e for a few days. With the senior detective incapacitated on a bed of pain, nobody could expect that things would progress with their usual elan and verve.

'I shall have to leave the leg work to you, laddie,' he had informed MacGregor from his pillows. He groaned pathetically as he reached for his grapes. 'I'll just have to lie here and do the thinking.'

Mr Tompkins proved a tower of strength. When he wasn't engaged on burying his wife or attending the coroner's inquest on her remains, he sat by the invalid's bedside and kept him amused. Dover had been reluctantly excused from personal attendance at the inquest. He had been allowed to submit his evidence, duplicating everything that Mr Tompkins had said about the discovery of the body, in writing.

Mr Tompkins, luckily, was one of those people who feel embarrassed if they visit the sick empty-handed, so Dover was kept well supplied with those little luxuries which make all the diffe ence. While Dover smoked Mr Tompkins's cigarettes and ate Mr Tompkins's chocolates and drank the occasional glass of Mr Tompkins's champagne, the two men chatted companionably about many things. Sometimes they even discussed the case of the poison-pen letters. Dover was prepared to talk about this otherwise taboo subject with Mr Tompkins because he had become quite fond of the inoffensi e little man. Besides, Mr Tompkins was still talking about establishing his own detective agency and naturally Dover (a detective himself, let it be remembered) was interested. Of course this project, so dear to everybody's heart, would probably have to wait until Mr Tompkins returned from his world cruise and might even have to be postponed until after the expedition to shoot grizzly bears in the Rockies, but Dover quite understood that the demands on the time of a rich man were many and varied.

Dover scrupulously obeyed the instructions of the physician, who was fetched to see him once a day in spite of his protests, all through Saturday, Sunday and Monday. By Tuesday he was beginning to get a bit bored. Not bored enough actually to get up, but bored all the same. Mr Tompkins was all right but a lot of him went a very long way. And then there was the fact that Dover had, when he'd nothing else to do, been thinking on and off about the case and one small point had struck him. When he'd had his nap after lunch on the Tuesday, he sent for MacGregor.

'Listen, laddie,' he said, heaving himself up on the pillows and making a mental note to ask old Hawnt about the danger of bed-sores, 'I've been going over the case in my mind while I've been lying here. I'm not sleeping very well at night, you know. Insomnia. And I've been wondering if you haven't been tackling this case from the wrong end, as you might say. Now, you've been looking at it from the angle of the women who've received these letters, haven't you?'

'Well, yes, sir,' admitted MacGregor. 'If you recall, sir, that was your theory right at the beginning. You said that the woman who was sending these letters would be sending some, probably a lot, to herself as well – a natural precaution. And you said that she'd never burn any of her letters, obviously. She'd make a point of taking them all to the police. And you said …'

'Oh, never mind what I said!' snapped Dover who was allergic to having his opinions quoted back to him in the light of a subordinate's hindsight. 'You've been working on those lines, haven't you? Well, where's it got you?'

'Not very far, I'm afraid, sir. I've interviewed practically all the women in the village now, sir, and really nothing significant has emerged at all. I concentrated on the ones you originally selected as being the most likely, but I haven't been able to turn up anything which points to one more than the others. You remember who they were, sir? Dame Alice, Mrs Tompkins, Mrs Crotty – the vicar's wife – and that girl who tried to commit suicide, Poppy Gullimore. Of course, Mrs Tompkins is dead now.'

'Of course,' said Dover who remembered it quite clearly. He remembered Dame Alice and that stupid little nit, Poppy Gullimore, quite clearly, too. 'What about this Mrs Crotty?' he asked. 'Did you get anything out of her?'

'Hardly, sir,' said MacGregor with a wealth of feeling. 'She's only just got back from hospital. She'd been there a fortnight so it's quite out of the question that she could have been writing and posting those poison-pen letters.'

'She's been ill, too, has she?' asked Dover with a great show of sympathy.

'Not quite, sir,' said MacGregor drily. 'She's just been having her eighth.'

'Her eighth what?' asked Dover, reaching under the bed and depositing his cigarette-end in the outsize receptacle provided.

'Child, sir. She's already got seven under seven, if you see what I mean. Of course, there is one set of twins.'

'Cripes!' said Dover who was not fond of children. 'Hasn't she ever heard of birth control?'

'Apparently not, sir.' MacGregor grinned slyly. 'They call Mr Crotty Brer Rabbit in the village.'

Dover thought this was funny and chuckled. 'Oh, well,' he said, 'I reckon you're right. She's obviously been too busy to get up to writing poison-pen letters. Besides, she doesn't sound the type of woman we're looking for. Scrub her! Now then, what were we talking about?'

'You were saying something about me having been wasting my time, sir.'

'Oh yes. Well, I wouldn't put it quite like that. We've got to explore every avenue and you mustn't despise dull slogging routine, MacGregor. It's what solves cases nine times out of ten,' said Dover pompously. He must have read it somewhere. 'Now then, to get back to the point. Have you ever considered the women who *haven't* been getting these blessed letters?'

'Well, of course I have sir,' said MacGregor, who might be bound body and soul with fetters of steel to the Chief Inspector, but who could still call this thoughts his own. 'Not counting the few teenage girls who don't seem to come into the picture, there's only one woman in the entire village who hasn't had at least one letter.'

'Two,' said Dover.

'Two letters, sir?'

'No, you fool! Two women.'

'Are there, sir? I only know of one – old Charlie Chettle's daughter. She's had a pretty rough time of it, one way and another. People have been hinting that the poison-pen letters only started a few months after she came to live here, and since she hasn't had any she must be writing them. You know the sort of thing. Personally, I don't think she's anything to do with it. But who's the other one, sir?'

'The absconding iss Thickett'

'Oh, yes.' MacGregor nodded his head and acknowledged this as one up to Dover. It didn't happen often and MacGregor felt he could affo d to be generous. 'I'd forgotten her. Incidentally, there's still no sign of her, sir. She seems to have disappeared completely.'

'Let's hope it stays that way,' grumbled Dover. 'I'm damned if I know what we'd charge her with if we did catch her.'

'We wouldn't need to charge her,' grinned MacGregor, 'not if Freda Gomersall finds her first. She's still threatening to make mincemeat out of her. But surely Miss Thickett couldn't be the letter-writer, could she? I shouldn't have thought she was well enough up in the local gossip. She doesn't seem to have mixed very much with the rest of the village – apart from Mrs Gomersall and Mrs Tompkins, that is.'

'No,' said Dover, trying to look enigmatic. 'The question you've got to ask yourself, laddie, is *why* neither Miss Thickett nor Charlie Chettle's daughter has had a poison-pen letter.'

'Oh,' said MacGregor, wondering whether he ought to point out that this obvious question had crossed his mind. 'Well, as far as Charlie Chettle's daughter is concerned, I just put it down to the fact that she's a comparative newcomer to the village. The same thing would apply to Miss Thickett, wouldn't it, sir? She's not been with Dame Alice for more than a few months.'

'Precisely,' said Dover, 'that's the crux of the whole matter. Now listen, why hasn't anybody been able to find that typewriter? Why hasn't anybody heard anybody else doing all that typing – and it's a fair amount, you know. Why hasn't anybody been spotted buying large supplies of Tendy Bond notepaper and stamps, too, if it comes to that? Why have no letters been sent to the only two women in the village who have lived here for less than a year?'

'I don't know, sir.'

'Well, I do, laddie! Up to now we've assumed that those letters have been written just before they were posted, haven't we? But suppose whoever wrote them got them all ready, typed, envelopes addressed, stamps stuck on – the lot – and got ready as long as – say twelve months ago?'

'I don't quite see, sir …'

'And chucked the typewriter away! Tha 's why we haven't been able to find it. Tha 's why nobody's drawn attention to themselves by sitting up all hours of the night typing with a pair of rubber gloves on. Tha 's why Charlie Chettle's daughter and Miss Thickett alone haven't had any letters. They weren't living in the village when the letters were originally written.'

'That sounds quite a bright idea, sir.' MacGregor's surprise was unflattering

'I thought it was,' agreed Dover smugly.

MacGregor searched frantically for objections. 'It makes the whole thing look very – well – deliberate and premeditated, though, doesn't it, sir?'

''Strewth!' said Dover. 'It looked that before, didn't it? She's an intelligent woman and she's thought out the whole business very carefully. The absence of fingerprints, the concealing of the typewriter – it all points the same way. If she did write those letters months and months ago, it just proves she is a bit cleverer and more cautious than we gave her credit for.'

'It doesn't sound much like the behaviour of a sexually disturbed, frustrated woman though, does it, sir?' said MacGregor doubtfully.

'It's what happened,' said Dover flatl . 'I'll stake my reputation on it. She's cut the risks down to a minimum. All she has to look out for now is not actually being caught posting the things.'

'Or being found with the unposted letters in her possession,' MacGregor pointed out.

'Easy enough to conceal,' snorted Dover, 'especially when nobody was looking for them. Much easier than hiding that bloody typewriter.' He helped himself to one of Mr Tompkins's liqueur chocolates. 'Only problem now is how do we catch her? If we set a watch on the pillar boxes she'd be sure to spot it, and just walk on with the bloody letters safe in her handbag.'

'I don't think there's much point in watching the pillar boxes now, sir,' said MacGregor. 'As a matter of fact, the letters seem to have stopped.'

'Stopped!' yelped Dover. 'Why the hell didn't you tell me about this before?'

'Well, we weren't really sure, sir, but there doesn't seem much doubt about it now. The e hasn't been an anonymous letter posted in Thornwich – or anywhere else, come to that – since last Tuesday. The day,' said MacGregor in case Dover had missed the point, 'before Mrs Tompkins killed herself.'

'Oh, help!' said Dover morosely.

'You see the implications, sir? The whole village is buzzing with it. They think that the poison-pen letter writer was Mrs Tompkins.'

'Poppycock!' said Dover, but his heart wasn't in it.

'Oh, but it's pretty obvious, sir, surely? As soon as she's dead, the letters stop. You've only got to put two and two together.'

'And you've only got to think like a detective instead of a blinking mathematician!' retorted Dover, gathering strength. He'd long ago made up his mind on whom he was going to pin the poison-pen letters, and he wasn't a man to give up his prejudices lightly. Winifred Tompkins was innocent. She'd got to be! 'Look, laddie,' said Dover, fighting strongly now that a matter of principle was at stake, 'you searched the Tompkinses' place from top to bottom, didn't you, when Mrs Tompkins killed herself? And you didn't find anything, did you? Not one bloody thing to connect her with these letters.'

'But, according to your theory, I wouldn't, would I, sir? If all the preparations had been made a year ago there wouldn't be any incriminating evidence lying around. It would all have been disposed of months ago. Even if she'd had a few letters left over, she'd only got to chuck them on the kitchen boiler before she killed herself. I'm afraid we've got to accept it, sir. It all fits '

'All fits my eye!' snarled Dover, tossing the bedclothes aside with reckless abandon. 'My God!' He started undoing the buttons on his pyjama jacket. 'If you haven't got somebody standing over you every fi e minutes, you go off like a berserk clockwork mouse! First you have me tearing about like a maniac all over the countryside over this baby buying business which proved to have no relation to anything, and now you're trying to pin the poison-pen letters on to a poor harmless soul who's dead and can't defend herself. You're damned well not fit to be walking the beat looking for lost dogs, never mind be a blooming CID man. Oh well,' sighed Dover, rummaging in his suitcase for a shirt, 'if you want something done properly, do it yourself. It's the old, old story!'

He reiterated his theme over lunch. 'Don't you worry, old man,' he informed an astonished Mr Tompkins, 'I'm back on the job now. I shouldn't be, I know, but there are some things that are more important than a man's health. I know your wife didn't write those letters and nothing is ever going to make me believe she did. Call it instinct, if you like,' said Dover generously, 'but it's an instinct I have learned, over many years of conducting successful criminal investigations, to trust!' Dover waved his knife and fork in the air to emphasize the point. 'Now then' – he pointed the knife accusingly at Mr Tompkins while shovelling a pile of potato into his mouth with the fork – 'you were her husband. You were living with her twenty-four hours a day. Did you ever suspect she was writing those poison-pen letters? No, of course you didn't! Did you ever hear or see your wife typing? No, of course you didn't! Ever see her buying large supplies of Tendy Bond notepaper – a brand, according to this genius of a sergeant here, she never used? No, of course you didn't! Did you ever see her popping out every fi e minutes day and night to post the letters? No, of course you didn't! How could she have ever kept a typewriter in your house without you knowing about it? Why, I don't suppose she could even type, could she?'

'Well, as a matter of fact,' admitted Mr Tompkins, 'she was a shorthand typist before I married her. She'd done a proper course and everything.'

'Well, that settles it, doesn't it?' demanded Dover triumphantly. 'The joker we're looking for used two fingers. Your wife would have used all ten!'

'She hadn't done any typing for a long time, Mr Dover. Perhaps she'd forgotten.'

'They never forget,' said Dover firml . 'It's like riding a bicycle. Once you know how, you know how.'

'Did Mrs Tompkins ever do any typing for you in the shop?' asked MacGregor, feeling the investigation could do with, a touch of common sense at this stage. 'I noticed you had a typewriter in your house.'

Mr Tompkins shook his head. 'Oh no, she said it used to damage her nails. She'd very brittle nails, you know, so what bit of typing there was to do in the business, I did.'

'Brittle nails!' snorted Dover. 'Well, that just about clinches it. She wasn't the poison-pen writer.'

'But what about the rubber gloves, sir?' asked MacGregor. 'We're pretty sure that whoever typed those letters was wearing rubber gloves – because of the fingerprints. That might make all the diffe ence. A touch-typist wearing rubber gloves might well resort to two-finger typing, it would be pretty awkward to do anything else. And, of course, rubber gloves would protect the fingernails f om getting damaged.'

Dover scowled at MacGregor. 'Why don't you keep your trap shut?' he asked savagely. 'When I want your half-baked opinions, I'll ask for 'em.'

But Dover didn't just leave it there. As soon as he'd had his lunch and a short nap to settle his digestion, he was off again. This time it was another visit to Mrs Poltensky, who greeted the two detectives like long lost friends. The laying out of Mrs Tompkins had eventually been entrusted to her and she felt, quite erroneously, that she had Dover to thank for a novel experience.

'I've never laid out a suicide before,' she informed them as she showed them into her front room. 'Quite a feather in my cap. I did an extra-special job on her, poor thing. I made her look quite nice, I really did. Well, considering what she looked like when she was alive. In fact,' – Mrs Poltensky beamed happily – 'she looked a jolly sight better in her shroud than ever she did when she was up and walking around, though I says it as shouldn't.'

Eventually Dover succeeded in stopping the fl w and got down to the serious business. It soon emerged (as Dover, a shrewd judge of character, if ever there was one, suspected it would) that very little went on in the Tompkins's ménage of which Mrs Poltensky was ignorant. Apart from Mr Tompkins's shed out in the back yard which neither she nor Mrs Tompkins ever entered for fear of being blown up, there was hardly a nook or cranny which was not thoroughly investigated at least twice a week by Mrs Poltensky in the course of her dusting.

She laughed to scorn the mere idea that anything as large as a portable typewriter could have been hidden from her. The suggestion that piles of Tendy Bond notepaper and sheets of stamps might have escaped her eagle eye was contemptuously pooh-poohed. 'When I clean a house, young man,' she told MacGregor, 'I *clean* it.'

Could the items under discussion have been concealed in the shop amongst the piles of merchandise?

They could not. Apart from the fact that Mr Tompkins would have been sure to have seen them, Mrs Poltensky frequently scanned the shelves since she was allowed to purchase her groceries at cost price. 'And that's another nice little perk I've lost myself,' she commented sadly. 'He sometimes used to give me them old tins when they got a bit battered and rusty. Oh well, I suppose I can always go on the Assistance.'

Dover had enough troubles of his own without worrying where Mrs Poltensky's next meal was coming from. 'Did you ever see any rubber gloves knocking around?' he asked.

'Rubber gloves?' Mrs Poltensky shook her head. 'I don't hold with 'em myself. If the good Lord meant us to wear rubber gloves he wouldn't have given us no skin, would he?' Mrs Poltensky chuckled just to show she wasn't being serious.

'What about Mrs Tompkins?' asked MacGregor. 'Did you ever see her wearing rubber gloves?'

'No, I can't say I have. The e wasn't a pair in the house or in the shop. On that I'll stake my dying oath. Not if you was to tear my tongue out with red-hot pincers would I say any diffe ent. What would she want rubber gloves for, anyhow? I did all the work round there, rough and smooth. And the cooking when her ladyship didn't feel up to it. Besides,' added Mrs Poltensky with a disparaging sniff, 'I seem to remember her telling me once she was allergic to rubber. Brought her out in spots, or something. She was always saying she was allergic to this, or that that upset her. I used to feel like telling her if she thought a bit less about herself she'd do a lot better, but it was a good job and it wasn't my place anyhow.'

'Right!' said Dover when they had finally escaped Mrs Poltensky's amiable clutches. 'Well, I hope you're satisfied '

MacGregor wasn't, not entirely, but it was clearly not a good moment to say so. 'It doesn't look very likely, I must admit, sir,' he said grudgingly. 'But, why should the letters stop as soon as Mrs Tompkins died?'

Dover didn't answer. If some people couldn't see what was staring them straight in the face, it was no good arguing with them. You might as well save your breath. He, personally, was quite satisfied that Mrs Tompkins was not the author of the poison-pen letters, and if that wasn't good enough for Clever-Boots MacGregor – hard blooming luck! Dover turned his mind to more important things. If he got a move on, he'd just have nice time for a nap before dinner.

Having settled the stupid, time-wasting business once, Dover was not pleased when MacGregor stirred the whole thing up again over the dinner table. Poor Mr Tompkins's being there only made MacGregor's insubordination – there was no other word for it – the more regrettable. With what Dover could only consider a lamentable lack of good taste, MacGregor harked back to the puzzle of why, if Mrs Tompkins didn't write them, the letters had stopped after her death.

If Dover had had any explanation he would have given it. As it was he had to resort to simple bullying and crude abuse.

'The e is one possible reason, sir,' persisted MacGregor who was getting a good deal above himself these days.

'I wish you'd hold your blithering tongue!' snarled Dover, red danger spots rising menacingly over his fi e o'clock shadow. 'Nobody's interested in your tin-pot theories.'

Mr Tompkins cleared his throat. 'Well, I must admit, I'd like to hear what Sergeant MacGregor has got to say, Mr Dover, being what you might call an interested party. Besides,' – he gave that admiring smile which Dover found so endearing – 'it really is fascinating to listen to you two chewing all the facts over and working things out. It's a real education for an old stick-in-the-mud like me.'

This put a diffe ent complexion on things. Dover managed to replace his scowl by something that could be taken as an indulgent beam, and MacGregor was allowed to proceed.

'Well, it's like this, sir,' he began, delighted to have the centre of the stage for once, and conscious he would have to pay for it later. 'Let's assume, for the sake of argument, that the late Mrs Tompkins *didn't* write the poison-pen letters.'

Dover blew down his nose.

'That means that somebody else w ote them.'

'Brilliant!' scoffed over.

'Here, give the lad a chance!' This was an interruption from Charlie Chettle who had come into the bar for his usual drink. Mr and Mrs Quince, who were both pottering about behind the counter, nodded their approval for this stand on behalf of the underdog.

Dover shrugged his shoulders and relapsed into a moody silence. The e were several more men in the bar, locals and passing lorry-drivers, all maintaining a respectful silence and all waiting impatiently for MacGregor to be allowed to continue.

'That means,' resumed MacGregor, 'that somebody else wrote them. Now, the question we have to ask ourselves is, why this other person, whom we will call Madam X, stopped writing the letters after Mrs Tompkins died.'

This statement met with general approval, but Charlie Chettle's whippet produced an enormous yawn. Very ostentatiously Dover patted the animal on the head.

'Now, so far we have been assuming,' continued MacGregor, quite unperturbed by Dover's petty attempts at sabotage, 'that the poison-pen letter writer was motivated by what we may call a package malice. In other words, she was lashing out indiscriminately at all the women in the village, or the vast majority of them at any rate. She had a grudge, or so we presumed, against all women in general. She hated them. She wanted to revenge herself on them for her own peculiar, twisted reasons.'

'Get on with it!' muttered Dover, bored to his back dentures.

'Why then should the death of one woman make Madame X stop? Why should the suicide of Mrs Tompkins make her put aside the typewriter for ever? The e is no reason, unless we change the basis of our original premise. Suppose the poison-pen letter writer ...'

'Whom we will call Madam X!' prompted Dover with a snigger.

'... Suppose she was not attacking *all* the women in the village. Suppose her spite was directed exclusively at Mrs Tompkins. Suppose all the other letters were just part of a gigantic blind to confuse and misdirect us. Suppose ...'

'Suppose you bloody well put a sock in it,' suggested Dover, playing it for a cheap laugh and, such is the fickleness of human nature, getting it.

'Well, it's an idea, sir,' said MacGregor, coming down to earth with a bump.

'Are you seriously suggesting,' asked Dover, 'that all this poison-pen mularky, damn near a hundred letters, was all set up just to drive Mrs Tompkins to commit suicide? It's a bit of a long shot, isn't it?'

'It's not beyond the realms of possibility, sir,' said MacGregor stiffly. 'I've heard of more elaborate plots.'

'Yes,' scoffed Dover with a broad wink at Mr Tompkins, 'and I should think you've invented 'em, too!'

'However,' said MacGregor, 'my theory becomes a good deal more logical if we work on the assumption that Mrs Tompkins did not commit suicide, but was murdered;'

'By Madame X?' asked Dover, grinning all over his face.

'Yes, sir.'

'Do you know what I think?' asked Dover nastily. 'I think Madame X isn't the only one who's barmy round here.'

'It's a theory that fits the facts, si .'

'Facts? 'Strewth, it's a fine time to be talking about facts! The fact is that Mrs Tompkins committed suicide. Exactly why we don't know and probably never will do, but there's no doubt that the poison-pen letters were part of the reason. Tha 's what the coroner decided, isn't it? And I'll give you a few more facts. Madame X has stopped sending obscene letters through Her Majesty's Postal Service (a) because she's got a guilty conscience about Mrs Tompkins's suicide which is probably a damned sight further than she intended things to go, and (b) because she's afraid of me! She thinks that by stopping now I shall lose interest in the case and the whole thing will be quietly dropped. Well,' – Dover addressed his ringing proclamation to the entire company – 'Madame X is just going to find she's wrong. I'm not the sort of man that gives up that easily!'

'Of course not, Mr Dover,' said Mr Tompkins soothingly.

'I've said it once,' Dover went on, 'and I'll say it again: Mrs Tompkins did not write those letters. And you can take my word for it, I shall not rest until I have brought the woman who did write them to book!'

'Well, I just hope,' said Mrs Quince to her husband, 'we've seen the last of those nasty letters, that's all. I'll be grateful enough if they just stop coming.'

'My dear madam,' said Dover, bowing graciously in Mrs Quince's direction, 'I think you may rest assured that the poison-pen letters have stopped, for the reasons I mentioned earlier. You won't be troubled by them again.'

Chief Inspector Dover was, of course, wrong.

Chapter Fourteen

MacGregor had the bitter-sweet task of breaking the news to him some thirty-two hours after the rather disgraceful public meeting in the bar of The Jolly Sailor. Dover met this set-back as he met most set-backs in his life: he lost his temper. Eventually, when things had calmed down, he announced that he would have his breakfast in his room. This was so that he wouldn't have to meet Mrs Quince, to whom the new anonymous letter had been addressed. When he had finished his breakfast, Dover sullenly consented to examine the evidence.

He took the letter which MacGregor had already enclosed between two pieces of transparent plastic so as to preserve any fingerprints. over gazed at it resentfully.

'But it's not the same!' he protested, as though it was MacGregor's fault.

'No, sir,' agreed MacGregor, 'but I think if you'll examine it, sir, you'll find it's been written by the same person. She's just had to change the format, that's all. Of course, if you're right about the original typewriter having been thrown away, it would explain why she's had to resort to this.'

Dover scowled miserably at the letter. It was on blue paper this time. The letter was not handwritten. Type-like characters in purple ink were arranged in smudgy and uneven lines. Dover read the contents. MacGregor was right. It was the same unrestrained outpouring of grammatical, well-spelt filth which had characterized the dozens of earlier letters, now reposing in Dover's file

'Don't you agree, sir?' asked MacGregor.

'Looks as though it's by the same woman,' admitted Dover grudgingly. 'What about fingerprints? Have you traced the notepaper? What's she using this time, another typewriter?'

'I only got the letter a couple of minutes ago,' MacGregor pointed out. 'I haven't had time to do more than read it and stick it between these sheets of talc.'

Dover, in spite of the severe shock he had just suffe ed, seized his opportunity with gratitude and both hands. 'Well, laddie,' he said more cheerfully, 'it's no good bringing it to me unless you've got the spade-work done, is it? You'd better get off to the County Headquarters and get the lab boys on to it, hadn't you? Once we've got the data we can get cracking, can't we? Here you are, laddie, and don't lose it.' He handed the letter back to MacGregor. 'You'd better get a move on. And do a thorough job, mind. The e's no point in spoiling the ship for a ha'porth of tar.'

The Chief Inspector's subtle plans for a quiet day didn't quite work out. Almost as soon as MacGregor had departed on yet another bus, there was a knock on Dover's door. He opened it and found Mrs Quince, arms akimbo, standing outside.

'Oh,' said Dover with an ingratiating smile, 'I didn't know it was time for coffee '

'It isn't!' said Mrs Quince in a manner which was definitely unfriendly. 'And if you want coffee they tell me you can get a perfectly good cup over at Freda Gomersall's for sixpence. I've told you before, I only took you two in to oblige and I'm much too busy to come traipsing up here with trays every fi e minutes. And too upset,' she added significantl .

'Oh,' said Dover.

'I thought you said we'd seen the last of these letters,' said Mrs Quince accusingly.

'Well …' said Dover.

'Well, nothing!' snapped Mrs Quince. 'You're like all the rest of 'em, say the first thing that comes into your head.' She folded her arms. 'The e's four ladies downstairs waiting to see you. They wanted to come up here but I told 'em I wasn't having any goings on, not in The Jolly Sailor. Shall I tell 'em you'll be down?'

'What do they want?' asked Dover.

'Your guts for garters, I shouldn't wonder! They want to show you what they found in their letter boxes this morning, Mr Dover. And Dame Alice phoned. She's had one, too, and she wants you to collect it as soon as possible.'

By the time Dover had got rid of Mrs Leatherbarrow, Miss Tilley and two other ladies whom he'd not had the pleasure of meeting before, the greater part of the morning had gone. After the second post which was delivered round about twelve o'clock he had three more callers. All of them were angry and two of them in tears. Dover's rash statement in The Jolly Sailor had received a wide circulation and the women were doubly annoyed that the poison-pen letter nuisance had started up again.

Dover rang through to the Headquarters of the County Police and, having traced MacGregor, told him what had happened.

'Oh Lord!' said MacGregor. 'Well, I'm not surprised. I didn't think Mrs Quince's would be the only one. I'd better come back and pick the others up then, sir, hadn't I?'

Dover weighed the pros and cons. 'No, don't bother,' he said, having reached his painful decision. 'I'll bring 'em in myself.'

'Really, sir?' MacGregor was surprised. He hadn't realized that the going in Thornwich was as tough as all that. 'Well, OK, sir. I'll be in the laboratory. Anybody'll tell you where it is when you get to the main building.'

Dover had his lunch – and a very scrappy affair it was, too – at The Jolly Sailor and eventually set out in pursuit of MacGregor. He'd plenty of time to think about things as the bus trundled slowly over the moors. It was a mess. Even for one of Dover's investigations, it was a mess. This was about as far as his meditations had got when the bus deposited him at the bus station in Castleham and he ambled over to a young constable to ask him the way to the County Police Headquarters.

MacGregor, happy as a sandboy, was installed in the laboratory helping with the detailed analysis of the letter which Mrs Quince had received. He took charge of the other letters which Dover had brought.

'Oh?' he said as he looked through them, handling them carefully because of possible fingerprints. 'Mrs Jones – that's Charlie Chettle's daughter, isn't it?'

'It is,' said Dover sourly. 'A poor widow woman, or so she told me. One who pays her rates and taxes regularly and thinks she's entitled to police protection in return. Fair make you sick, some of these people! You'd think we'd nothing else to do except run around looking after them.' He stared around with some distaste at the long benches packed with odd-looking machines and equipment. 'How are you getting on?'

'Well, we're still eliminating at this stage, sir,' explained MacGregor, 'but it's going quite well. We shan't have anything definite for th ee or four hours yet.'

'Oh,' said Dover.

'Are you going back to Thornwich, sir? Because, if not, you can use Inspector Tedlow's office He's going to be out for the rest of the day.'

Dover wasn't one to hang around where he wasn't wanted. Besides, the laboratory had a funny smell which made him feel quite queasy. He'd no intention of going back to Thornwich until he had MacGregor to protect him and, somehow, he didn't fancy sitting all by himself in Inspector Tedlow's offic with nothing to do. He decided to go to the pictures and eventually passed quite an enjoyable afternoon, sleeping fitfully through a double feature horror programme.

'Oh, here you are, sir!' said MacGregor brightly when he at last ran Dover to earth in the police canteen. 'I think I'll have a bite to eat, too. I didn't get any lunch, and we can't get a bus back to

Thornwich for nearly a couple of hours. Can I get you another cup of tea, sir?'

'Well, have you got the answers?' asked Dover when MacGregor returned to the table with a tray full of food. 'Ugh! You've spilt my tea in the saucer!'

'Sorry, sir,' said MacGregor. 'Here, take mine! Yes, I think we know where we are now, sir. Not that what we do know looks as though it's going to be any more helpful than it was with the last lot. The letters were all posted in Thornwich again, some time yesterday. It looks as though Madam X posted them in two or three batches, but we'll have to do a thorough check with the Post Offic to get anything more definite. Of course, these letters don't look like the last lot, so the postmen who were doing the collections won't have been on the look-out for them. And, once again, sir, it looks as though we're going to draw a complete blank on the fingerprints. The 're still working on them but I don't think for a minute she's been careless at this stage in the game. Incidentally, sir, it's just struck me that the woman who's writing them must be wearing gloves when she posts them. I don't know whether this might help us spot her.'

'Everybody wears gloves at this time of year,' grunted Dover, helping himself to a piece of MacGregor's bread and butter. 'Got a cigarette, laddie? I seem to have left mine behind somewhere.'

'Well, sir,' MacGregor went on, dutifully wielding the cigarette-case and lighter, 'the writing paper is Tendy Bond again, but blue this time. I've got the local boys asking questions in the towns nearest Thornwich, but I don't suppose that'll get us anywhere. The shops sell far too much of it to remember anybody who buys the odd packet.'

'What about the way the letters were written?'

'Oh yes, I was just coming to that, sir. Really, it's the most interesting part. Highly original. And clever. Do you know what she used, sir?'

'I wouldn't bloody well be asking if I did!' snarled Dover. Two thick-necked policemen at the next table exchanged knowing winks and grinned at each other. 'Glad I don't work for that old baa-lamb!' muttered one of them.

MacGregor hastily resumed his narrative in an attempt to avert a punch-up as an ugly red flush sp ead over Dover's features.

'The letters were printed with one of those children's printing sets, sir. You know, the ones they sell in little cardboard boxes.'

Dover's face remained blank.

'Like this, sir.' MacGregor fished around in his brief-case and produced a small cardboard box. 'You can get them in diffe ent sizes but we think this is the one she used. You see, sir,' – MacGregor took the lid off – 'you get all these little rubber letters and you insert them in the order you want in this little wooden holder.' With some difficult MacGregor composed his surname. 'You'll see, sir,' he said, fumbling enthusiastically away, 'it's a fiddly sort of job and I doubt if you could do it with a pair of rubber gloves on. With a bit of luck – oh, thank you very much, constable! The e's another one under that chair, if you wouldn't mind – she may get careless and give us the present of a nice fat fingerprint. The e you are, sir! I've got it set up now. All you have to do now is get this little inking pad, press the line of type on it – so – and then' – MacGregor hunted in his brief-case for a sheet of paper – 'you stamp it – so!'

Solemnly the two men stared at the result. The e was MacGregor's name, smudgy but quite legible, in purple ink on the paper.

'Hm,' said Dover with interest. 'Here, do one with my name now.'

'The only trouble is, sir,' said MacGregor, fastidiously dismantling his own name and setting up the Chief Inspector's, 'that it's very slow, as you can see. But it serves its purpose. The e's no question of us being able to identify the author by any handwriting tests. In the bigger boxes you get more of the rubber letters and a bigger stick thing to hold them in but, judging by the way our poison-pen letters have been done, this is probably the box she used.'

'Where do you buy them?' asked Dover, happily stamping his name in purple ink all over the paper.

'Practically any toy shop, sir. This model only costs a few bob. I'm having the local boys check around. It's a better lead than the writing paper at any rate. If our Madam X bought one of these in the last few days, I think we've a good chance that the shopkeeper might remember.'

'She's been pretty far-seeing so far. She might have bought it months ago, maybe in London or somewhere like that.'

'Well, in that case, sir, we haven't a hope of tracing it. Still,' said MacGregor, who was a great one for looking on the bright side, 'we've got a few advantages in our favour this time.'

'Such as?' said Dover.

'Well, sir, it looks pretty obvious that this second batch of letters is a sort of challenge, don't you think? You said in The Jolly Sailor on Tuesday night that she was more or less too scared to write any more letters.'

'So?' said Dover cautiously.

'So here she is proving you wrong! It's an act of defiance, sir, don't you think? But, and here's the point, she didn't expect that she would have to send this second lot, otherwise she would have done them on the typewriter. Obviously this kid's printing-set method is a matter of improvisation. If you're right, sir – and clearly you are – the first lot of letters were written well in advance, and the typewriter was disposed of long before any letters were sent. Obviously she couldn't use it again. Hence the printing-set, but it's very slow and clearly second-best. The point is, sir, she must actually be writing these letters *now*. Don't you agree? She must have this lot of writing paper and her printing-set in her possession *now*.'

'As a matter of fact,' said Dover, idly trying to lick some purple ink off the tips of his fingers, 'that's why I said what I did in The Jolly Sailor. I was just trying to goad her into action. Seems as though I've succeeded.'

Several months and a few unsolved cases earlier MacGregor's jaw would have dropped, and other signs of frank incredulity would have passed over his handsomely chiselled features, but not now. Now he was too accustomed to the Chief Inspector's awe-inspiringly accurate rear vision, and just ignored it.

'If we could organize another house-to-house search in Thornwich, sir, we might catch her purple-handed.' MacGregor laughed at his little joke.

Dover didn't. He looked at the little cardboard box as it lay on the table. 'Not very difficul to hide,' he commented, always happy to pour cold water on other people's ideas. 'As soon as she got wind of the search she could chuck it on the fi e. And, knowing Thornwich, sh 'd probably know about it before we did.'

'The ubber would smell,' said MacGregor hopefully.

'Pshaw,' said Dover.

And that, for some considerable time, was that. For the next few days, as the obscene letters continued to arrive in Thornwic 's letter boxes, the local police, goaded by MacGregor, pursued their investigations. They didn't succeed in tracing the purchase of the blue Tendy Bond writing paper or of the child's printing-set. Inquiries were made to see if any one had bought suspiciously large supplies of postage stamps but, not unexpectedly, this too proved a complete waste of police time and led to yet another dead end. MacGregor tried to organize a discreet watch on Thornwic 's two post boxes, but the Chief Constable regretted that he just couldn't spare the surprisingly large number of men required, and Dover said that, if MacGregor thought he was going to stand out in the cold and rain for twenty-four hours at a stretch, he'd got another think coming. MacGregor tried a few hours of guard duty on his own but soon gave it up as a bad job.

Dover virtually retired from the case. After long hours spent having a quiet think in his room, he would emerge from time to time with some cock-eyed suggestion which involved other people in a great deal of work and achieved absolutely nothing. Had it not been for the continued presence of his sister-in-law under his roof he would have packed the whole case in long ago. The atmosphere in Thornwich was unfriendly and Mrs Quince, under the new onslaught of poison-pen letters, became less and less obliging. Her cooking deteriorated, and her fondness for bingo became a positive addiction. Day after day Charlie Chettle made the perilous double crossing over the main road to bring pie and chips for Dover and MacGregor. Dover's digestion suffe ed and he hinted darkly that Freda Gomersall was trying to poison him.

Negative reports on every new line of investigation continued to pour in. Madam X wasn't making any mistakes. In spite of the considerable handling that the use of the printing-set involved, the letters remained unsullied by any fingerprint which couldn't be accounted for. Depressed and thoroughly bored, Dover hung doggedly on. After all, he consoled himself, it was better than going home.

The idea of a house-to-house search was abandoned for the time being. As Dover told MacGregor, he knew where to start looking all right but, if nothing was found, there would be a great deal of unpleasantness and – give the woman credit for some intelligence – nothing would be found. The e was no point in antagonizing the local population more than they had been antagonized already. Indeed, much of the fury which had been directed at the poison-pen letter writer in the past was now being unleashed in Dover's direction. Even the loyal Mr Tompkins seemed to be avoiding him these days, and spent a great deal of time over in his grocer's shop, getting it ready for what he hoped would be an immediate sale.

It was Monday morning, well over a fortnight since Dover had first burst upon the Thornwich scene, when two things happened which spurred on the Chief Inspector to a most uncharacteristic burst of energy.

He received a particularly disgusting poison-pen letter addressed to himself, and his wife telephoned to say that, at long last, the coast was clear.

Chapter Fifteen

Dover was reduced to jowl-quivering fury by the poison-pen letter. Mrs Quince brought it in to him as he and MacGregor were sitting waiting for their breakfast. Dover had started coming downstairs for breakfast again in an unsuccessful attempt to mollify Mrs Quince's displeasure. When she got upset it seemed to go straight to her cooking and Dover's stomach couldn't stand much more of her culinary onslaughts.

'The e you are!' said Mrs Quince as she slapped down the blue envelope with Dover's name and address printed on it in purple ink. 'You've got one all to yourself now. Let's see how you like it!'

Dover picked up his knife and with considerable reluctance slit the envelope open. 'Perhaps it's a confession,' he said.

'And perhaps it isn't!' snorted Mrs Quince as she plonked Dover's breakfast on the table. It consisted of one small, cold, parboiled egg which Mrs Quince had been saving for several weeks for just such an occasion. 'Well?' she demanded triumphantly, seeing the answer already in Dover's expression as he read the letter. 'Is it?'

'Is it what?' said Dover.

'Is it a confession?'

'No, it isn't.'

'No,' said Mrs Quince sardonically. 'I didn't think it would be. Well, come on!' she said as Dover hastily stuffed the letter back in the envelope. 'Aren't you going to hand it round? You were pretty keen to have a good snigger over those everybody else was getting. Strikes me it's only fair to give us a chance now you've got one.'

'Tha's entirely diffe ent,' said Dover, getting very puce round the ears.

'Oh yes,' – Mrs Quince nodded her head – 'yes, it would be, wouldn't it? Well, what's sauce for the goose is sauce for the gander, that's what I always say.'

'Do you?' inquired Dover unpleasantly. He put the letter in his inside pocket and buttoned his jacket firmly over it. The letter had accused him not only of advanced satyriasis in connection with some of the less attractive women in Thornwich, but also of running an affair with MacGregor as well. As far as Dover was concerned, nobody, but nobody, was ever going to clap eyes on that letter.

Mrs Quince recognized defeat and retired with a flounce to her kitchen where she evolved a really nasty idea for Dover's lunch.

'I'll tell you one thing, laddie,' said Dover, gazing with dismay into the depths of his egg, 'I'm getting sick to death of women! The world, in my opinion, would be a happier place without them.'

'Oh, I don't know, sir,' said MacGregor, inevitably, 'they do have their uses.'

Dover snorted.

'Er – what about your letter, sir?' asked MacGregor, who was dying to read it. 'It is a genuine poison-pen one, isn't it?'

'Yes,' said Dover shortly. 'Cheeky bitch! I'll get her for this if it's the last thing I do!'

'I suppose I'd better have it for the usual tests, sir, just in case,' said MacGregor hopefully.

'She's gone too far this time,' muttered Dover sourly. 'I've been trying to handle things diplomatically, trying to avoid a scandal, you know. I could have barged in days ago and thrown my weight around and bust the whole thing sky high, but I didn't. I thought it would be very embarrassing for a woman in her position, a Justice of the Peace and chairman of this and president of that. I thought I'd give her every chance to just drop the whole matter quietly. But that's not good enough for her. She's got to reduce the whole thing to a personal level.'

'Do you think I could have a look at your letter, sir?' asked MacGregor, realizing that subtlety was going to get him nowhere.

'She's got to be stopped,' said Dover, manfully finishing off Mrs Quince's egg and reaching for the burnt toast. 'The general public's got to be protected from people like her. Here! – he licked the end of the butter knife suspiciously – 'I think that old cow's given us margarine!'

'I don't think we can make a case against Dame Alice, sir,' ventured MacGregor, fairly confident that he had interrupted the Chief Inspector's ramblings aright.

'No,' said Dover glumly. 'She's been very clever. Of course,' he added thoughtfully, 'we could, maybe, break her down a bit and get a confession out of her. All women are cowards when it comes to the push.'

MacGregor could feel the blood drain from his cheeks. Dover's tendency to resort to his fists when more orthodox methods of investigation had failed was one which MacGregor had had to contend with before. Sooner or later, in practically every case he was concerned with, the point came when the Chief Inspector deemed it advisable to thump or rattle the truth out of some unfortunate individual who had not taken his fancy. MacGregor shuddered at the thought of what would happen if these strong arm, fist-in-the-ear tactics   ere employed on Dame Alice.

'I don't think that would be very advisable, sir, really I don't,' he said feverishly. 'She is a woman, you know.'

'Worse than the men,' grumbled Dover, 'and tougher, most of 'em.'

'She's a magistrate, too, sir, and Chairman of the Standing Joint Committee.'

'I don't care if she's the Queen of Sheba,' replied Dover haughtily. 'It's my job to crack down on criminals whoever they are and I pride myself, I don't mind telling you, that I carry out my duties without fear or favour.'

'She's a friend of the Assistant Commissioner, sir!' MacGregor was getting frantic. 'If you start leaning on her and you don't make the poison-pen business stick good and proper, she'll crucify you!'

'Garn!' scoffed over. 'I know what I'm doing, laddie.'

'But you've absolutely no proof, sir, none at all! You haven't got one single thing to connect Dame Alice with those poison-pen letters.'

Dover frowned. 'Well,' he admitted, 'nothing that we could actually produce in court.'

'You haven't anything that you couldn't produce in court either, have you sir?'

Dover's frown deepened. His mean little eyes regarded MacGregor sulkily. 'All the more reason to push her around a bit until she confesses,' he said without much conviction. He wiped his mouth with the back of his hand and pushed his chair away from the table.

'You're not thinking of going up to see her now, are you, sir?' asked a horrified acGregor.

'As a matter of fact,' said Dover with great dignity, 'I was just going to the toilet.'

'Oh,' said MacGregor, sweating gently with relief.

'When I come back we'll have to talk over what we're going to do.' Dover scratched his chin. 'I wonder if we could infiltrate Mrs Poltensky? If we could get her installed in Friday Lodge as a charwoman or something, she'd be sure to ferret out the evidence for us. She might,' he added thoughtfully, 'even plant it there for us.'

MacGregor looked shocked.

'Oh, for God's sake, laddie,' said Dover crossly, 'it's been done before and it'll be done again. It's not as though we were framing an innocent woman. It's just a matter of helping things on a bit and making it a bit clearer for the judge and jury.'

MacGregor was totally unconvinced. 'I think it would be very dangerous, sir, apart from being highly unethical. You'd be putting yourself and your career right in Mrs Poltensky's hands. Suppose she decided to talk? You'd never be able to trust her.'

'No,' said Dover with a sigh. 'Maybe you're right. Well, the only other thing I can think of is an intensive, round-the-clock watch on Dame Alice. If we could just catch her posting one of those letters we'd have her cold. Of course it'd mean a lot of work for you, laddie. We'll not get any help from the local police, that's for sure. Well, you just kick it around and think about it.' Dover got to his feet. 'I'll be down in a minute.'

He was half-way up the stairs when the phone rang. It was his wife.

'She's going home this afternoon, Wilf,' said Mrs Dover.

'And about time, too! I was beginning to think she'd taken up residence for life.'

'She's been very good, Wilf, I don't know how I would have managed without her.'

The e was a snort from Dover.

'How have you been keeping, Wilf?' asked his wife hastily.

'Rotten,' said Dover. 'My stomach's still not right, you know. I think I'll have to see a specialist. These ordinary doctors just don't seem able to get to the root of the trouble. I have this sort of dull ache all the time, you see, and as soon as I've had anything to eat – not that I've got any appetite, but I force myself – I've got to keep my strength up, haven't I? Well, when I do, I get the most terrible shooting pains. Agonizing, they are, and they needn't tell me it's wind. I've had wind and ...' Dover talked with enthusiasm until the pips reminded him that the call would be appearing in due course on his telephone bill.

'Oh dear,' said Mrs Dover when, at last, she could get a word in, 'I am sorry you're having such a rotten time, Wilf. I've been feeling a lot better these last couple of days but ...'

'Some people have all the luck,' said Dover. 'When's she going exactly?'

'She's catching the afternoon train.'

'Right,' said Dover. 'I'll be home tomorrow morning.'

He replaced the receiver and turned to MacGregor who was still sitting at the breakfast table. 'I was going to do something when the phone rang,' he said. 'What was it?'

'You were going upstairs, sir.'

'Oh yes,' said Dover. 'Well, we've no time for that now. I want this case wrapped up today, one way or the other. We're going to catch the night train back to London. I've had enough of this crummy dump. Well, for God's sake, what are you sitting there for? Lost the use of your legs or something? Nip upstairs and get my hat and coat. We've no time to lose!'

'Are we going to see Dame Alice, sir?' asked MacGregor. It was a rhetorical question but Dover answered it.

''Strewth! Don't you ever listen to anything that's said to you? Of course we're going to see Dame Alice! We agreed on it not fi e minutes ago, didn't we?'

By the time MacGregor came downstairs clutching Dover's bowler hat and long black overcoat, the Chief Inspector had got things humming in the bar of The Jolly Sailor. Mr and Mrs Quince had been pressed, without too much difficul , into organizing Dover's return home. It was a complicated business and Dover had no intention of tackling Dame Alice until he'd got his lines of retreat secured. MacGregor surveyed the – to him – premature hustle and bustle with dismay. The e was no doubt about it. Dover intended to leave Thornwich and The Jolly Sailor that night, and in the lurch, if needs be. Mrs Quince was giving him sterling support. It took half an hour of acrimonious argument before it was finally established that the two detectives would have to catch the six o'clock bus into Cumberley, change there with a thirty minute wait on to another bus to Grailton and then wait two hours before catching the through train to London at a quarter to one in the morning.

'You'd do much better to wait and catch the ten o'clock bus to Bearle in the morning,' said Mr Quince. 'Then you could get a local train to Wellchester and from there you could get another bus to …'

'No!' said Dover and Mrs Quince in unison.

'I've got to get back to London urgently,' said Dover. 'They need me. We'll have a high tea at fi e o'clock, Mrs Quince, and catch that six o'clock bus.'

Mrs Quince had intended to go to bingo that afternoon but, under the circumstances, she was prepared to forgo the pleasure. Anything to get rid of this fat lazy old devil.

MacGregor helped Dover on with his overcoat and handed him his hat.

'Where are you off to n w?' asked Mrs Quince curiously.

'Never you mind,' Dover snubbed her. 'You'll hear all about it soon enough.'

'Are you going to make an arrest, Mr Dover?' asked Mr Quince.

'Well, now,' said Dover, smiling enigmatically, 'that'd be telling, wouldn't it?'

The pull up the hill, from The Jolly Sailor at the bottom to Friday Lodge at the top, didn't get any easier or shorter. Dover was all for getting at Dame Alice as soon as possible but it wasn't long before he was reduced to his usual panting crawl. When they were half-way there the rain, which had been threatening all morning, began to fall.

'Maybe we should have phoned first to see whether she was in, sir?' said MacGregor, who was praying quite hard that the good Lord, in His infinite me cy, would ensure that she was out.

'What? And tip her off that we were after her? Not on your nelly!' The rain-water dripped off the brim of Dover's bowler. 'Surprise, that's what we want. Catch her unawares. Chuck the accusation at her before she's had time to think up some cock-and-bull story. Let her have it straight between the eyes, right out of the blue.'

It'll be right out of the blue all right, thought MacGregor and wondered despondently what occupations or professions were open to an ex-detective sergeant who had been discharged with ignominy. Dame Alice would have their heads on a charger if Dover did one half of the things he was threatening to do. She wasn't some old lag you could push around as the fancy took you. She was an experienced, well-educated woman of the world with friends in some very high places, and she'd go off like a rocket the minute Dover plonked one of his flat feet out of line. It wasn't even, MacGregor told himself miserably, as though there was a chance in a thousand of her being guilty. All the evidence they had so far was that Dover didn't like her face, and hadn't since he had first laid e es on it.

'Thank the Lord!' said Dover with genuine fervour. 'We're here at last. 'Strewth, my feet are killing me!'

They turned into the drive. Dame Alice's car was standing outside the front door.

'Oh well, it looks as though she's in,' said Dover, hobbling painfully across the gravel.

MacGregor silently cursed his luck. 'Perhaps, sir,' he said, grasping at a pretty soggy straw, 'you'd sooner tackle her by yourself, without a witness, I mean? I could wait out here. I don't mind at all.'

'No,' said Dover generously. 'You come along and see the fun. Besides, if there are any repercussions it'll be much better two against one. With you and me telling the same story, they'll just put it down to another malicious attempt to blacken the good name of the police.'

As they approached the steps leading to the front door Dame Alice's dog came bounding round the house with its usual jubilance. Dover bent down and grabbed a lump of stone from a near-by rockery. The dog stopped dead in its tracks as though unable to believe its eyes. Dover took careful aim. The dog didn't wait. With an outraged yelp and its tail tucked well between its legs, it shot round the comer and disappeared from sight.

'Pity,' said Dover as he dropped his stone back in a fl wer-bed. 'Right! Ring the bell, laddie, and let's get cracking.'

MacGregor rang the bell and they stood waiting.

Dover rang the bell.

Dover hammered on the door panels with his fists

Dover kicked the door.

'I think she must be out, sir,' said MacGregor, grateful for an answer, however belated, to his prayers.

'Fiddlesticks!' said Dover and peered through the coloured glass panels. 'She must be in.' He stepped back. 'Here, try the door and see if it's open.'

Reflecting, and not for the first time, that the Chief Inspector had a positive genius for unloading the dirty work on to younger and less canny shoulders, MacGregor tried the door handle. The door was not locked.

'Well, don't hang about, man!' hissed Dover. 'Get inside!'

MacGregor, hesitating naturally at entering private premises, got a good thump in the small of the back for his scruples, and the two detectives tip-toed cautiously into Dame Alice's hall. Everything seemed very quiet and perfectly normal.

'Hello!' called Dover, feeling a bit of a fool. 'Is there anybody about?'

The e was no answer.

'Just have a look around, laddie,' suggested Dover casually. What are subordinates for if not to take risks?

The e wasn't a sign of any occupant on the ground floo .

'She might be upstairs, sir,' said MacGregor with muted urgency as he saw Dover heading like a homing pigeon towards the alluring haven of Dame Alice's desk.

'Well, keep a look-out, you great fool!' snapped Dover, his fat paws already rummaging in the desk drawers.

Working quickly and ignoring MacGregor's ever more pathetic protests, Dover gave the whole of the downstairs part of Friday Lodge a good going over. He knew what he was looking for and stout-heartedly ignored side issues such as a detailed study of Dame Alice's bank statement and a bundle of letters tied up with ribbon at the back of one of the drawers. But nowhere, not in the kitchen, nor the dining-room, nor the drawing-room, nor the downstairs lavatory, nor the hall, did he find a little cardboard box containing a well-used child's printing-set. He didn't find any Tendy Bond writing paper either.

'Sir!' MacGregor came creeping back from his post at the bottom of the stairs. 'I think there's somebody up there. I can hear the bath water running.'

'Bath water?' said Dover, a most unpleasant suspicion crossing his mind. 'Are you sure?'

'I think so, sir,' replied MacGregor, beginning to get worried in his turn.

'But, nobody takes a bath at this time of the day,' whispered Dover, his brow furrowed with anxiety.

MacGregor swallowed hard, 'Mrs Tompkins did, sir.'

Dover crinkled his nose. ''Strewth,' he said, 'you're a cheerful Charlie!'

'They do say things go in threes, sir,' MacGregor pointed out unhappily. 'Poppy Gullimore, Mrs Tompkins, and now, this.' He jerked his head in the direction of the stairs.

'She must know we're on to her,' agreed Dover slowly. 'I wouldn't put it past her to try and take the easy way out.' He scratched his head thoughtfully, pushing his bowler hat farther back. 'I wonder if we ought to hang on a bit and give her time to make a proper job of it?'

'Oh, sir,' whispered MacGregor in deep reproach, 'we can't do that!'

'I don't know what you're in such a flaming hurry for, laddie,' grumbled Dover. 'It won't be a pretty sight, I can tell you. She'll have got into a hot bath and slit her wrists. They always reckon it's a very comfortable way to go, but I can't say as how I've ever fancied it. Just slowly bleeding to death and all that pink water! Ugh!' he shivered. 'It's a horrible mess for them that's got to fish 'em out!'

'We haven't any choice, sir,' said MacGregor stoutly. 'I mean, her life may be ebbing away now, while we just stand here talking about it.'

'Oh, all right,' said Dover grudgingly. 'Come on! And I just hope you've remembered something of your first aid. If we've got to wait for old Hawnt to get here we might as well save ourselves the trouble of going upstairs.'

Still whispering and walking on tip-toe, MacGregor and Dover, each trying to let the other go first, made their way unenthusiastically up to the first floo . It didn't take them long to identify the bathroom. They could hear the bath water gurgling away inside, and periodically there was a shattering series of heavy thumps from the antique water system.

'You'd better knock,' said Dover, nodding at the heavy mahogany door.

'She's keeping the water running a long time, sir, isn't she?' said MacGregor as a trickle of sweat ran down his temple.

'She may have cut her throat,' Dover suggested. 'Tha 'll be even worse. Quicker, of course, if you do it properly but most people tend to botch it. It takes some doing to draw a sharp blade clean across, nice and steady and cutting deep enough.' He illustrated his point with a chubby forefinger ac oss his own neck.

MacGregor gulped and tapped hesitantly on the door.

They listened intently. The e was only the sound of the water pouring from the bath taps.

Dover shook his head. 'I reckon we're too late,' he said. 'You'd better go in.'

MacGregor turned the handle. The door opened a fraction of an inch. He glanced back at the Chief Inspector. Dover nodded his head. MacGregor steeled himself and opened the door wider. He stepped over the threshold with Dover close behind, treading on his heels.

It took them a fraction of a second to get their bearings. Th bathroom was enormous. Over on the far left, gushing out great clouds of steam, stood a huge old-fashioned bath. Both taps were full on.

''Strewth! You could drown an elephant in that,' breathed Dover as he and MacGregor moved forward instinctively to investigate whatever horrors the billowing steam might conceal.

They were well into the bathroom before a movement on the right attracted their attention. Only a few wisps of steam had managed to cross the vast tiled expanse so that the view was clear and unobstructed. The e was Dame Alice, clothed in nothing but a fl wered plastic mob cap, cavorting and preening herself in front of a large tarnished mirror. As the two detectives stood with gaping jaws, Dame Alice twisted herself into a creaking, shaky arabesque. Had she been thirty years younger it might have been a sight to stir the blood. As things were, it wasn't.

Dame Alice regarded herself in the mirror with quite unwarranted satisfaction. She smiled at her reflection and, taking a deep breath, spun into a pirouette. On the second time round, shortage of wind and an obscure intuition that something was wrong made her hesitate. She peered towards the door.

Dover's hand went to his bowler hat, a gesture of courtesy that was as incongruous as it was untypical.

Dame Alice opened her mouth and screamed. Being a lady of good family and impeccable connections, she then clutched herself desperately in the appropriate places. For the first time in her life, perhaps, she regretted her exquisite, tiny, small-boned hands. They were totally inadequate for the task modestly demanded of them.

Dame Alice screamed again, but by this time the two masculine intruders were in full and fearful retreat. Even MacGregor, a great one for smoothing over little social awkwardnesses, decided to postpone the abject apologies which the situation clearly demanded. He fought valiantly with Dover for the honour of being first through the bathroom door. Neck and neck they pounded down the stairs and across the hall. MacGregor, forging slightly ahead, got the front door open in time for Dover to surge through unchecked. With winged heels they fl w down the front steps and along the gravelled drive. Dame Alice's dog, a bewildered look on its face, came round the side of the house only in time to see them disappearing through the gates. It sat down and had a good scratch, wondering in its dumb way what the hell was going on.

But there was no rest for Dover and MacGregor. They pounded resolutely on, down the hill to the sanctuary of The Jolly Sailor. From time to time MacGregor, younger and fitter than his Chief Inspector, turned round to see if they were being followed. Dover, eyes popping, jowls wobbling, concentrated all his energies on putting as much distance as possible between himself and Dame Alice. Sweat poured off him, and his face acquired a glow like that of the rising sun. Had The Jolly Sailor been another fifty yards farther away, it is more than likely that Dover's undistinguished career would have ended in apoplexy there and then.

They reached the bar parlour. Dover flopped panting for dear life into the nearest chair. But the old war-horse still maintained a firm grasp on the essentials

'Lock the door!' he gasped. 'And give us a fag!'

Chapter Sixteen

It must have been a good ten minutes before either Dover or MacGregor returned to something like a normal state. The cigarette which Dover had insisted on having did little to restore his physical condition, but it may have helped steady his nerves. When MacGregor had got his breath back, he lit one for himself.

'Do you think she recognized us, sir?' he asked anxiously.

Dover, still speechless, still scarlet in the face and coughing dangerously, shook his head to indicate that he really didn't know.

'It was actually quite dark in the bathroom, wasn't it, sir?' asked MacGregor hopefully. 'And there was quite a lot of steam where we were standing. She can only have caught a glimpse of us for a split second. And she hadn't got her glasses on. I should think she's probably as blind as a bat without them, wouldn't you, sir?'

Dover gulped down another lungful of air and tobacco smoke and went on coughing. MacGregor looked at him with some concern. The last thing he wanted at this particular moment was to be left alone to face the wrath to come.

'Are you all right, sir?' he asked.

Dover regarded him with bleary, bloodshot eyes. 'Gemeadrink!' he croaked.

'A glass of water, sir?'

Dover raised an exhausted head from the table on which he had laid it. 'You bloody fool!' he groaned.

Feeling much happier MacGregor went behind the counter and helped himself to a couple of large whiskies. The bar was locked but MacGregor knew where the Quinces hid the key.

'Should I go and have a look to see if she's coming, sir?'

Dover shook his head again. 'No,' he said. 'We've just got to behave normally. If she did spot us our only hope is to deny it. Swear we've never been near the place. It'll be our word against hers, and everybody knows what funny fancies some women get at her age.'

MacGregor looked dubious. 'But, suppose somebody saw us, sir?'

'Hallucinations!' snapped Dover. 'And if you've got any better suggestions, let's be hearing them! If it hadn't been for you and your crack-brained ideas we'd have never gone upstairs in the first place. Things always go in threes! She's cutting her wrists in the bath! By God, MacGregor, if there are any repercussions from this, I'll break you! So help me, I will!'

MacGregor meekly bowed his head. He knew that Dover could turn very nasty when needs be, and that he had a solid reputation at Scotland Yard for wriggling out of tricky situations with a whole skin while his innocent subordinates found themselves being fla ed alive.

Suddenly Dover chuckled. It started him off coughing again. He soothed his throat with another mouthful of neat whisky. As the minutes went by he began to feel more and more secure. If a rampaging Dame Alice was going to appear on the threshold of The Jolly Sailor, she would appear quickly. It couldn't take her more than ten minutes to get dressed and be down at the pub, and already a quarter of an hour had passed since Dover and MacGregor had returned.

'Mind you,' said Dover with a grin, 'I shouldn't think she'll be too keen on the idea of having this spread all round the blooming county, even if she did recognize us. Prancing about in her birthday suit like a water nymph! In front of a mirror, too. Damned disgusting, I call it, at her age. 'Strewth!' he chuckled again. 'The look on her face when she spotted us!

MacGregor smirked. 'I must say, sir, you're very observant,' he twitted Dover. 'It wasn't her face I was looking at!'

'You dirty-minded young pup!' Dover's tone dripped with masculine indulgence. 'And her a Dame of the British Empire, too!'

This set them both off laughin

'Come to think of it, sir,' said MacGregor, sniggering like a smutty-minded schoolboy, 'she hasn't got a bad figu e, not considering she's a bit past her prime. Quite – er – full, she was. In parts!'

'Oh, do you think so?' said Dover, now thoroughly relaxed and enjoying himself hugely. 'I thought …' – he broke off for a guffaw and a cough – 'I thought things had slipped a bit here and there!'

MacGregor sniggered again and made some vulgar remark to which Dover responded with equal coarseness. They were both laughing almost uncontrollably as the conversation grew bawdier.

'What she should have done,' said Dover, mopping the tears of mirth from his eyes, 'was use that little plastic hat she was wearing. Properly placed it would have covered a lot of her embarrassment!'

'Yes,' agreed MacGregor, 'her hands were far too small – from her point of view, of course, not ours. I thought that purple stuff on her fingers provided the final kinky touch, didn't you, sir? It clashed so gloriously with the blush which, if I remember correctly, reached right down to her …'

'What purple stuff?' asked Dover sharply, his face sinking back with relief into its usual sullenness as he wiped the smile off

'Oh, I suppose she'd burnt her finger or something, sir. She'd dabbed some of that gentian violet stuff on it. I remember it quite distinctly. I'm surprised you didn't notice it, sir. It was on her …' – MacGregor jiggled about with his hands as he repeated Dame Alice's modest gesture – 'right hand.'

'My God!' Dover stared with fascination at his sergeant. 'My God!' he repeated fervently. 'Are you calmly sitting there, you great nincompoop, telling me that Dame Alice had gentian violet daubed all over her hands!' His voice cracked on an outraged bellow.

'Well, yes, sir,' said MacGregor.

'Gentian violet!' roared Dover. 'You damned fool, it wasn't gentian violet! It was purple ink!'

'Oh, *no*, sir!'

'Purple ink from a kid's printing-set, you blithering halfwit! The stuff the second batch of poison-pen letters was written with. We've got her! By all that's holy, we've got her!' Dover gave a whoop of triumph and slapped his hand down painfully on the table to emphasize his point.

'Oh, *no*!' said MacGregor.

'Don't you say "oh, no" to me!' yelped Dover. 'Call yourself a detective! You couldn't see a frying-pan if it was held right under your nose. I told you she was responsible for those poison-pen letters. I told you so right from the beginning. Of course you didn't believe me. You had to go haring off after a lot of red herrings all over the place. Black-market babies, my Aunt Fanny! Well, thanks to me we're home and dry now. It's a good thing one of us has got some brains.'

'It might really be gentian violet, sir,' muttered MacGregor unhappily. 'People do burn their fingers '

'Only when they play with fi e!' retorted Dover. 'And that's what your Dame Alice has been doing. Cheek of the woman, getting me sent down here. I suppose she thought she was being very clever. Well,' – Dover smirked complacently – 'he who laughs last, laughs longest!'

'What are we going to do now, sir? asked MacGregor timidly. 'We'll have to get her along to the police lab and get the stuff on her fingers analysed. If we can prove it's the same ink as was used in the letters, well, she'll have some explaining to do, won't she?'

Dover scowled. Time was getting on. He was going to be out of Thornwich on that six o'clock bus if it was the last thing he did, Dame Alice or no Dame Alice.

'If,' he said cautiously, 'the old cow knows it was us in her bathroom, she'll know that we spotted the purple ink on her fingers. And, if she knows I've seen it, she'll know I'm going to do something about it. Right?'

'Er – yes, sir,' agreed MacGregor doubtfully.

'So, what'll she do? She'll wash it off, wo 't she?'

'Er – yes, I suppose so, sir.'

'The e's no suppose about it!' snarled Dover. 'The woman's not a complete fool. She'll have that stuff off in two shakes of a lamb's tail if she's got to amputate every finger she's got to do it. And then where shall we be? Right back where we started!' Dover's jowls dropped sulkily and his lower lip stuck out like a bad-tempered child's. 'We know who it is and we haven't an ounce of proof, nothing that'd stand up in court for fi e lousy seconds.' Dover's voice dropped pathetically. 'It's too bad, really it is.'

MacGregor maintained a tactful silence. It was difficul and possibly dangerous to find anything to sa .

'No.' Dover shook his head sorrowfully as he got into his stride. 'It's no good kicking against fate. We're never going to be able to bring Dame Alice before the Bar of Justice. These things happen, laddie, even to the best of detectives. In our profession you've just got to learn to take the rough with the smooth.'

'Oh, I don't know, sir,' said MacGregor with the selfish optimism of youth, 'I dare say if we poked around a bit ...'

'No!' said Dover categorically. 'I know when I'm beaten and I hope I'm big enough to accept it gracefully. Further investigation would be an unjustified waste of the taxpa ers' money.'

'It still may not be Dame Alice, sir,' ventured MacGregor. 'I mean, everything's very circumstantial, sir, isn't it?'

'It's Dame Alice,' said Dover crossly. 'Don't start up another argument about that!'

'But if you abandon the case now, sir,' MacGregor protested, 'it means she'll get clean away with it. Apart from all the trouble and distress she's caused, she may even have been responsible for driving Mrs Tompkins to her death, though of course – as you know, sir – I've always thought there was something more ...'

'I said we couldn't get a conviction in court,' Dover broke in quickly before MacGregor started dragging all that business up again, 'but there is, however, still the Bar of Public Opinion.' He permitted himself a sly, wicked, smile. 'Lead me to the telephone, laddie. I am about to cook Dame Alice's goose!'

It was Miss Tilley who answered with a twitter of delight when she heard Dover's rumbling voice throbbing in her ear. 'The Chief Constable, Mr Dover? I'll look his number up for you right away. It won't take me a minute. Just hang on will you?'

'If there's any difficult about putting me through,' said Dover portentously, 'just tell 'em I wish to speak to Mr Mulkerrin on a matter of the utmost importance in connection with the case I have been investigating here in Thornwich'

The e was another gurgle from Miss Tilley and Dover gave MacGregor a broad wink. 'Wild horses wouldn't keep the old dear from listening in after that!' he observed complacently.

Miss Tilley was indeed in such a flur y of excitement that it was several minutes before she got the Chief Constable on the line. Her hands twitched nervously over the keys on her switchboard and it was only by the grace of God that she didn't cut him off again. 'You're through!' she whispered and, from long practice, gave a convincing click on the wires as Dover identified himsel .

Chief Inspector Dover spoke fluently and at length. Mr Mulkerrin at the other end seemed to have lost his voice.

Eventually, when Dover had had his say, he found it. 'Are you sure?' he said weakly.

'Without a shadow of doubt,' said Dover firml . Then, feeling that politeness doesn't cost anything, he added a fractionally belated 'sir'.

'I just can't believe it,' said the Chief Constable, floundering as his world was turned ruthlessly upside-down. 'Dame Alice writing poison-pen letters? It's completely incredible!'

'You can't get away from the facts,' said Dover. 'My sergeant and I have no doubts at all.'

'But surely you're not just going to throw up the case at this stage?'

'No choice, sir. She's not going to make a slip now. Your men can keep an eye on the situation, if you like, now they know where to look, but I doubt if they'll catch her Dameship.'

'Well, it's all very unsatisfactory,' grumbled the Chief Constable. 'You're going to let me have a written report, I hope?'

'Er – no,' said Dover, 'no, I think not. The whole case has been handled on a very unofficia and irregular level, as you know. I don't think it would be a very good idea to have anything on paper at this stage, especially in view of Dame Alice's position.'

'It's precisely Dame Alice's position that's worrying me,' said the Chief Constable tartly. 'It's most unsuitable that she should be allowed to continue as a County Councillor and Chairman of my Standing Joint Committee. Most unsuitable! Why, the woman's nothing more than a common criminal of the most disgusting kind.'

'Tha's why I thought I ought to let you know, confidentiall , what conclusions my sergeant and I had come to. Perhaps you can find some wa , behind the scenes, you know, of easing her out.'

'The e is such a thing as slander,' said the Chief Constable.

'Oh, quite,' said Dover. 'You'll have to be careful. But I didn't want you to think that I'd just been unable to solve the case.'

'No,' said the Chief Constable. 'No, of course not.'

Dover replaced the telephone receiver and turned with great satisfaction to a goggle-eyed MacGregor. 'The e are more ways of killing a cat, laddie,' he observed gleefully. 'Tha 'll teach the old baggage to come the high hat with me! And now' – he looked at the bar clock – 'I think we've just nice time to pack and have something to eat before we catch that bus.'

As departures go, it was a rather ignominious one. Mrs Quince obliged, for the last time and with no visible signs of regret, with a high tea consisting of tomato soup and kippers – a very popular combination with walkers and cyclists from all quarters of the country. Charlie Chettle and his whippet dog came along to see the two detectives off, and Mr Quince flatly refused to hear any hint that he should carry the bags downstairs. Only little Mr Tompkins was missing from those who had come to know Chief Inspector Dover most intimately during his short stay in Thornwich

'Don't ask me where he is,' said Mrs Quince unhelpfully. 'He went off somewhere this morning before you were up and he didn't know what time he'd be back.'

'It's very odd,' said Dover, who would have liked to tie up a few loose ends with Mr Tompkins before he left. 'Well, ask him to drop me a line at the Yard, will you?'

'If I think on about it,' said Mrs Quince.

'He didn't say where he was going, did he?' asked Dover.

'No, he didn't,' said Mrs Quince, observing with a rejoicing heart that it was now only fi e minutes to zero hour. 'And if you want to catch that bus you'd better be getting a move on. They run a bit early sometimes, and he won't stop if he doesn't see you there.'

Dover settled his bowler hat squarely on his head and MacGregor picked up the two suitcases. Unmourned, they left The Jolly Sailor for the last time and ventured out into the darkness. It was raining again, a fact they had ample time to appreciate because not only was the bar clock fast, but the bus was late as well. When, at last, it arrived they clambered on board.

The overnight express from Grailton to London was running smoothly. The e were no sleepers on the train but Dover and MacGregor had a first-class compartment to themselves so the journey was not going to be too uncomfortable. Very few people seemed to be travelling down to London that night, and nobody had even tried to invade the detectives' sanctuary.

Not long after two o'clock in the morning the train was rocking along merrily at high speed. MacGregor and Dover were sitting at diagonally opposite ends of their compartment. MacGregor was scratching a few desultory notes in his notebook and worrying about his future. Dover, staring glassyeyed in front of him, was wondering anxiously about his wife. He sincerely hoped she had fully recovered her health and strength under the administrations of her horrible sister, because he had an idea she was going to need both in the near future. His stomach didn't feel at all good. Maybe it was Mrs Quince's parting kipper, or maybe it was those sausage rolls MacGregor had bought him at the station buffet, or maybe he'd caught a chill with standing about waiting for all these buses and trains. It could, he thought, be almost anything, knowing his stomach. But, whatever it was, he was sure it was going to force him to take to his bed for the next six or seven days. By the time he reported fit for duty, the worst of the unpleasantness which was sure to come would have blown over, and the Assistant Commissioner (Crime) and his various underlings would have found something else to tear their hair about.

You could regard the Thornwich poison-pen case either as a qualified success or a qualified failure, depending on your personal point of view and standards. Dover didn't think that, in the circumstances, he had done too badly. God knows, there were plenty of occasions when he'd done a hell of a lot worse. But his superiors were a carping, fault-finding crew and it might be pleasanter all round if he didn't turn up at the Yard for a few days.

And his stomach really did feel queasy. Slowly he heaved himself to his feet. What a life! Nothing but go, go, go! MacGregor looked up from his notebook.

'I'm just going down the corridor,' explained Dover as he pushed open the sliding door.

MacGregor's eyes dropped back to his notes and he sighed.

Dover sat moodily in the little room at the end of the corridor for a good fi e minutes. It was warm and comfortable there and he'd nothing else to do. From time to time a faint grin passed over the broad expanse of his face as he thought of Dame Alice's discomfitu e, past and present. The investigation had not been entirely without its minor satisfactions.

Eventually he decided it was time to be getting back. MacGregor might be getting worried. With a sigh and a grunt he twisted the lock from 'engaged' to 'vacant' and opened the door. Immediately outside, to Dover's vast astonishment, stood a steely-eyed, grim-faced Mr Tompkins holding a large revolver in his hand. The revolver was pointing unwaveringly at the dead centre of Dover's stomach.

''Strewth!' said Dover, backing away instinctively.

Mr Tompkins stepped towards him into the toilet and, still not removing his eyes from Dover's face or his gun from pointing at Dover's stomach, locked the door behind him with his left hand.

For a long, dramatic moment the two men stood staring at each other.

'You think you've been very clever, don't you, Mr Dover?' said Mr Tompkins in a quiet voice.

'Eh?' said Dover, glancing despondently at Mr Tompkins's gun.

'It's a Colt .36,' explained Mr Tompkins helpfully. 'The US Navy model. It's over a hundred years old but it'll still blow the living daylights out of you if you so much as move a muscle.'

'Oh, quite,' said Dover, swallowing hard. 'You won't have any trouble with me.'

'Good,' said Mr Tompkins. 'Now, what was it we were talking about? Oh yes, you think you've been very clever, don't you? Well, you've just got to realize that, this time, you've not been quite clever enough. I saw you get on the train at Grailton, you know. You thought you were going to catch me unawares, didn't you? But I saw you getting on the train and I've had time to make a few little arrangements of my own.'

'I don't know what you're talking about,' said Dover as soothingly as he could. 'Why don't you just put that gun thing away and come back to my compartment and have a quiet little chat about it, eh?'

'Don't give me any more of that dumb ox act!' retorted Mr Tompkins impatiently. 'You've fooled me all along the line with that! The e was me thinking you were just a great fat stupid lump – all this complaining about your stomach and spending half your time in bed … oh, you really pulled the wool over my eyes!'

Dover looked unhappily at Mr Tompkins's gun which was now being waggled up and down in a rather excitable manner.

'It's not fair,' complained Mr Tompkins. 'If they'd just sent an ordinary detective down, I'd have got away with it. Even you've got to admit, it was a brilliant plan.'

'Oh, yes, it was,' said Dover, smarmily eager to agree. 'Really brilliant!'

'It didn't deceive you, though,' Mr Tompkins pointed out crossly.

'Oh, well,' said Dover with a deprecating smile.

'I'd worked it all out very carefully,' insisted Mr Tompkins, 'and I took my time about it. I think patience is a great virtue, don't you? I typed all the poison-pen letters out months and months ago – in my shed out at the back. Nobody ever went in there. It took me a long time, just a few letters every day. Then, when I'd finished, I destroyed everything: the typewriter, the notepaper, the rubber gloves, everything! I just kept the letters, all stamped and addressed and sealed up.'

'Quite,' said Dover, nodding his head slowly and trying not to look as though all this was news to him.

'The timing was most important,' said Mr Tompkins. 'As soon as she started this business of trying to adopt a baby, my first instinct was to get cracking and finish her off there and then. With a baby in the house I'd never have managed to get away. But I restrained myself. It was important that I shouldn't appear to have a shadow of a motive. You do see that, don't you?'

Dover nodded his head again.

'Well, when things quietened down again I started posting the letters. I always carried a few on me and whenever a favourable opportunity presented itself I slipped them into one of the post boxes. Too easy, really, because nobody ever suspected *me*. Well, it worked like a dream, everybody getting all upset and panicky and blaming everybody else. Lovely! Just what I wanted! I knew that sooner or later they'd call the police in, but I'd taken my precautions. They wouldn't find any incriminating evidence within a hundred miles of me.'

Dover sighed and leaned wearily up against the wall. God, he'd caught a ripe one here, all right! Mr Tompkins watched him suspiciously.

'Don't try anything funny!' he warned Dover. 'One false move and I'll let you have it.'

'You've nothing to worry about from me,' Dover assured him earnestly. 'I won't move a muscle, I promise you.'

Mr Tompkins sniffed. 'You'd better not! I've killed once and I'll kill again. I've got nothing to lose now.'

'Your wife?' asked Dover, his mouth suddenly becoming very dry.

'Of course.' Mr Tompkins frowned. 'You needn't waste your time trying to trick me into making a confession, you know.' I'm only talking to you in here to give you the satisfaction of knowing all the details before it's too late. Not that it'll do you much good,' he added and Dover broke out in a cold sweat. 'Now, where was I? Oh yes, the murder of Mrs Tompkins. Of course I'd got the general plan worked out long ago. I had toyed with the idea of a shooting accident, me cleaning one of my guns, you know, but I think that one's been done a bit too often, don't you? In the end I settled for the gas fi e. Simpler, really. And it's the stupid sort of thing that happens every day. If it hadn't been for you I might have made it just a simple accident – the light blowing out on the gas fi e, somehow. Mind you, I had thought about a fake suicide but when you told me just how to do it, well I decided that was the best way after all.'

'I told you?' said Dover.

'At The Jolly Sailor after the Poppy Gullimore fiasco' agreed Mr Tompkins. 'Of course, at the time I just thought you were one of those stupid, bragging oafs who can't keep their mouths shut after a couple of drinks.' Mr Tompkins gave a wry little laugh. 'I need hardly say that I underestimated you! Anyhow, I'd got to go through with it right away. I'd already set the poison-pen letters in motion and I knew she was fixing up something about that black-market baby – she didn't tell me but I put two and two together.

The e was no time to lose so I decided on suicide for her. All your tips were most helpful and I flatter myself I did a p etty good job. I'd a bit of difficult persuading her to take a bath on Wednesday morning, but otherwise everything went like clockwork. I was very lucky about that suicide note. I'd been saving that for months, just on the off-chance. It was part of a letter she'd been writing. I'd slammed a door – by sheer accident, of course – and made her jump, so she had to start a new sheet.'

Dover, swaying gently as the train roared and rattled on its heedless way, regarded Mr Tompkins sourly.

'I knew she'd ask for a glass of brandy,' Mr Tompkins went on, blithely unaware of the anguish and suffering his words were inflicting. 'She always did. I'd got it all ready and waiting for her. With an overdose of sleeping pills mixed up in it, naturally.'

'The e was no trace of the sleeping pills in the glass,' said Dover. 'We had it analysed. The e was only brandy.'

'Oh, but I changed the glass,' said Mr Tompkins brightly. 'When we went into the shop together I'd smelled the gas long before you did. I thought you were never going to mention it. Well, when at last you did, I rushed to the sitting-room door and told you it was locked.' He smiled shyly. 'It wasn't, of course. I rushed round outside and broke into the room through the window. Then I pushed the suicide note under the body, and substituted the innocent brandy glass I'd been carrying around all afternoon for the one Mrs Tompkins had drunk from. Tha's all there was to do, really.'

Dover wrinkled his nose and wondered how much longer that young nit MacGregor was going to go on sitting on his backside before coming to find out what was the matter. Dover sighed. He decided to work on the principle that yack-yack was better than bang-bang. 'But how did you turn the gas on in the first place?' he asked wearily. 'According to Mrs Poltensky, you never went near the sitting-room.'

'No more I did,' said Mr Tompkins proudly. 'Don't you remember I told you that just before the two of us, Mrs Poltensky and me, left the shop, I went back into the kitchen to get some stamps? Well, while I was in there I just turned all the gas off at the meter. Mrs Tompkins was fast asleep and, of course, she didn't notice when the gas fi e went out. Exactly one minute later I turned the main gas tap on again. Tha 's all there was to it.'

'Ingenious,' observed Dover bitterly.

'But not ingenious enough,' said Mr Tompkins with some regret. 'You obviously spotted it or you wouldn't be here now, would you?'

Dover managed a half-hearted smile. 'No, I suppose I wouldn't, would I?'

'It was your sergeant who first started putting the wind up me,' mused Mr Tompkins. 'He's not a patch on you when it comes to playing the village idiot, is he? When he got on to all that baby buying business, I began to get really worried. I mean, he was heading straight for the core of the whole affai , wasn't he? But you did a wonderful cover-up job, pretending you just couldn't see what was staring you straight in the face. Oh, you fooled me all right! You must have been laughing yourself silly deep down inside. Of course, I can see now you were just biding your time, giving me enough rope to hang myself, eh? You're a proper card, Mr Dover, you really are! I was a fool ever to think that I could outwit you, though, really, I think you've got to give me full marks for trying.'

'Oh, I do,' said Dover sincerely, 'I do.'

Mr Tompkins looked pleased. 'Coming from you that's a real compliment, Mr Dover. Thank ou!'

'Don't mention it,' said Dover, moving uncomfortably from one foot to the other. He nodded his head at the only seat available. 'Do you think I might sit down?'

'Oh no you don't!' said Mr Tompkins cunningly. 'I don't trust you. You just stay where you are. We shan't be much longer. Anything else you'd like to know?'

Dover searched his memory frantically. 'Why didn't you want to tell us where you were on the Wednesday afternoon?' he asked.

Mr Tompkins waved the gun about vaguely. 'Oh, that was just a bit of over-elaboration,' he explained. 'I thought it would look more convincing if you found out about Louise de Gascoigne for yourselves. Anything else?'

Dover thought about scratching his head but decided that Mr Tompkins, who was really behaving in a most peculiar manner, might misinterpret this innocent gesture. 'I'm not absolutely sure, you know,' he said cautiously, 'exactly why you had to kill your wife. It seems a bit drastic. Why didn't you just leave her?'

'Oh,' exclaimed Mr Tompkins looking both surprised and shocked, 'I couldn't have done anything like that! She relied on me absolutely for everything, you know. What sort of a life would she have had if I'd just skipped off with all the money? The shame and humiliation would have killed her. How could she have faced all those people in Thornwich? Oh no, I may be selfish and a murderer, but I'm not *cruel* – nobody could ever accuse me of that! Tha's partly why I had to start writing that second batch of poison-pen letters. Your sergeant really scared the pants off me when he started hinting that the whole of the poison-pen scheme was aimed at getting rid of Mrs Tompkins – I suppose you put him up to that, you cunning old fox! Naturally, I had to start writing a new lot of letters to scotch that idea. But I did it for Mrs Tompkins's sake too, you know. I couldn't have them all saying that she'd been writing all those disgusting letters. She was absolutely incapable of doing anything like that and it was up to me to clear her name and her memory. You do see that, don't you?'

Dover nodded his head. He wasn't really listening too carefully to what Mr Tompkins was saying. He was fully occupied wondering how long all this was going on, and how it was going to end.

'It's funny,' Mr Tompkins went on, 'but up to Friday night I was quite confident I'd got away with it. Over-confident, I suppose.' He smiled wanly. 'And then suddenly I just saw the whole thing in a flash: how you'd been playing with me like a cat playing with a mouse. All this comic blundering around and pretending to get tiddly and making believe you'd be my partner in a private detective agency – well, on Friday night I suddenly couldn't see how I'd ever been taken in by it! I felt such a fool!'

'So you decided to run for it?'

'Yes. I'd got everything pre-planned of course, just in case. I worked out a new identity and even got myself a false passport – and that was dead easy, I don't mind telling you. Somebody ought to do something about it – criminal it is! Still, I did a brilliant job, though I say it as shouldn't. I defy anybody,' pronounced Mr Tompkins truculently, 'to connect me now with Arthur Tompkins of Thornwich! I've covered my tracks perfectly. I've ...' His face fell suddenly. 'But you found me, didn't you?'

Dover cleared his throat modestly.

'You found me or you wouldn't be on this train. Oh dear' – Mr Tompkins looked quite crestfallen – 'I haven't been as clever as I thought, have I?' He sighed. 'You've not left me much choice, have you? I'm not going to let you clap a pair of handcuffs on me and lead me off quietly, you do realize that, don't you? I don't suppose you'd call my family exactly distinguished, but we've always kept ourselves decent and I'm not going to be the first one to besmirch our good name. You do understand that, Mr Dover, don't you? I'm very sorry for your sake, but there it is.'

'Now, look here, old chap,' said Dover in a hoarse but fatherly voice, 'just take your time about this and think it over. There's no hurry. If you pack it in quietly now, they can only give you life and, a chap like you, why you'd be out as free as a bird in eight or nine years, honest you would. You don't want to go making things worse by killing me, now do you?'

'Kill you?' asked Mr Tompkins in great surprise. 'What on earth made you think I was going to kill you? Oh well,' he admitted ruefully, 'I must confess that the thought did cross my mind, but there's your sergeant, too, isn't there? And then, if I shot you now in here, I'd never get this door open, not with a brawny, well-built chap like you sprawled over the floo . The really ought to make these toilet doors open outwards. And anyhow,' – Mr Tompkins rubbed his free hand wearily across his face – 'I've had enough. The whole thing's sort of gone sour on me. I thought I'd solve everything by killing Winifred. I'd start a new life and it'd all be wonderful and diffe ent, but it isn't. And the odd thing is, I miss her somehow. No, I'm going to kill myself. I just wanted to talk to you first and make sure you'd got everything straight. I could have left a note, I suppose, but I think I'd sooner do it this way. I know I can rely on you, Mr Dover. You will see that they identify me properly, won't you? I might have been a bit too clever there. I'd like to be buried next to Winifred, if you could arrange it.'

'I'll do what I can,' said Dover, who had relaxed visibly when the true nature of Mr Tompkins's final solution had become clear. 'Er – all things considered, I think maybe you're doing the right thing.'

'Well, *I* think I am,' said Mr Tompkins with an apologetic smile, 'but I've been wrong before, haven't I?' He seemed to hesitate for a moment. 'Well, I'll be saying goodbye, then.'

Under Dover's amazed eyes Mr Tompkins unlocked the toilet door and opened it – a manoeuvre which brought him stomach to stomach with the Chief Inspector – and slipped out into the corridor. Dover's reactions were never lightning fast, especially when he had a loaded revolver pointing at his midriff. Almost before he had pushed himself off his supporting wall, Mr Tompkins was out in the corridor. In a flash he'd got the outside door open and was standing in the pitch-black opening with the wind tearing at his clothing. He gave a final, brief little smile, put the muzzle of the revolver in his mouth and pulled the trigger.

The noise of the shot was lost in the roar of the train as it sped furiously on its way. Mr Tompkins disappeared from the doorway into the inky darkness beyond. As he released his grip on the corridor door it swung back with uncanny precision and shut itself with a slam. Dover was left staring, pop-eyed, at a perfectly empty, perfectly innocent and perfectly normal train corridor.

With shaking hands he pulled out a grubby handkerchief and wiped his forehead.

He looked up and down the corridor. The e was nobody about. He checked the inside of the toilet. No sign that Mr Tompkins had ever been there. He stood and thought. Then he made up his mind. He took a deep breath and walked slowly back to his compartment.

MacGregor looked up as the door slid open.

'Are you all right, sir?' he asked. 'I was wondering what had happened to you. I say, you do look a bit seedy, sir.'

Dover flopped heavily back into his seat and let his body sag. 'It's my bowels,' he said. 'I reckon I'll be on the trot all night. You haven't got a drop of brandy on you, I suppose?'

'I'm afraid not, sir.'

'Trust you!' grumbled Dover. He settled himself down in his comer, propped his feet up on the opposite seat and closed his eyes. In a few moments his jaw dropped open, the snores started and he was fast asleep, but with his lips, metaphorically speaking, sealed.

After all, he had got his reputation to think of.

Preview

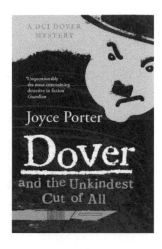

When Mrs. Dover witnesses a young policeman's suicide and has the bad taste to report it, Dover's vacation ends abruptly at the seaside wasteland of Wallerton.

As he sluggishly investigates the matter, an earlier case of murder and mutilation turns up as well. Suspecting that the town's Ladies' Club may be oddly involved, Dover devises an elaborate and utterly wicked trap.

His bait: his overworked, unsuspecting assistant MacGregor.

A Dover Mystery, Book 4

Also Available

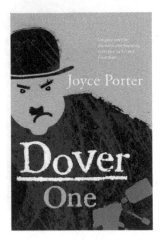

For its own very good reasons, Scotland Yard sends Dover off to remote Creedshire to investigate the disappearance of a young housemaid, Juliet Rugg.

Though there's every cause to assume that she has been murdered – she gave her favours freely and may even have stooped to a bit of blackmail – no body is to be found. Weighing in at sixteen stone, she couldn't be hard to overlook.

But where is she? And why should Dover, of all people, be called upon to find her? Or, for that matter, even bother to solve the damned case?

A Dover Mystery, Book 1

OUT NOW!

About the Dover Series

Detective Chief Inspector Wilfred Dover is arguably the most idle and avaricious hero of any novel, mystery or otherwise. Why should he even be bothered to solve the case?

The full series –

Dover One

Dover Two

Dover Three

Dover and the Unkindest Cut of All

Dover Goes to Pott

Dover Strikes Again

It's Murder with Dover

Dover and the Claret Tappers

Dead Easy for Dover

Dover Beats the Band

Dover: The Collected Short Stories

About the Author

Joyce Porter was born in Cheshire, England and educated at King's College, London. In 1949 she joined the Women's Royal Air Force, and, on the strength of an intensive course in Russian, qualified for confidential work in intelligence. When she left the service in 1963 she had completed three detective novels.

Porter is best known for her series of novels featuring Detective Inspector Wilfred Dover. Dover One appeared in 1964, followed by nine more in a highly successful series. Porter also created the reluctant spy Eddie Brown, and the "Hon-Con", the aristocratic gentlewoman-detective Constance Ethel Morrison Burke.

Note from the Publisher

To receive background material and updates on next releases in the Dover series, sign up at farragobooks.com/dover-signup